MONDA
WASHING DAY

Book One: Grace
Duty and Responsibility

ELIZABETH HUGHES

To Sarah Thanks for your support. Best Wishes EAHughes

Monday is Washing Day is a work of fiction. Names, characters, businesses, organisations, places, events and incidents are either the products of the author's imagination or are, if real, used fictitiously. Any resemblance to any person, living or dead, is purely coincidental.

Publisher: Cyclamen Press.   ISBN 978-1-7397834-2-6

First Edition 2022

For Glyn Hughes, Poet, Author, Artist, Mentor,
Friend and Love of my life.
The only love who is my sweetheart still.

I hope you're waiting for me on some Astral Plane
somewhere out there, with a large glass of single malt.
I'll see you there. *'Thee mine, I thine, forever.'*

Also by the Elizabeth Hughes:

Monday is Washing Day Book Two: Audrey – Escape and Surrender

Monday is Washing Day Book Three: Kathryn – Control and Release

Monday is Washing Day Book Four: Charlie's Story

CONTENTS

PROLOGUE 1949

As Grace Parsons stowed away the galvanised washtub, mangle, dolly and wooden tongs in the Anderson shelter, she mouthed a silent prayer of gratitude. Never again would she, Ned and the girls have to spend a night in this monstrosity. Shivering with cold and terror, dressed in their nightclothes, with feet hastily shoved into waiting wellington boots and wrapped in blankets to ward off the cold. Reading was almost impossible with only a paraffin lamp to shed light, but anyway, who could concentrate?

They had simply waited, listening for the bombs aimed by the Luftwaffe at Vickers' Shipyard and the railway lines into Barrow-in-Furness. Praying that the blackout would be sufficient to keep them safe, hoping the planes would miss the Yard and the town in the darkness, giving thanks at the sound of the 'all-clear' siren.

She shuddered as the memories came, then banished them with a shake of her head. Always pragmatic, she scolded herself for being silly: it was all over now, thank God, and had been for a few years.

Grace was a sensible, practical, middle-aged housewife and mother. She had never been what most people would call attractive, and at almost forty-nine, her hips and breasts relied on good foundation garments. Even then, her figure had spread into what would be politely called 'matronly' and what her younger brother, Freddie, called 'Fat and Fifty-ish'. Bloody cheek of the man! Her mop of brown hair, kept imprisoned in tight curlers and covered with a headscarf, was beginning to show the intrusion of grey. Behind the hated wire-framed spectacles, the

1

crows' feet were starting to win the battle against her nightly regime of Pond's Cold Crème. However, her startling blue eyes had lost none of their sparkle and sometimes revealed a deeply hidden sense of humour.

Like many of their neighbours, the Parsons had decided to keep the corrugated iron shed erected, not just to store her washday equipment and Ned's gardening implements. It also served as a constant thankful reminder that the family had survived the war more or less unscathed. Unlike some, they hadn't lost anyone to the war machine. Her menfolk had been in reserved occupations and had remained at home whilst thousands of others fought the enemy face-to-face, many never to return.

Grace bolted the green wooden door and gazed with satisfaction at the lines of sheets and clothing stretching the 30 yards to the bottom of the back garden at 25 Amphitrite Street. The dark blackcurrant hedges made a stark contrast with the brilliant whiteness of the laundry. 'Putting Dolly Blue in the final rinse makes all the difference between having bright whites and shameful dingy ones,' she thought. Her next thought was that she sounded like an advert in the Barrow News even to herself. It was true, though; she could hold her head high – our Sally next door couldn't criticise the Parsons' laundry even if she were her sister-in-law!

When Grace rose at six that Monday morning, she'd been glad to see the brilliant sunshine streaming through a crack in the curtains. She had left Ned sleeping for another half-hour. She liked to get a head start on washday in the hope of getting everything out on the line to dry enough for ironing on Tuesday. It was always a blessing to get a dry Monday. Fortunately, it was pretty windy here on Walney Island as usual, so it wouldn't take too much time to dry. So far, so good. She left the peg bag and wicker wash-basket on the lawn and entered the kitchen through the 'back' door; a misnomer, as it was at the side of the house. As she went in, she heard the door opposite open and Sally's voice calling out, "Are you making a brew, our Gracie?"

Damn it! Just when she was getting on so well and ahead of the game too! But there was no avoiding it: "I was just about to! Give me five minutes to shape up, then come on over, love."

She knew the house was already immaculate. She was proud of the smart semi with its 'sunshine' double-lounge that let in light through both front and rear windows, and she kept it spotless. Nevertheless, she plumped up the cushions on the settee just to make sure there would be no cause for gossip if Sally should get talking to the neighbours.

In her kitchen, Grace lit the stove under the kettle, feeling she deserved a tea break after all her efforts outside. When it had boiled, she swilled some steaming water into the earthenware pot and emptied it before spooning in the tea leaves and filling it up again. She set china cups and saucers on a tray with a snowy white embroidered cloth as the tea brewed. She took the tray into the living room and sat at the dining table. She didn't want Sally getting too comfortable by sitting in the easy chairs; Grace had far too much to do to waste the day in gossip. As she sat surveying her domestic domain, she heard the distant slam of a door and her sister-in-law's shuffling slipper-clad footsteps as she crossed their adjoining drive to come into the kitchen.

"How are things, our Grace?" Sally asked. "Everything settled down after the engagement party?"

"Oh yes, it was a good night, wasn't it?" said Grace, "We're very happy for them, though I must confess I do think our Thelma is a bit young yet! She's only just turned 20, after all. But Tom is a nice lad, from good, respectable stock, and he works hard. He thinks the world of her, and that's not a bad start to married life. I'm glad they're waiting until after his National Service will be up, though. It gives us a chance to save up a bit for the wedding. Also, I believe his first posting is to Egypt, and God knows what could happen out there. But at least he can rest easy, knowing that she'll be waiting for him. It's official now, so he won't have to worry about her going off with anyone else! And by the time he finishes in the Army, she'll be a bit older and more ready for marriage."

"Did you say he's already bought that plot on Biggar Bank to build them a house when he gets back? It'll be useful to have a builder in the family, won't it?" asked Sally, pouring a little tea from her cup into the saucer, blowing to cool it down before taking a delicate sip.

"That's right, he's been saving hard ever since he started working, and I think his folks have helped him out a bit moneywise. He's already talked to an architect to get the plans sorted out. From what he said, it'll be a lovely little bungalow when it's finished. Just two bedrooms, but I suppose once they start having babies, they'll be able to add on. The garden plot's big enough!"

After a short time talking together and as soon as Sally had finished her tea, Grace stood up and put the china back on the tray. "I'm sorry not to offer you a refill, love, but I've got such a lot to do today. I have to nip to my Mam's to see if she needs anything; she wasn't too well yesterday when she came for dinner. I'll see you later, all right?" Grudgingly Sally got up from the table and let herself out of the kitchen door.

As Grace washed up the tea things, she checked the bucket under the sink, where two milk bottles stood, one unopened and the other just over half full. There might even be enough to make a rice pudding to take for Mam. She ran the cold tap into the sink and replaced the water in the bucket. If only they had an icebox to keep the milk fresh in this warm weather!

She opened the pantry door and brought out the makings of the evening meal. Monday was always the leftover beef from Sunday, minced and cooked with chopped root vegetables to make a cottage pie, topped with mashed potatoes mixed with cabbage and any other leftover vegetables, as a sort of 'bubble and squeak'. This week, there was also enough cheese left to put on top to make it even better. Ned loved it when it came out of the oven, with the cheese golden brown and bubbling. As she prepared the food, she was deep in thought about her family and how life was gradually improving for them all. The girls were getting old enough to need less looking after now they were both working.

Thelma had started at the hospital at 16 as a post girl, and after only four years, she was already in charge of the reception office. She'd met her fiancé, Tom Armstrong, at the Abbey Musical Society, an amateur dramatics group that put on a musical play each year at the Public Hall.

Thelma and Audrey, Grace's younger daughter, had attended dancing classes from being very young. Though she was no relation, 'Auntie' Rene (pronounced 'Reeny' in the local dialect) had recently taken on Thelma as her assistant at the 'Rene Rawlinson School of Dance'. Both girls religiously went to class every Saturday.

Thelma had also taken her dancing talents to the Abbey Musical Society, known locally just as 'the amateurs', where she danced in the chorus and often helped with the choreography. Tom, a handsome dark-haired young man, had a magnificent tenor singing voice and thus more often than not found himself in the leading male roles, reminiscent of a young Mario Lanza. Their mutual love of performance had led to them courting, but Tom had recently had his call up for National Service. He had asked Thelma to wait for him and promised they would be married on his return.

The young couple had announced their engagement to their friends and colleagues after a rehearsal for their next show. There had also been the party; Grace and Ned's parents, siblings and assorted cousins that lived close by had all turned up. Except that is, for Grace's sister Joy, who lived in Milnthorpe with her husband Maurice and their children. Already part of the family, Tom, coming from North Yorkshire, had no relatives living nearby, but Ken had attended, his best friend and soon-to-be best man, as had Thelma's maid-of-honour to-be, Sylvia. A very happy occasion ensued, ending with everyone singing along as Ned's sister Florrie played the piano to his accompaniment on the violin.

Yes, thought Grace, Thelma was all set, her life sorted for the foreseeable future at least.

Grace worried about Audrey, though. Since being a toddler, the girl had a very dry skin condition which caused her skin to flake and became sore if not moisturised constantly. Now Audrey was older; the ailment seemed to be improving, and she could administer the cream herself, but even so, cold winters were still a trial. Then the skin on her legs cracked, sometimes bleeding and becoming painful. Grace had to visit the Headmistress at Barrow Girls' Grammar School to get special dispensation for Audrey to wear silk or nylon stockings. Otherwise, the thick woollen socks of the school uniform would stick to her cracked skin, making it torture to undress. More than once, Audrey had been pulled up in the school corridors by one teacher or another, demanding to know why she wasn't in the proper uniform, and she hated the humiliation of having to explain.

Audrey had hated school anyway. She was intelligent enough but daydreamed a lot and was always in trouble for not paying attention. There had been many arguments about it; Ned had finally taken her out of school, his daughter was so unhappy. She had become very withdrawn and had taken to staying in her bedroom sewing and embroidering rather than spending time with the family. She justified her behaviour by accusing Grace of constantly picking on her and favouring Thelma.

Thinking about it, Grace realised it must have seemed that way to the lass. After all, with Thelma working and courting, Audrey was left with chores like helping with cooking, baking, and doing the dishes each evening. And especially with all the fuss over the engagement, she must have felt her nose pushed right out. Grace resolved to try and make amends with her young daughter as soon as she could.

Audrey had found herself a job, working as a stock girl at Pass's department store, opposite the Town Hall. The motto was 'Everything from a pin to a piano', and the building was indeed a very imposing sight on Duke Street opposite the Town Hall. Audrey was beginning to get over her initial shyness and make friends. As her sister had rather unkindly put it, "At least she's not trailing around after me anymore!" Thelma could have a sharp tongue on her sometimes!

Thinking of the engagement 'do' had brought to mind some of the parties they'd had during the War for various reasons when friends and nearby neighbours would donate from their rations. Grace would make a 'pie and peas' supper; vast potato and meat pies topped with shortcrust pastry and huge cauldrons of mushy peas soaked overnight. The pies were light on meat, but potatoes were plentiful from Ned's vegetable plot and dried peas very cheap. There was always lots of singing and dancing at these events, which did a great deal to raise morale in Amphitrite Street. They often ended up like street parties until the Air Raid Precaution wardens sent everyone home as darkness fell.

ARP wardens supervised the Blackout; their primary purpose was to patrol the streets to ensure that no light was visible to give a target for the Luftwaffe bombs. If the curtains showed even a glimpse of light, it would earn the reprimand 'Put that light out!' To be caught regularly could even incur a fine.

In 1941, during what became known as the 'Barrow Blitz', one of the bombs exploded close to the railway. The blast had blown out the windows of many of the surrounding houses and damaged a lot of property, including the gable-end wall of the large end-of-terrace house at number 1 Warwick Street. The house belonged to her husband's sister and brother-in-law Florrie and Raymond Thompson, where they and Florrie's parents, Edward and Florence Parsons, lived.

The house had been designated unsafe, so the whole household had moved into Amphitrite Street until they could carry out the repairs. At the same time, Herbert Hodgkins, a fireman from Hull, had been billeted with Ned and Grace whilst covering night shifts in the Shipyard.

The Parsons' house was new and semi-detached but had only two bedrooms and a boxroom, and with two young daughters also at home, it was a tight fit with sleeping arrangements. The elder Parsons occupied one of the double rooms, Grace and Ned shared the other and Florrie and Ray had slept on a mattress in the living room, stowing it behind the settee when they rose each day. Thelma and Audrey 'topped and tailed' in a single bed in the boxroom, and as they rose for school in the mornings, Herbert arrived home from his night shift and got into their empty but still warm bed. It had been a challenging period with everyone forced together and not a moment's privacy for anyone.

Ray and Ned had both been electricians, and even Florrie had been driving cranes in the Shipyard, sometimes working 12-hour shifts and coming home too tired to do anything but eat and sleep. The elderly parental couple had pottered around the house and garden, but most of the domestic work had fallen to Grace. All the cooking, cleaning and washing for nine people and looking after her two small girls had left her exhausted at the end of each day.

Then, when the war had ended, all the men demobbed from the military and returned to Vickers. Repairs on the Warwick Street house were complete, and the elder Parsons and Thompsons had moved back home. Florrie had lost her job in the yard and gone to work as a laundress at one of the posh hotels in town, the Imperial on Cornwallis Street.

It had taken time to get used to having a quiet, tidy house again after having so many people to stay, and Grace very much appreciated the peace and space now that the world was gradually returning to normal. It was much less work for her too. It was almost too easy just to be looking after her small brood.

Not that Grace wasn't used to caring for a houseful! As the eldest girl and second oldest sibling of eight children, she had always helped her mother, Kate, to look after the younger ones and do chores in the little terraced house in Cameron Street that they had moved to in 1903 from Hull where the clan originated. They'd been packed in like sardines by the time the Great War started - the three youngest girls in cots in Mam and Dad's room. The three older girls had a double bed, and the two boys were in a homemade bunk bed that Albert had built, all squeezed in the second bedroom with hardly space to hang a big curtain across for privacy!

But they'd had fun and were a close family all pulling together. Grace could wish for nothing better for her own two girls...

CHAPTER ONE 1903 - 1914

Grace had been born in Hull in 1900 to Kate and Albert Tunstall, a little sister for Charles aged two. Her father, a foundry worker by trade, had heard in 1903 that the Shipyard in Barrow, recently taken over by Vickers, were looking for experienced tradesmen to complete the building of HMS Princess Royal and their next contract to build the HMS Emperor of India. The company were crying out for skilled men, and as an experienced brass-moulder, he would be sure to get employment. Armed with this knowledge, he'd moved his family from the East to the West coast of England.

They found a small house to rent at Buller Street on Walney, a small two-up-two-down red-brick terraced house, more or less identical to hundreds of others in the town, recently erected to house the expanding workforce at Vickers.

Pregnant with her third child, Kate made the little house habitable for her family. She was a tiny woman, barely five feet tall, often commented upon when she walked alongside her 6-foot 2-inch husband. Or rather, she trotted alongside, trying to keep pace with his great loping stride. But Kate was a devoted wife and mother, and it gave her nothing but pleasure to look after her 'big man'. Theirs was a love match; he wanted no more than to love and protect his pretty little wife. She returned his love, showing how much, she cared in a hundred small ways. Albert was a gentle giant, his muddy-brown hair always unruly and a pair of piercing blue-grey eyes that were his best feature. He was a placid man, slow to anger, which was helpful with two small children constantly under his feet whenever he was at home.

As she grew, Grace worshipped her older brother; Charlie could do no wrong in her eyes. She was a willing participant in all his games. She preferred playing in their backyard to 'playing out' in the streets with his friends. Some of them complained about her tagging along, But Charlie always included her in their play. Mam would be having the new baby soon and found it an effort to keep up with her energetic children. Charlie's job was to look after Gracie, and he took it very seriously.

They were a happy little household whose numbers increased as the new century progressed. The new baby, Faith, was followed two years later by another girl, Joy. Charlie was delighted when at last, his little brother Frederick arrived in 1908. After another two years, the twins, Hope and Constance, came. Then in 1911, another baby girl, Prudence, was born after an uncomfortable pregnancy and difficult breech birth. Kate had been in labour for fourteen hours before she delivered the baby at last, and the doctor said there should be no more children if Kate wished to survive to bring up her already sizeable brood. After eight children in twelve years, this news brought Kate a sense of relief, tinged with guilt and sadness that her fecundity was at an end.

By this time, the family had moved to 51 Cameron Street, Barrow Island, just a short walk from Vickers' gates. Times were hard enough even with Albert working at the Shipyard; with eight bairns of 12 and under to clothe and feed, Kate still needed to take in odd sewing jobs to help eke out the housekeeping. But she was slow to recover from her birthing ordeal and became quite delicate, lacking stamina and often unequal to carrying out those domestic tasks that required any strength. Thus, many of the household chores fell to Grace, by this time, aged ten.

Kate didn't have a favourite child, they were all precious little souls to her, but Albert's pride and joy was Charles, their firstborn. At 12, Charlie was tall like his dad and already towered over his mother's tiny frame.

Charlie had done his best to help his family, becoming a paper lad and messenger boy before and after school. He'd even gone to some of the posh houses on Ocean Road, offering his services doing chores and gardening. At first, he'd had a hard time at school, but he could hold his own and had won them round with his prowess at sports and intelligence at his lessons. Yes, it was easy to see that Charlie would make something of himself.

Grace didn't mind in the least becoming 'little mother' to her siblings. She found it easy to manage the younger children, keeping them occupied so as not to bother their mother. Day by day, Grace ensured the children were washed, dressed and fed. Thankfully the Infants and Primary Schools were a short walk away on Island Road, which meant she could escort everyone to school, though often she did not attend her own lessons. Leaving Mam to cope with the tiny ones was too much for her, even for a few hours.

Grace enjoyed the shopping each day; the local shopkeepers got to know her and admired how the young girl was helping her folks. She would even barter with them if she thought an item was overpriced, so they often kept bargains for her or gave her discounted prices. Grace also liked cooking the meals and had become a dab hand at making large quantities. She would make big pans of soup and stews, braising the cheapest cuts of meat slowly until tender and adding lots of vegetables when the meat was sparse.

She wasn't that keen on the cleaning and the laundry, but there was no help for that; someone had to do these things. So, she hummed merry tunes as she heaved the rugs into the backyard to be flung over the washing line and beaten clean. She blackleaded the grate and the kitchen range and scrubbed and polished the front doorstep and the brasses. She sometimes struggled with the laundry and had to get Charlie to help out with the mangle for sheets and blankets, but running the house was her domain for the most part.

She ruled her siblings with a loving rod of iron and brooked no tantrums or mutiny. Sometimes, she came across as a bit cold and unemotional, but she'd found that it created more work if she was soft and let the little ones get away with their mischief. To relieve the burden on her mother, Grace had learned that it was best to chase them along to get on with their tasks. Being matter-of-fact and practical had become second nature to her; she had no time for whimsy and fairy-tales.

Kate felt guilty at the amount of responsibility heaped on her eldest daughter's shoulders and that her schooling was so often interrupted or neglected. She worried that Grace would resent her weakness and frailty, but Grace was always strong and cheerful. "Don't fret so, Mam," she said one evening after Kate had voiced her worries. "I love looking after the kids, and doing the housework is good practice for when I have a home and children of my own." The look of relief and gratitude on her mother's face was enough reward for Grace.

In June 1911, as the country celebrated the coronation of the new King, George V, the Tunstalls were forced to move to another house. The owner of the current property, Miss

Muncaster, was sister to a Duke and therefore aristocracy, some of whom had no regard for the plight of the working classes.

Miss Muncaster required the house in Cameron Street for other purposes, so Albert, Kate and their family had no choice but to relinquish their home. However, Albert struck a blow for rebellion by removing all the wallpaper and spoiling the new paint in the house, much to Miss Muncaster's chagrin. Her fury at his actions was impotent, though; Albert had recently redecorated all through the house, but at his own expense, so she had no retribution.

Fortunately, a friend of Albert's knew of a vacant property for rent in Crellin Street, in the town centre, so the Tunstalls moved lock, stock and barrel within the matter of a few days. There was naturally some upheaval. As well as settling into the new house, the children had to change schools and attend at Thwaite Street, leaving their old friends behind in Barrow Island.

As she grew out of her cute babyness, it became apparent that Grace would never be a beauty. She had inherited her father's looks rather than her pretty mother's. Together with quite prominent teeth and her father's tousled mud-coloured hair, the girl had Albert's blue-grey eyes but also had a slight squint that meant having to wear spectacles, which the girl hated. She often lamented to her mother that her name could not be more inappropriate as she was tall for a girl and gangling, which made her clumsy sometimes.

When Faith had arrived, all giggles and smiles, followed by Joy, an equally beautiful child, Grace was a little jealous. She had been quite glad when the next baby arrived, at last, a boy,

Freddie, but the twins, Hope and Connie, were born a year later. There had been much concern over the new babies; both were sickly, and the doctor didn't expect them to survive. However, with Kate's and Grace's care and devotion, they soon began to thrive and were out of danger.

All four little girls were cherubs with curly hair and big blue eyes, pretty smiles and dimples, tiny duplicates of their mother. Grace very much felt the ugly duckling of her family and prayed that in time she would emerge as a beautiful swan.

Even Freddie was cute. He was an imp of a boy, with a mischievous and twinkling grin that won everyone's heart. He wasn't clever like Charles but was bright enough and took pleasure in entertaining people and clowning around, never taking anything seriously. Freddie was also Grace's favourite sibling, although Charlie still reigned supreme in her estimation.

As they had grown up, with Charlie concentrating on his schooling and earning the necessary funds to help out, he had become more distant than when they were younger. Grace's domestic responsibilities helping out her Mam meant she elevated him onto a pedestal, still worshipped and adored but in whom she no longer confided. Instead, young Freddie made her laugh with his cheeky ways and could always cheer her up when the four little girls seemed hard work. Grace and Freddie would be close all their lives, even living next door to each other in the far distant future.

Last of all was baby Prudence, who was delicate and pale, with a cloud of thick dark curls unlike any of her siblings. She had large luminous blue eyes tipped with long thick lashes that Grace coveted; hers were short and sparse, not noticeable behind the hated specs. Despite Prue's dramatic arrival and the after-effects on her mother, she was adored by all. She was a quiet baby who rarely cried and, even when she did, just grizzled in her crib until she got the attention she needed.

And so, life went on. The Titanic sank in April 1912, and Albert found yet another new house for the family. They moved to Delhi Street; finally, they were back on Walney Island, where they belonged. As her sisters grew older, Grace taught them to help around the house, thus reducing her load somewhat, which eased Kate's worries a little. Even young Freddie could be coaxed into some chores, as mischievous as he was.

Then the world seemed to explode, changing the lives of every person in Britain forever. It was 1914, and their country was at War.

CHAPTER TWO 1901 - 1914

Edward Parsons Junior, affectionately known as Ned, was born in Stone in Staffordshire in April 1901. His father, Edward Senior, had been a shopkeeper, selling pottery and household goods, but Stone was a relatively small market town just a few miles from Stafford, and the shop didn't do all that well. Edward had heard that Barrow was becoming a boom town and expanding rapidly. So much so that it was becoming known as the Chicago of the North. Thousands of houses were being built to cater for the expanding workforce, both in Vickers shipbuilding and the Hematite Steel Company, which was currently the biggest in the world. It seemed sensible to take his business somewhere it might thrive instead of dwindling to nothing as he feared it would if they stayed in the Midlands.

His wife, Florence, had trained as a tailor before their marriage, which was quite unusual in those days. Most women who earned their living sewing were seamstresses, sewing gowns and shirts, but her father had been a bespoke tailor. In Peterborough, where she was born, Henry Edmonds had taught his daughter all he knew.

Florence agreed with her husband's reasons for relocating and persuaded him that he might also include rooms over the shop where the family could live as one of the factors when he searched for new premises. Perhaps there might even be room for her to start her own small tailoring business if it was possible. After all, the many thousands of men flocking to work in Barrow would need jackets and trousers for work as well as a Sunday

Best suit for church. And, of course, they would have families who would need garments as well, which she could also make.

After much searching, Edward finally found a place in Cavendish Street in the town centre, just off the main shopping street, Dalton Road. It had a large bay window, perfect for displaying the crockery, and upstairs were two other floors. The uppermost was suitable for bedrooms, a large double for the adults and two smaller rooms, one a bedroom for Ned, and a spare room for storage which could double as a room for visitors. There were three rooms directly above the shop, one of which could be used as a sitting room, the other a kitchen and scullery and a large space perfect for Florence's tailoring business.

The Parsons managed to get their businesses set up with little difficulty, although neither attracted the large turnover they had hoped for immediately, but it was early days yet. Hopefully, with suitable advertising in the local papers, eventually, the trade would come.

In 1905, Florence gave birth to a daughter named Florence Primrose; the little girl was known as Florrie to avoid confusion. After being an only child, Ned was happy to have a sibling at last and couldn't wait for her to grow up enough to play with him.

The children were close; with their parents both busy all day plying their trades, Ned and Florrie had to entertain each other in their mother's workroom above the shop. Florence was there to keep an eye on them and make sure they didn't get into too much mischief, but concentrating on her cutting and sewing meant her attention was mostly elsewhere. This was especially the case when she had a customer sent upstairs by Ned when she would have to measure carefully and make copious notes about cut, materials and style. At those times, the children soon learned to keep out of the way and be quiet.

They rarely ventured into Edward's domain, the shop downstairs. There was on display too much delicate porcelain and glassware, bought by the better-off folk, and the everyday earthenware crockery used by most of their customers to have children playing in the shop.

As they grew and started school, their horizons broadened somewhat. Ned was quiet, studious, and quite shy, but he made a few friends among his classmates. Four years younger, Florrie was a vivacious child, a chatterbox with an infectious laugh, and she quickly became a favourite with her classmates and teachers. In addition to their school education, Florence decided the children should take music lessons, so Ned opted for the violin as his instrument. Florrie learned to play the upright piano that had been a wedding gift to her parents from her maternal grandparents, Henry and Hattie Edmonds.

Both of the children loved their music – it had been instilled in them from an early age that they must practice every day. It was another means of keeping them occupied whilst their parents tended to business. Both Ned and Florrie were to play all their lives, accompanying each other at family gatherings and parties. Ned spent what money he had on sheet music and was garnering quite a collection of the popular songs of the day.

When he was quite young, his parents had bought him a small magic lantern toy with various slides, and he liked to entertain his sister with a picture show, shining the lantern onto a sheet spread across the backs of two chairs to create a screen. His interest developed further when early cinema arrived in Barrow when his father would take the family out regularly to watch the latest films. Ned became fascinated with the mechanics of film, and eventually, as he grew, he became friendly with the projectionists at several of the theatres, who would sometimes let him watch them work.

Tragedy struck the family one night in 1914, shortly before the war started. Edward and Florence had taken the children to a film show at the newly renamed Tivoli Theatre in Forshaw Street, the next street to their home and shop. They had enjoyed the show, which had been several reels of 'shorts' featuring the comic antics of Charlie Chaplin and *'The Perils of Pauline'* as well as newsreels, including one showing the King and Queen on a state visit to Paris.

They made their way out of the picture house at the show's end and started the short walk back to Cavendish Street. There seemed to be some kerfuffle going on further down the street, and as they drew near, they realised that there was a fire, with a Fire Tender in attendance and countless people milling about. Getting even closer, they were horrified to find that the fire was at their property!

"Floss, you and the children wait here, where it's safe. I'll go and see what's happened. No, Ned, I mean it!" Edward's voice was stern as he held back his son, "Wait here out of harm's way with your mother and sister. I need to find out what's going on."

Florence did as she was bade and stood a good distance away from the disarray with an arm around each child. She watched as her husband approached the firemen, who seemed to have got the blaze under control. As far as she could see, the fire was dying down, and clouds of steam rose from the smouldering wreckage as the water doused the flames, sending up showers of sparks and loud hissing noises that they could still hear, as far away as they were.

Edward's heart sank as he got closer to the scene, and a burly fireman stopped him from getting any closer. "Sorry, mister, but you need to stay away. We've got it under control, but it's still very dangerous."

"But it's my property – my shop, my home! What happened? Do you know how it started?" Edward couldn't help himself; he was near tears and had a lump in his throat that caused his voice to sound strangulated.

"Oh right! Is it your place? Then you need to speak to the Fire Chief – he'll want to get some details from you." The fireman led Edward through the crowd of onlookers until he found a tall, powerfully built man with a large handlebar moustache, issuing orders to several firefighters armed with shovels and buckets. The man looked at Edward, puzzled, then nodded quizzically at the fireman.

In answer to his chief's unspoken question, the fireman said, "This chap says it's his shop, Sir. I thought you'd want to question him?"

"Good fellow," said the Fire Chief, "just go back and make sure no one else gets any closer. We don't need any casualties." The fireman saluted and turned back to go to his guarding position. The Chief continued, "Now then, we'd better talk, Mr – ah -? "

"Parsons," said Edward. He barely acknowledged the chief's presence, his eyes inexorably drawn towards the shell of what had been his business and his home.

"Righto, Mr Parsons. First things first, was there anyone home, to your knowledge? We haven't completed our search yet, but so far haven't found any…" the Chief searched for an appropriate word, "ah, victims, shall we say?"

"No, there was no one at home. I had taken my wife and children out for the evening to the picture house – the Tivoli. They're all standing down the street there, quite safe, thank God."

"Thank God indeed, Mr Parsons," the Chief nodded, "property, belongings – they can all be replaced. Loved ones cannot. I'm very glad to hear that your family is safe."

"Do you know what caused it? Will you be able to find out, Mr, er, Chief – sorry, what should I call you?" Edward looked at him.

"Burns. Yes, I know, ironic, isn't it? Mr Burns the fireman, like in the children's card game. There will be an investigation, Sir, and we may be able to ascertain the cause of the fire if we can find the point of origin. I should think right now, though, that it's more important that we find somewhere for you and your family to stay, at least for tonight. Get some rest, and we can start the investigation properly tomorrow. Do you have any relatives or friends you could stay with tonight?"

"No relatives, I'm afraid. I have a friend, Mr Wood in Forshaw Street, the furniture dealers? He may be able to help. Otherwise, we can stay at a hotel, I expect?" Edward cast around in his mind for the best option. "I'll discuss with my wife as to what we should do."

"Probably best, Sir, I daresay Mrs Parsons and the children are going to be upset by all this. I will need to speak to you in the morning, though."

"I'll come down to the Fire Station and see you. What would be the best time?" said Edward.

"Whenever is convenient for you, Mr Parsons. You're going to have a lot to deal with. May I ask if you have insurance?"

"Yes, being a business, I thought it best to take out insurance, to cover the stock and such. But whether it will be enough to rehouse us and to provide for us whilst we get back on our feet is another question." Edward's forehead creased with worry. At the moment, the future looked very bleak.

"It looks like your wife has company, Mr Parsons. Will I leave you to sort things out for tonight and see you in the morning? I'd say good night, sir, but that doesn't seem appropriate right now." Burns turned and walked back towards the wreckage of the shop where black-faced firemen clambered amongst the rubble.

Edward looked to see Florence, Ned and Florrie waiting for him. He could see a man and woman talking to them but could not make out who the couple were at that distance. He walked over, and as he got closer, he recognised the man he'd spoken to Burns about, Joseph Wood, from Wood's Furnishings and Auction House in Forshaw Street. This business was next door to the picture house where the Parsons family had spent a happy evening just a few hours earlier.

"Eddie!" Joseph held out his hand to his friend, "Fanny and I heard something was going on here, so being nosy, we came to see what the excitement was about. I never thought I'd find poor Floss and the children standing here, watching your home burn!" He clapped his friend on the back. "Do you know what happened?"

"No, Joe, not yet. There's to be an investigation, and I've to go to the Fire Station tomorrow to give them some information. But the immediate concern is to find somewhere for us to stay tonight. I thought perhaps the Theatre Hotel might be useful, just down from here, being so close. Tomorrow I'll have to go and see what, if anything, can be salvaged from our belongings."

Frances Wood, Joseph's wife and Florence's dearest friend interrupted, "I won't hear of you going to a hotel. Floss – you must come and stay with us until you can sort something out. Mustn't they, Joe? You tell Eddie, they must stay at our place – we've plenty of room above the shop. And I can sort you out anything you might need in the way of clothes and washing things. It will be much more comfortable than a hotel! Do come! I insist!"

"Fanny's right, Edward; you must stay with us." Joseph nodded in agreement with his wife. "Come on, let's go and get a nice hot drink and some supper organised. Everything will look brighter in the morning. You'll see!" With that, Joseph offered Florence his arm.

Frances tucked her hand into Edward's elbow. She beckoned to Ned and Florrie, "come along, children. This is turning into quite an adventure, isn't it?"

Ned took hold of his little sister's hand. At only nine years old, she was frightened by all the chaos, and he could see she was bewildered. "Come on, Florrie. It'll be all right. You'll see," and they followed the older couples towards the next street.

CHAPTER THREE 1914

The Wood family made the Parsons very welcome in their home. Joseph Wood had a business selling furniture and household goods, and, like the Parsons, his family lived above the shop. As might be expected, being in such a business, their home was well-furnished, and Frances kept it in immaculate condition. In the living room, every wooden surface, whether a table, sideboard or bookcase, was highly polished and gleamed in the glow of the many lamps scattered hither and yon about the place.

Joseph was a successful businessman; he had started with a market stall, selling second-hand goods, but had such an eye for quality that it didn't take long for him to do so well as to move to the shop on Forshaw Street, from which he started selling new furniture as well. With the town's expansion, his business also expanded, and he bought the shop next door, merging the two premises but keeping them separate internally. Using the original shop for the brand-new goods, Joseph catered for the well to do, stocking the best quality furniture. He created an auction house in the larger adjacent premises and dealt in second-hand household goods. With plenty of space to display the goods around the walls, he used the remaining middle floor space to make an auction floor. He provided benches for prospective customers to sit and make their bids in relative comfort at the weekly sales, each Saturday afternoon when most workers began their weekends. The sales were very popular among the poorer sections of the town, usually workers from Barrow Island and the Scotch Buildings. They could go to Joe

Wood's and buy whatever they needed to furnish their flats at bargain prices, and also, should it become necessary, they could sell it back to him when money grew short.

He also trained his son, Osmond Percival Wood, to recognise household goods of quality from a young age. Ossie was around the same age as Ned, and was considered capable of carrying out house clearances without his father's supervision. He would take the Wood's horse and cart used for delivering large items like armoires and brass beds to customers' homes, and with a helper or two, he would clear out a property on behalf of the landlord. This was a regular happening, for example, if the residents had done a 'moonlight flit' or died without family members to claim the goods left behind. In those cases, the landlord paid for the service and received a part of the goods' value when Joseph sold them at Auction. This benefitted both parties; it increased Joseph's stock and emptied the properties that could then be rented out again, without any effort on the landlord's part towards clearing and storing the goods and selling them on.

So business was booming for Joseph; he and his family lived well and were happy to help out the Parsons family who had suffered such bad luck. Although Edward and Florence were naturally upset at the loss of their home and business, they could rely on their good friends' hospitality for a little while at least. Frances provided them with comfortable beds, nightclothes and nourishment that would see them through until the morning when they could go and survey the wreckage.

The next morning, Joseph insisted that Edward should have a good breakfast; then, they would walk together to the next street and see if they could salvage anything from the burnt-out premises before visiting the Fire Station as arranged. Meanwhile, Frances encouraged Florence and the children to make themselves at home until the men came back with some idea of how the family might move on.

The news was not good, though not as bad as it might have been. It seemed the fire had started in the kitchen – perhaps an ember from the fire, damped down for the evening, had dropped onto the rag rug in front of the hearth where the cast-iron range still stood. The fire had then spread throughout the living quarters and upstairs to the bedrooms, consuming all the wooden and soft furnishings, leaving very little undamaged. In Florence's workshop, there was nothing salvageable aside from a few pairs of scissors and shears. Even the needles and straight pins had melted into a few small tangled spots of metal. Most of the fabrics were reduced to ash. Any that escaped the fire were ruined by the firefighters' attempt to save the building.

Downstairs in the shop, however, the outlook was slightly brighter – there were a few stacks of crockery still intact, though filthy with ash and smuts of soot, but they would probably still be saleable once washed. The best part was that careful Edward had purchased a small iron safe which he kept in the back of the shop. The safe had survived the conflagration and was squatting in amongst the debris, unopened. It contained a reasonable amount of cash from both the tailoring and the crockery businesses waiting to be banked on Friday and the cash drawer used in the shop holding the takings from yesterday. So at least the family weren't completely destitute. Edward would have to visit the Insurance company and arrange for the assessor to come and look. Eventually, there would be a pay-out that would keep the family going for a while, hopefully until they could decide how to progress from the current situation. But for the time being, at least, it didn't look like they'd all be forced into the workhouse.

The first thing to do was to salvage everything possible from the shop. Now aged 14, Ned was old enough to help out the clearing up. He and Edward borrowed a hand cart from the Wood's shop and trundled it down Cavendish Street, stopping where their beautiful bay window had once displayed the crockery and glassware that sparkled whenever the sun caught the plate glass of the shopfront. In the blackened mess that remained, they tramped through the shards of pottery and glass that littered the floor and gradually loaded up the cart with the few stacks of plates, soup dishes, saucers and cups that remained on the very back shelves that had avoided the flames. Between them, they also manoeuvred the small heavy safe onto the cart. Edward had already removed the money from it, but Joseph had offered to buy it from him for his own business use, and the few pounds it brought would be useful.

When they had retrieved everything that remained intact from the shop, they returned to the furniture shop. Ready and waiting in the scullery were Florence and Florrie, with buckets and pans of soapy water, ready to wash the soiled crockery and ensure that it was saleable. Edward had decided to sell his remaining stock in Joseph's next auction, and Joe had agreed not to charge any commission on those sales to try and help muster finances for the Parsons family. Edward was worried that even with the payment from the insurance company, there would not be enough money for them to start again from scratch. He would also have to find somewhere for them to live very soon; he didn't want to prevail upon his friend's good nature. So, he would start by finding a house to rent for the time being, then see what they could do from a business point of view.

But Joe Wood was better than just a friend; he could see potential in Edward that might be useful to his own business. In the world of buying and selling household goods and furniture, he often came across quality glass and ornaments. He knew his friend had a good eye for these items, so he had been thinking of asking Edward to come and work for him in the capacity of glassware and ceramics advisor. But he said nothing for the moment; it might well be that Edward would have enough to start over. He would wait and see what the prospects were then they could discuss it together.

Within a week, Edward had found a house for his family at 12 Thomas Street, not far from the new Town Hall. It was two-up, two down, which was far from ideal. With Ned growing fast into a young man, it was not appropriate for him to share a room with nine-year-old Florrie, so they would have to forego having a separate parlour or sitting room downstairs. Instead, the ground-floor front room would be Ned's bedroom; they would live in the large kitchen with separate scullery and an outhouse lavatory in the backyard; Florrie would have her own bedroom upstairs, next to her parents' room. Until things improved, they would just have to manage. Joseph gave them good prices to furnish the new house with everything they needed, from a double brass bed for the grown-ups to the smallest teaspoon for the kitchen. He would have given them everything gratis, but Edward would not hear of it – he was grateful for his friend's help but would not accept charity and insisted on paying his way.

Florence set to making clothing for her family; she bought bolts of cloth from the market and made everything from suits and workwear for Edward and Ned, dresses for herself and Florrie, right down to shirts and underwear. They may not have much, but she was determined that her family would look presentable. As she cut and sewed, she started to teach little Florrie, who occupied herself hemming and embroidering handkerchiefs for the family.

Though the cinema entranced him even at 14, Ned thought it unlikely he could make a living in that way. He decided that he was grown up enough to leave school and get an apprenticeship to contribute to the family finances. Thus began his career as an electrician. Edward was quietly disappointed – he had wanted his firstborn son to have opportunities, an education and perhaps even entry to a university where he could become a professional in law or medicine. But as things were for the family, it was certainly more practical for Ned to start his working life, and Edward supported Ned in his choices. Electricity was a new and exciting field; the talk was that eventually, all houses would have electric power, and a good electrician would always find work, even one trained in a shipyard.

As anticipated, when it arrived, the insurance pay-out was not sufficient to set up in business again from scratch. Although the Parsons were living in their own home by then, Edward had some decisions to make. The money would not last long with his growing family, even though Ned was paying into the family finances. Edward decided to accept Joseph's offer of a job – at least there would be a weekly wage coming in.

If they managed to save enough, perhaps eventually he might be able to go into trade for himself again, but that would not be for the foreseeable future, especially with a war currently going on. Edward quickly became adept at estimating prices on all sorts of household goods, not only glassware and ceramics, and soon became part of Joseph's trusted team of employees. Life moved on, and compared to those poor men fighting at the Front in France and Belgium, they all had a great deal to be thankful for.

CHAPTER FOUR 1914

13-year-old Grace burst through the back door into the kitchen of 24 Delhi Street and went to her mother, sitting in her usual chair by the side of the kitchen range. The fire was getting low, so Grace lifted the brass scuttle and poured on a few nuggets of coal. Even though it was midsummer, the fire was the only source of cooking in the house, and because Kate's health had been delicate, even though it was improving, she still felt the cold somewhat.

"Thank you, love." Kate could see from her daughter's shining eyes that she had some news to impart. "Now, what's all the excitement about?"

Since the difficult birth of Prue, it had taken four years for Kate to start feeling stronger, and at last, she was on the mend. She was still very much reliant on Grace, but she hoped as time went on, she would get back to normal and once again be able to take over the reins of running her household. Kate still felt guilty that her eldest daughter had missed out on so much of her childhood and schooling to take charge of the house and family. But Kate was proud of Grace; the girl had never complained about her responsibilities and undertook each new challenge with a cheerful and competent attitude.

She was almost breathless with excitement. "Mam, I heard they're taking on girls in Vickers to work in the airship hangar, sewing the fabric that covers the airships! I want to go and see if I can get a job! Is it all right? Do you think our Dad will let me?"

"Oh, Grace, love! Don't you think you're a bit young to go out working? And I still need you here to help with the housework and the children until I'm properly better. How would I manage without you?"

"I know, but I'm nearly 14, and our Charlie started working with Dad when he was that age!" Grace pleaded, "Please, Mam, let me go and see if they'll take me on at least? Our Faith is eleven now, she can do some of the chores I do, and Joy and Freddie are big enough to help out more. Please, Mam? Think of the money I could earn!"

She had been practically running their home for so long and asked for so little in return that Kate was reluctant to refuse her request, "Let's wait and ask your dad; see what he says. Will that do for now?"

Grace bent and kissed her mother's cheek, "Thanks, Mam! I'd better get the tea served up, the kids have been home from school for a while, and they'll be starving, no doubt." She had set a big pot of stew to cook slowly in the range oven earlier that day, so a delicious aroma wafted around the kitchen when she opened the oven door. She got a spoon and scooped out a chunk of carrot to taste. "Hmm, a bit more salt, I think, then it's ready. Do you want yours yet, Mam?"

"No, love, I'm not very hungry yet," Kate replied, "I'll wait till Dad gets in."

Grace set the lid back on the pot and pushed it back into the oven. She set the big kitchen table with seven places and sliced up a large loaf freshly baked that morning. "I'll bring the kids in for theirs, and then they can go back out to play for a bit so you, Dad and Charlie can have yours in peace." She went to the back door, stepped outside and shouted, "Faith, Joy, Freddie! Bring your sisters and come and get your tea!"

Before long, the young rabble had gathered in the kitchen, noisy and hungry. Grace sat at the head of the table after settling little Prudence in the seat next to her. Prue, at four, was too big for a high chair but just too small to reach the table without being propped up on cushions. Grace ladled the stew out into bowls, which the children passed around until everyone had one. They each grabbed a slice of bread and tucked into their meal. Grace had made sure to leave plenty of meat and vegetables in the pot to ensure her father and brother came home to a hearty meal.

First to finish was Freddie, "Is there any more?" As a healthy growing boy of seven, Freddie was always hungry.

"Not yet," replied Grace, "you'll have to see what's left when Dad and Charlie have had theirs. You can take another slice of bread if you're still hungry."

"That'll do! Can I have some butter or jam?"

"Give it here; I'll dip it in my gravy for you," his big sister took the slice and passed it back, dripping slightly. "Put your hand underneath it, Freddie! I don't want it dripping on the tablecloth and leaving a mess for Dad to sit down to!"

Within seconds, Freddie had wolfed down the bread and said, "I'm finished! Can I go back out to play?"

"What do you say first?" Her mother had taught Grace to be a stickler for manners.

"Please may I leave the table?" he responded.

"Yes, you may."

One by one, his sisters finished their meal and asked permission to get down from the table. Grace assented each time and finally lifted Prue down from her perch. The little one ran outside to catch up with her siblings. Kate had been watching all this and smiled at her daughter, "You've trained them well, Grace. They're such well-behaved children!"

Grace laughed, "It's a good job you don't see what they get up to while they're out playing, or you wouldn't say that, Mam!"

She cleared the table, reset it with three places, and then set to work washing up the dirty bowls and spoons in the big Belfast sink. She refilled the kettle and set it back over the fire so the water would be good and hot for her dad to have a wash and shave before eating, and Charlie too, who was an apprentice brass-moulder with his dad. Theirs was a hard and dirty job in the Vickers foundry; their faces and upper bodies were always caked in dirt and sweat when they got home.

After his meal, Charlie would be off out to his St John's Ambulance Brigade that evening. He was doing very well with them and had just got his Ambulance First Aid Certificate. He was also a member of the Vickers' Ambulance unit, and he would be expected to go out with the Ambulance should any incidents require first-aid treatment. It was not something that appealed to Grace, but Charlie seemed to enjoy it.

Grace waited until her father washed, fed and settled down for the evening before she looked at her mother, her eyebrows raised quizzically. It was a quiet moment; the children were still out playing as dusk was yet to fall, then they would all be inside, raising the roof as usual. Kate nodded her agreement at Grace; she thought it was a good moment.

"Dad," said Grace, "I have something to ask you."

"Yes, love, what is it?" Like Kate, Albert appreciated everything Grace had done in the last few years with little reward, so he was open to any reasonable request.

"I heard that they're taking on girls to work in Vickers' airship hangar, sewing the covering fabric, and I wondered if you would let me try for a job."

"A job? You're only 13, lass! That's a bit young for going out to work, isn't it? And what about the house and your mam – you're needed here more." He knocked the ash out of his pipe on the fender, pulled his tobacco pouch out of his pocket, then started to refill the pipe.

"Oh please, Dad! I'm fourteen in October, and our Charlie started work at that age! And as for the house, our Faith and Joy and even our Freddie are old enough to help out a lot more. And Mam is starting to feel stronger now. Please, Dad, at least let me try for a job? I'll be bringing a wage in, and that will surely help?" Grace pleaded.

"What do you think, Mother?" Albert looked at his wife, "Should we let her have a go?"

"It's all right with me, if you think so, Albert. I am starting to feel stronger, and the younger ones are not so little; we should manage between us. And the money would certainly be helpful."

"I'll tell you what. I'm going to take your mam to see the family in Hull come the shipyard holidays, so you and Charlie will be here looking after the rest of the bairns. When we get back, you can see if they're still looking and apply then. Does that sound fair?" Albert smiled.

Grace threw her arms around her father's neck in a huge hug, "Aww thanks, Dad, yes, that's grand!"

Kate was also pleasantly surprised. "A visit to the family? What a lovely idea. It's been so long since we've seen them."

"Aye, well, I think we'd better go soon because it might be a while before we get another chance. The papers are all talking about War, and it looks like it might be happening soon." Albert shook his head grimly.

Kate looked horrified, "You won't have to go and fight, will you, Bertie?"

"No, love, don't you worry about that! I'm too old for a start; they'll be taking the young single men first. Besides, I think as a foreman moulder, my job will be classified as a reserved occupation because they'll be wanting us to build new warships as quickly as we can."

Grace asked, "What about Charlie? He's too young to be taken, isn't he? And if he works with you, he won't have to go, will he, Dad?"

"No, he's far too young to be called up, so don't worry your head. They reckon it'll be over by Christmas anyway, so it will all be finished before Charlie gets to the age for conscription." Albert looked at his pocket watch, "Well, time's getting on. I think I'll just go for a last pint at the King Alfred before bed. Don't wait up for me, Katie; you need your rest. You're looking right well, lately; I'm glad you're starting to feel a bit better. It's about time you got the children in, our Gracie; it's starting to get dark!"

As Albert kissed his wife goodnight, Grace scurried out to the backyard door shouting for the children to come in, and in short order, had them all washed and ready for bed. "Off you go, you lot! Kiss your mam goodnight and get up those stairs, no messing about!"

Connie tugged at her big sister's sleeve, "Can we have a story tonight, Grace?"

"Perhaps, if you're all good. Go on; I'll be up in a bit to tuck you all in."

When the children were asleep, Grace came back to join her mother at the fireside. "It'll be nice for you and Dad to get away for a bit, eh Mam? We haven't seen any of the Hull relatives since Grandpa Turner walked all the way here from Hull to find work a few years ago. All that way, then he ended up driving the biggest crane in Vickers before deciding he'd had enough and disappearing again! It was nearly a week before we heard he was back in Hull! Do you remember?" They both laughed.

"Aye," said her mother, "he always was a character, your grandpa! Now, then, about us going away. I think we'll take the three littlest ones with us. The twins are six, and Prue is old enough to behave without being too much work. It will be a bit less responsibility for you and Charlie if there are only five of you to bother about."

"You can leave them all for me, Mam, but just as you like, if it makes you feel better. We'll be all right – Charlie is 15 and sensible enough. We'll manage just fine, don't you worry."

A few weeks later, the last week in July, Kate and Albert were ready for their visit to Hull with the three youngest children, Hope, Connie, and Prue. All dressed in their best, Albert ushered them all out of the door as Kate issued last-minute instructions. "Come on, woman! We'll miss the tram, and if we do, we'll miss the train an' all!" he urged.

"Yes, I'm coming, Bertie! Children, go with your dad. Grace, Charlie, you should have plenty of money there for the time we're away; be sure not to spend it all the first few days! And if you should run out, tell Mr Clarke at the grocers to put whatever you need on my account, and I'll sort it out when I come back. Right, yes, I'm coming, Bert! Goodbye, children, be sure to do what Charlie and Grace tell you!"

The remaining children followed out into the street to wave off their parents and sisters. "Right, our Grace, what are we having for dinner? Set to, there's a good girl!" said Charlie, once they went back indoors. He sat in his father's chair and made to put his feet up on the fender, only to have them brusquely knocked away by his sister.

"Let's get something straight, right now, Charlie Tunstall! You needn't think you're going to Lord it over the rest of us, bossing us around while Mam and Dad are gone! They left both of us in charge, and you are not the boss of me! We'll eat when it's ready, not before, so you can get that idea out of your head. You can make yourself useful, take our Freddie and go to the allotment to fetch some vegetables. When I've got them back here, I'll start thinking about cooking when I'm good and ready!" Grace stood over him, threateningly.

Charlie had the grace to look abashed, "All right, all right Gracie, keep your hair on! Come on, Freddie, let's go and see what we can find."

Freddie looked at his brother, "By 'eck Charlie, our Grace is going to make a wonderful wife someday; she's got the nagging sorted already!" He ducked, laughing, just in time to miss Grace's outstretched hand moving to slap him, and ran out with Charlie following. Grace sniggered to herself; Freddie was a cheeky monkey, but you couldn't help but laugh at him.

All was proceeding nicely for the first few days with no accidents or dramas when the news came in that War had finally been declared. Grace was worried, but Charlie told her not to be scared; nothing would happen in the first couple of weeks, and Mam and Dad would be back before anything serious occurred. She took some reassurance from that; after all, her parents had already got their return tickets booked, they wouldn't be able to change them without spending a fortune, which, if Charlie were right, would be unnecessary.

She soon came across the greatest difficulty that she would have to face. When shopping at Clarke's grocery and greengrocers, she discovered that the stock prices had doubled overnight. When she asked why she was told, 'There's a war on, you know! Things are going to get scarce, and when that happens, prices always go up."

Grace tried to argue, "but this is stock you already had, bought in at the usual prices! There are no scarcities yet, so why have prices gone up already?"

"That's just the way it is. You can always shop elsewhere," came the reply. The prospect of walking further to other shops on Walney or taking a tram into town then having to carry heavy shopping back home was not one she wished to contemplate, so she bought only the absolute necessities. At this rate, no matter how much she scrimped, the money would be gone in a week!

Grace was right; the money ran out long before her parents were due back, so she had Charlie and Freddie bringing home as much veg as they could dig up, and anything else had to go on the account. She dreaded to think what her mother would say and felt guilty, even knowing it wasn't her fault. When Kate and Albert returned, Grace shamefacedly reported what had happened. Her dad gave her a big bear hug and resolved to go and sort Mr Clarke out, man to man. His wife disagreed. She said this was a serious case of fraud, and she would report it, which she duly did, to the local police officer, PC Morris, who then visited Mr Clarke unofficially. Mr Clarke agreed to make reparations and promised not to take advantage again, on pain of having his crimes made official and the penalty more severe.

'That's that sorted,' thought Kate, 'now we only have to deal with the War.'

CHAPTER FIVE 1914

True to his word, Albert allowed Grace to inquire about going to work in Vickers. Many of the shipyard workers had already enlisted into the military, and numerous women were recruited to fill their jobs, so it was a foregone conclusion that Grace would be taken on. However, her father stipulated that she could only accept employment in the Airship division where she would be safe. At nearly fourteen, she was far too young to work in the munitions section, which was growing apace, nor did he want her welding or riveting, or any of the hard physical trades; sewing airship fabric would be a much safer option.

Grace rushed into the house; ignoring her siblings' clamour, she flung her arms around Kate and said, "I start on Monday, Mam! They said I could join the girls in the Airship Hangar at half-past seven, and they'll give me some training so I can start work proper on Tuesday. It's shift work, but I'll first be on days because of my age. When I turn 16, I'll have to do nights as well. But that's two years off yet - hopefully, the War will be over long before then!"

Kate laughed, "I never saw anyone so happy to start working! It will be hard work, you know, and you'll have to do as your told. You won't be in charge like you are here, lording it over the little 'uns!"

"I know, Mam, but I feel like I'll be making a difference, doing something worthwhile for the war effort. And I'll be getting paid too! They're paying 11/6 a week; just think what we can do with all that extra money!"

"How many hours do you have to do for that?" Kate asked.

"Only 54; nine hours a day, six days a week," Grace replied.

"Only? You say only? That's almost as many as your dad! And you just a slip of a girl. I'm not sure this is such a good idea, Gracie. I'm having second thoughts about letting you do it." Kate shook her head doubtfully.

"Oh, Mam! You can't change your mind! Please let me give it a try? If it turns out too much for me, I'll pack it in, I promise, but you've got to let me try at least?" Grace pleaded.

She seemed to have her heart set on it, so Kate shook her head and sighed, "Oh, all right then! But I'll be keeping an eye on you!"

"Thanks, Mam, you won't regret it, I promise!"

"We'll see about that!" her mother sighed.

On Monday morning at seven o'clock, Grace was already at the Works' Gate at Cavendish Dock, asking at the gatehouse where she should report to for her first day. Following the man's directions, she found herself in a vast hangar and stood bewildered, looking about her at the sheer size and scale of the place. As she was trying to take it all in, a group of girls walked by, heading towards the middle of the hangar. One of them noticed the young girl looking lost.

"You a new starter, are you, love?" the girl called to Grace.

"Aye, that's right. The man on the gate told me to report here but didn't say where exactly. I thought I'd find it easily, but I never expected anything like this!" Grace's eyes were like saucers behind her glasses, wide with amazement.

"Come along with us, love; we'll see you right. My name's Flo, what's yours? You're only a bit of a kid. How old are you?" she smiled.

"I'm Grace, and I'll be fourteen in October."

"Just a babe in arms! Well, don't worry, Gracie, your Auntie Flo here will show you the ropes all right. First things first, let's get a cuppa before the Dragon arrives!" Flo linked arms with Grace and drew her to an alcove where there was a canteen of sorts.

"Who's The Dragon?" asked Grace, soon cradling a mug of hot tea.

"Take no notice of Flo," another girl leant over and helped herself to a biscuit from a big tin, "I'm June, by the way! The Dragon is Mrs Simpson, our supervisor here at work, and she's our housemother at the hostel. She's a bit overbearing, but if you behave well, she's all right. It's just that Flo misbehaves and gets the sharp end of her tongue."

Grace was full of questions, "What's the hostel? What is it that Flo does to get told off? Why…"

But there was no time for answers. The gaggle of girls fell suddenly silent as a middle-aged woman in a tweed suit walked towards them, "That's enough chatter ladies, finish your tea and get to work. Who are you?" her beady eye fell on Grace.

"Grace Tunstall, Missus. I was told to start today." Grace held the older woman's gaze, confident but not defiant, as she didn't want to be seen as a child but also knew those first impressions were important.

"Well, Miss Tunstall, no one told me you were joining us today. Miss Taylor, would you take this young lady under your wing for the time being. Sort her out with a place and a machine; show her where everything is. In the meantime, I will attempt to find some lodgings for you, though goodness knows where; the hostel is already completely full!"

Grace raised her hand. "Excuse me, Mrs Simpson, but I don't need lodgings. I live on Walney with my family."

The relief on the older woman's face was palpable, "Thank heavens for small mercies! Good, well, you do as June shows you. I'm sure you'll soon settle in."

By the end of the first day, Grace was tired. They'd finished their shift at five-thirty, and she was feeling marginally less confused but still overwhelmed by the vastness of her surroundings. When the airship was built, it would just about fill the hangar, but the project's enormity was beyond her imagination.

She'd enjoyed herself though; the girls seemed nice and friendly. When they'd had their breaks for dinner and tea, they all seemed interested in her. She'd found out that 'The Hostel' Mrs Simpson had spoken about was a large building up at West Shore, nicknamed the Manx Hostel. It was so named because it housed over a hundred girls brought over from the Isle of Man to work on the coverings for the Airships. It would be months before they went home, but the money was good for a woman's pay, and they were doing this for their families. Most of them had left family behind and missed them.

When Grace got home, Kate had already prepared the very welcome evening meal. It seemed a long time since the half-hour dinner break and the dripping sandwich from yesterday's roast beef. The girl had wanted to wait and eat with her father and brother, but as her head drooped, Kate suggested she eat first then go and lie down; she could always see the family later. Grace accepted the suggestion and gratefully sank into the big double bed that she would share later with two of her sisters. In a few moments, she was fast asleep.

CHAPTER SIX 1915

Like most families, much of their day-to-day existence was mundane; each day was the same - just normal family life, but there was some drama in ensuing months when a series of incidents relieved the boredom.

The first was a fire on the *SS Vedra*, an oil tanker currently in port in Barrow. As a St John's First Aider, Charlie went aboard the tug, *Cartmel*, which went out to the ship to see if they could offer any assistance. Unfortunately, out of a crew of 38, there was only one survivor; he was one of three men who jumped ship and tried to swim through the flaming oil. The man was so traumatised he never spoke again, though he lived the rest of his life in Barrow. Afterwards, back at home, Charlie didn't say very much about the incident; he was very quiet for some time.

His father took him to one side and asked if he was all right and wanted to continue in the Ambulance Service. "No one would blame you if you'd found this too much, Charlie. It's a terrible thing for a young lad such as you to deal with."

But Charlie was resolute; "On the contrary, Dad, it's made me even more determined to help in these situations. I feel like I'm doing something worthwhile."

Albert had never been more proud of his eldest son.

Not long afterwards, the family gathered for their evening meal, but Charlie was missing. Kate began to worry; it was not like her son to miss out on food. "Where on earth can he be?" she asked no one in particular.

Grace said, "I know he was doing a shift at Fort Walney for the St John's. Maybe there was an accident, and he's stayed behind?"

At the head of the table, Albert decided, "No point in letting good food get cold. Serve it up, Katie, but save him some. I daresay he'll be famished when he gets home."

"But what if something's happened to him?" asked Kate, her imagination giving rise to some awful predicament.

"If he's hurt or in trouble, we'll hear soon enough about it, love. Let's just wait and see before we start imagining the worst, eh?" said her husband.

By the time Charlie got home, it was just about time for bed, all the children upstairs already. Kate was pacing the floor, unable to sit quietly until she knew what had happened to her firstborn. As he came through the back door, she almost flung herself upon him, trying to find out if he was hurt.

"It's all right, Mam; I'm not hurt or anything. I've just had a bit of an experience, that's all." He hugged Kate and ushered her to her chair. "Is there anything left to eat? I'm starving!"

"Grace, warm the stew up for your brother while he tells us his tale," Albert said, lighting up a cigarette with a taper from the fire. "Go on then, Son, tell us what happened?"

His eyes shining with excitement, Charlie sat at the table to wait for his sister to serve his dinner, "You'll never believe what happened to me! I'd finished my shift at the Fort and was coming home over the fields. I saw a few mushrooms, so I was bobbing about all over the place collecting them when suddenly this soldier was standing over me pointing a rifle and telling me to put my hands up or he'd shoot!"

As Grace put a steaming bowl in front of him, he lifted his spoon but didn't get it as far as his mouth in his urgency to tell the story, "He thought I was a German spy! He didn't believe me when I explained why I was there, and he and his squad marched me back to the Fort. They locked me up in this little room with bars on the windows and a guard outside the door. I had to wait there for ages until somebody came and took me to the CO's office. The CO and a sergeant were questioning me, trying to catch me out in a lie, but obviously, they couldn't because I was telling the truth! In the end, they sent for the St John's shift supervisor to vouch for me, which he did, so they let me go and here I am! I won't be stopping to collect mushrooms again, that's for sure!" He was laughing, but Albert could see that the episode had shaken him up.

Grace had only been working in the airship shed for a few months when a strange incident brought some drama. She and her colleagues had moved from the hangar on Cavendish Dock to a new, larger site built on Walney. It was not far from West

Shore, where they were building a new airship design. One of the new design innovators was Barnes Wallis, then a Sub-lieutenant in the Royal Naval Air Service and later famed for inventing the 'Bouncing Bomb' used in WW2 in the 'Dambusters' raids in Germany.

Although the airship design was different, the materials covering it were the same, so Grace's job had hardly changed. She enjoyed the banter with the other girls and had made some good friends. She was happy in her work, a world away from the domestic drudgery at home. While she loved her family and would do anything for them, the endless housework and chores had bored her, so she was glad to have the opportunity of trying something different.

She was not so keen though, in the New Year. On 29th January, a submarine was sighted just off the coast at West Shore. It was not unusual, as Vickers built many submarines, but it always created some excitement to see the result of the worker's labours at Vickers. A couple of the girls on a tea break had seen the sub and told their friends about it when they went back into the hangar.

Shortly afterwards, the girls were surprised to hear several explosions which sounded very close to their workplace. Thinking it was an Invasion Drill, the girls left their workstations in the shed and went to their shelter. They heard several larger bursts, and then, to their surprise, they heard answering gunfire which appeared to come from Fort Walney. The barrage did not last for long, but it was only later when they emerged from the shelter, they found that it had been a real attack – the submarine was German U-boat 21 that had been attempting to blow up the airshed but had fortunately fallen short of their target.

Rumour had it that the U-boat was sunk, but a few days later, there were reports of several attacks further up the coast and some shipping casualties attributed to U-21. It was the closest Grace had ever come to danger, but when she excitedly told the tale to her family, it became just another worry for Kate that one of her children might be injured in this war.

The St John's Brigade had been asked to provide trained volunteers to join the Royal Army Medical Corps, and Charlie was desperate to go. As soon as Charlie turned 16, he asked his superiors at St John's Ambulance if they could arrange for him to go overseas to join the battlefront. However, they turned him down as too young; they would not accept volunteers under eighteen, which greatly relieved his mother and eldest sister.

"It's just not fair!" Charlie exclaimed, "I want to get out there and see some action. By the time I'm 18, it will be all over."

"Aww, Charlie, don't take on so," responded his mother. "I know you're keen for the adventure and excitement, but I'm glad they've turned you down. I know we're all supposed to be patriotic and be happy to send all our menfolk away, but I would not be happy to think of either you or your dad on some terrible battlefield somewhere. I'm glad you're too young, and he's too old! Maybe that's selfish of me, but I can't help it."

Kate had got herself into quite a state over the mere thought of it, but Grace agreed with her. "I'm glad too, Mam! I couldn't bear it if anything happened to any one of you!" She put her arms around her mother to comfort her.

"It makes no sense!" spluttered Charlie, "there's my dad and me, both strong and able-bodied, yet the only one doing anything for the war effort is my little sister! It's just not right, I tell you!"

Albert caught the end of this tirade as he came into the room. "Now then, Charlie, calm yourself." He put his hand on the boy's shoulder, "I know how you feel; with some of the men we work with already gone to War. That they were already in camp with the territorials when war was declared was their good fortune, if you see it that way. But you have to think of it, that we at home are already doing our bit too – if we're not there to build the submarines and warships and make the munitions, England has no chance of winning against the Germans. The brave men in the trenches and the Navy couldn't possibly fight without us. So don't think of it as doing nothing. We're the backbone of England and are as necessary to the fight as an active soldier or sailor."

Subdued, Charlie ruefully acknowledged that his father was right. Working in the foundry was essential war work, after all.

"Besides," Albert continued, "They're bringing some lads back from the front because of the lack of skilled men in the Yard. So even if you'd gone, you'd probably have been brought back anyway."

A little later, after the family meal, when the younger children were in bed, Kate, Albert, Charlie and Grace spent a quiet evening together. Albert, his feet up on the fender as he smoked and read the local paper, suddenly let out a hoot of laughter. "Hey Charlie, you were right! It seems that women are getting stuck into the action. Listen to this!"

He sat forward in his chair and read aloud, "It says here that a woman disguised herself as a man by cropping her hair, wearing men's clothes and a false moustache and got herself taken on as a labourer in Vickers' timber yard. She worked there for nearly three days before anyone became suspicious. It seems she's twice been widowed, and apart from being patriotic, she needed the money to take care of her family. She's quoted as saying that she would go up in an airship and bomb the Kaiser herself if she could!"

Kate looked aghast. "That poor woman! Fancy being driven to do something like that to look after your family. She must be so brave."

Albert realised that perhaps the story wasn't quite so funny after all. He would hate for his Katie to be in such desperate straits that she would have to do such a thing. He continued, "Fair play to the woman; she lasted for two full days before being found out. She'd worked from six o'clock in the morning on both days and did overtime till 8.20 pm on the first day and until 5.00 pm on the second before they stopped her. It was no easy job either; she was lifting heavy timber all day with a gang of men. I have to say I admire her guts, if nothing else."

Grace, who had been listening quietly to her father, chose this moment to pipe up, "While we're on the subject of women working, Dad, there are going to be some changes at work for me too. They will be moving the airship operation up to Flookburgh before long because the sheds here aren't big enough for the new design they want to work on. It won't be for a while yet, months probably, but they've said I have a choice about what I do. I can move up to Flookburgh to work, which means living in a hostel with the other girls. Or I can stay here and move into munitions. What do you think I should do?"

There was a silence in the room as her family took in the news. Charlie was the first to break it, "I don't think you should do either one! You're not sixteen yet, and too young to work in munitions. It's too dangerous! Just give up and stay at home."

"I'm not asking you, Charlie!" Grace turned on her big brother. "You're a fine one to talk about doing dangerous stuff! Not five minutes ago, you wanted to go off to the front with the RAMC! You're only a year older than me, so what's the difference?"

"The difference is that you're only a girl," Charlie retorted. "You're not meant to be working like that."

"Stuff and nonsense!" Grace fired back, "I wouldn't be doing anything thousands of other girls aren't doing. Why should it only be men who get to do anything for the war effort? Women are doing all sorts of things they didn't used to, now that there are so many men away fighting."

"That's enough, both of you," Albert stepped in to stop it from developing into a full-blown argument. "Charlie, Grace is quite right; women are doing more than they've ever done before while their menfolk are away. It's something to be proud of, not to denigrate. But Grace, munitions? If it's a choice between the two, I'd rather know that you were safe in Flookburgh. What do you think, Kate?"

Kate wiped away tears that had formed before they could spill down her cheeks. "I don't know what to think yet. I kind of agree with Charlie; neither option is one that I would choose for my girl. Grace, I think your dad and I need to talk a lot more about this before we make a decision."

"I understand, Mam, and of course, I'll do whatever you both agree on. But I don't want to stop working. And if my choice holds any sway, I'd rather work on munitions and come home to my family every day rather than live up the coast and not see you. I think I'll go to bed. Good night, all." Grace kissed her parents and punched Charlie's shoulder before going upstairs.

"You're not going to let her do it, are you, Dad?" Charlie rubbed his shoulder; Grace could pack quite a punch when she wanted!

"She has a point, Son. England will not win this war unless we all pull together and do our bit. Grace and all the others like her will be hard-pressed to join and do whatever they can. It's not as if they can go to the Front and fight, is it? Yes, I'd rather she sat at home and knitted socks, like your Mam here, but Grace is a strong, healthy, intelligent girl who feels like she is playing her part to help win this awful war. I can't take that away from her any more than I can stop you from wanting to go and fight. You're both cut from the same cloth, strong and brave, and I'm proud of you both. I think it's time we all went to bed; it's a working day tomorrow!"

Albert and Kate talked long into the night; both realised that their loyal, dependable daughter had a greater use than tending to family responsibilities. They decided that Grace could choose which action she would take; either would have their support.

Grace was up first the next morning; by the time the others rose, she had started breakfast and made lunches for herself, father and brother to take to their days' labours.

Spooning porridge into bowls, making sure to leave enough for the little ones when they got up for school, Grace sat at the kitchen table, an expectant look on her face. As Albert took his seat at the head of the table, she looked at him, "Well, Dad? Have you made a decision yet?"

"Aye, love. Your mam and I have decided that you can choose what you want to do. Neither of us is happy that you have to make such a choice, but whatever you decide, you have our blessing."

Grace's grin stretched from ear to ear, "Oh, thank you, Dad! You won't regret it, I promise!"

"Go and take your mam a cup of tea before she gets the children up, will you? Let her have 10 minutes peace." As Grace sped up the stairs, he watched after her and said to himself, "I hope not, my girl, I hope not."

CHAPTER SEVEN 1916

Grace moved into the munitions shop to begin work, as she'd chosen. She got home after the first day, still bewildered at the changes in her environment. Albert and Charlie weren't yet home from work, so she tried to explain what the job was like to her mother. "Everywhere you're surrounded by the appalling din of machinery; there are so many lathes running, you can barely hear yourself think! It's pointless trying to talk because unless you shout at the top of your voice, no one can hear you."

Grace's eyes shone with excitement as she continued, "And wherever you look, all around you are shells. Some are complete, waiting to be loaded onto trucks that take them away for shipment; others are rough turned, waiting to be finished and yet more, rows and rows and rows of them waiting to be filled, which is what I'm going to do. There are loads of us girls in our overalls and caps. It's very strange to be wearing trousers, but I've sort of got used to them, and they're quite comfortable. But we're not allowed to have any metal on us in the shop. No brooches or fasteners, even hairpins aren't allowed. Any spark could cause an explosion, so we have to be really careful."

She stopped to take a breath and realised that her mother looked horrified. "Of course, it sounds much worse than it is, honestly, Mam! I'm just trying to get you to understand that they have all sorts of rules and regulations to keep us safe! For example, there's no smoking allowed, not even outside the shed. Anyone caught with matches is subject to a hefty fine or even dismissal. Someone told us that one girl was caught when a match fell out of her pocket; she wasn't only fined, they sent her to prison! Not that I would do anything like that because I don't smoke, but some of the girls do. They were moaning about having to leave their cigarettes and matches in their lockers."

"It all sounds very dangerous to me, love," said Kate, "Are you sure you want to work there? Do you have to work shifts?"

"Yes, the shell shop works 24 hours a day, so there are three shifts; from 6:30 am to 2:30 pm, 2:30 to 10:30 pm and 10:30 pm to 6:30 am; we change shifts every week. We're lucky here because our shifts are only eight hours – I've heard they do a 12-hour shift in some factories! Though until I'm 18, I don't have to do nightshifts, which I'm glad of! We have three weeks of training on the early shift; after that, I'll be on both day shifts."

Kate shook her head, "That sounds like a lot of very hard work, Grace. Are you sure it's what you want to do? I'm sure there's plenty of other work you could do that isn't so dangerous!"

"Mam, I'm happy to do it! If I were a boy, I'd be just like our Charlie, dying to get away to the front line to fight! But that's never going to happen. So, I'm doing my bit in a way that I know will help our boys over there."

"Well, I'm very proud of you, love. I'm scared to death something dreadful might happen to you, but I'm so proud too." Kate put her arms around her daughter and squeezed hard. It was hard to believe her precious baby girl was a working woman doing the same work that men had previously only done. It seemed a far cry from sewing in the Airship hangar, much more dangerous, and Kate couldn't help but worry.

Grace returned her embrace, "You don't need to worry about me, Mam, I'll be all right. I'll make sure that I wear the masks and gloves they give us. They use stuff to fill the shells, a new explosive called TNT. It can make your skin turn bright yellow, and you can't wash it off. That's why they call us 'Canaries', but mostly we're called 'Munitionettes'. I do have to warn you, and again, you're not to worry if it happens, but I might turn yellow! But once you're off the production line for a while, you go back to normal."

Kate begged, "Please, Grace, don't tell me anything more! I'm worried enough about you, but each time you tell me something new, it makes things much worse!"

Grace laughed, "All right, Mam, I'll say no more for now. The one good thing you won't mind is that the money's much better than when I was on airship work! I can earn up to a whole pound a week once I'm trained! You'll be able to put my board up a bit; that'll be good, won't it?"

"Yes, love, it will," Kate smiled. Little did her daughter know that the weekly contribution she made to the housekeeping was being put aside as a nest egg which hopefully one day would pay for Grace's wedding if and when she met someone special. She was far too young yet, of course, to be thinking about marriage and children, certainly, while she was working for the war effort. But it was something that might happen in a far-distant future.

Kate had been 28 before she married Albert, so Grace, at only fifteen, had plenty of time ahead of her before she needed to think about that.

Little did Kate know that Grace was indeed starting to think about her future. As the weeks passed, she found that she had a new sense of being. She was no longer just Albert's daughter or Charlie's sister; she was Grace Tunstall, a person in her own right. Working alongside other girls and women, some much older than her, she began to feel responsible for herself. Whilst it was true, she had still to do as her supervisors told her and follow the safety rules, she was doing so because she wanted to.

She was trusted to work in this highly dangerous environment without being watched every minute like a child. Her life depended on it, as well as those of her workmates – all looking out for each other. Not only that, the work was of vital importance to the war effort too. In the early days when the conflict had started, the army could not fight because of the shortage of armaments, so Grace was only too happy to put in the long hours and harsh conditions to help.

Despite the discomfort and danger, she enjoyed her work life; she was making friends with her colleagues. At first, just shyly watching and listening to the women talk during their rare breaks, but eventually joined in occasionally when she felt she had something worthwhile to add to the conversation. It was practically impossible to have a proper conversation while they worked; for a start, the noise of the machinery was so loud to hear without shouting, so they all gradually learned to lip read.

One slight slip and you could overfill the shell; or hit too hard with a hammer when damping down the chemicals in the shells, and it was easy to cause an explosion that might take off a few fingers or even a whole hand or worse! In any case, to keep safe, it took real concentration to carry out the work.

Much of the conversation, of course, revolved around men, or rather, the lack of them. Many of their loved ones – husbands, boyfriends, brothers, cousins and even fathers – were at the front, fighting for King and Country in the trenches of the Somme. But although the women were missing their menfolk, or at least most of them were, it didn't prevent them from having fun, socialising, entertaining each other. There was great camaraderie between the girls.

Grace had never had many friends; she had been too busy with her household responsibilities whilst her mother was frail, so she had not had the carefree childhood enjoyed by her siblings. Her schooling had been sporadic at best, so her friends had been few, though those she did have were close. Most of the girls she knew were working; they were in all sorts of jobs that would have been unthinkable before the war. Ideally, a woman's place was in the home, caring for her family and home. That was how it had always been.

But this was a different situation. So many young men had gone to war this time – thousands and thousands of them – and someone had to keep things going. So, the women stepped in, doing work that they couldn't have dreamed of before. It was not unusual to see female postmen and tram drivers. Women were being trained as mechanical engineers to look after motors of all sorts which would have been unthinkable a few years before. There were female doctors, architects and scientists. Women were currently doing most of the unskilled work in Vickers.

It was natural that they should take the few rest hours they had and indulge in pleasures that had also been denied them in the past. There were even some women playing football against each other – several 'Munitionettes' teams in the North had formed a league and were having lots of fun, especially the team at the top of the league, "Dick Kerr's Ladies" from Preston. Those men still left at home thought it sacrilege at first, but if they wanted to follow their favourite sport, it was women or nothing, so it was gradually catching on.

That was not for Grace, though; she'd never been particularly sporty. She met with friends outside working hours to go to the many cinemas recently sprung up in Barrow. One of her favourites was the old Music Hall, 'The Star Varieties' in Forshaw Street, newly renamed the Tivoli. They still had the musical variety shows that she loved, and they also showed films. The girls liked to watch the Newsreels reporting back from the Front, some of them even searching the sea of soldiers' faces to see if they could spot their menfolk. Grace particularly loved the movies with Charlie Chaplin and Buster Keaton. It was something to raise their spirits and take her mind off the war.

Grace had arranged with Edna Fenton, a colleague, to go to the cinema one evening. Edna was very pretty but not very bright.

Grace was quite envious of Edna's looks, but she was such a lovely little thing, almost like one of her sisters, so Grace couldn't help but like her. Edna often attracted wolf-whistles from the men in the shipyard, even when dressed in overalls, hair tucked into their caps. Edna had quite an eye for the boys, and sometimes Grace had to keep reminding her friend to concentrate on her work instead of flirting. One wrong move could cause an explosion, so it was necessary to focus constantly.

Edna also lived on Walney, in Buller Street, so they arranged to meet outside the new Walney Theatre and Picture House on Natal Road to see the latest programme of newsreels and comedy films. The theatre had been built in 1915 with a proper stage so that live theatre could also be performed there. But most of Grace's friends and colleagues went for the cinema.

Edna was late; Grace had been waiting outside for her for what seemed like ages. When she did finally arrive, she was dressed as if for a dance, all made up and her hair styled into long ringlets that hung down her back. It didn't improve Grace's temper that she felt dowdy and frumpy, in an old dress and her wild hair pinned into submission. She'd thought her appearance wouldn't matter when they would just be sitting in the dark.

The auditorium was quite full, and the girls had to squeeze into two seats in the middle of a row to sit together. Somehow Edna managed to get seated next to a rather good-looking boy and a couple of his friends. Throughout the show, Edna and the boy were whispering loudly to each other to the annoyance of the audience sitting around them. Grace had become even more annoyed with her pal and had demonstrated her anger with a few choice digs to Edna's ribs with her elbow.

Towards the end of the programme, Edna suddenly turned and whispered in Grace's ear, "I need the lav! I'm going to see if I can get out past the rest of the row. Since it's nearly finished, I won't bother returning to my seat. I'll wait for you in the foyer." Grace nodded, grateful that her pal would no longer annoy the people nearby. There were mutters and grumbles as Edna moved along the row, but Grace was thankful that she was gone.

It was only when the credits rolled, and everyone stood to listen to the National Anthem before the lights went up, that Grace noticed that the boy who had been sitting next to Edna was no longer in his seat either. Embarrassed, she realised that the two of them must have sneaked off together for some canoodling. Nevertheless, Grace stood in the foyer as the crowds streamed out of the theatre into the night air, waiting to see if Edna would come back to meet her. Deep down, she knew she had seen the last of her so-called friend, but still, she waited until the last person had left the Auditorium. She wasn't quite sure if she should continue to wait – Edna and her beau could still be in the theatre somewhere for all she knew, hidden in some cupboard or storeroom. She didn't think that her friend would abandon her like that, to walk home alone.

She heard a door slam in the distance and voices – male voices – coming in her direction. Two men - well, one older man and a youth – came into view from around a corner, talking.

"You did well tonight, Ned. I'm going to be able to leave it all to you very soon," the older man said, patting the lad on the shoulder.

"Do you think so, Mr Blake? That would be grand! If you think I can handle it?"

The conversation stopped as they spotted Grace standing alone in the foyer. Mr Blake smiled, "Are you all right, Miss? You look a bit lost."

Grace felt foolish. Of course, Edna had gone and left her. She was an idiot for thinking otherwise. "I was waiting for my friend, but she seems to have left without me. I just wanted to be sure I hadn't missed her before I left, but I can see that she must have gone. I'm sorry, I'll go now." Blushing, Grace put on her coat and fastened it, heading for the door.

"It's Grace, isn't it? Grace Tunstall?" the lad said.

She turned back and looked at him, "Do I know you?"

"Oh, well, you probably don't remember me; it was a while ago. I'm Ned Parsons; we were at Thwaite Street School together a few years ago."

"The name sounds familiar, but I'm sorry, I don't recognise you," she said, embarrassed.

"That's all right – I'm instantly forgettable!" Ned laughed. "Since your pal seems to have deserted you, can I see you home? A nice young lady like you shouldn't be walking out by herself at this time of night."

"No, it's all right. I don't live far, just in Delhi Street."

"What a coincidence! I live in Liverpool Street, so we're going the same way. Is it all right if I walk with you?"

Grace gave in. It would be churlish to refuse. Anyway, he was more or less an old schoolmate, so it might be nice to have company on the walk home. "All right," she agreed, "we might as well walk together."

Ned said his goodbyes to Mr Blake and held open the outer door for Grace. She did not notice the wink the two men swapped before the door closed.

The walk home was pleasant enough. Ned was quiet and seemed a little shy, and she could tell he was trying to think of a topic of conversation. To help him out, she said, "Do you work at the cinema then?"

"Just as a hobby at the moment. I'm doing an apprenticeship in the Yard. When I finish, I'll be a fully qualified electrician. But it's the cinema I enjoy most. Mr Blake has taught me to be a projectionist, and I love it. Tonight, he even said I'm almost ready to take over the whole programme! At the moment, he lets me sort the reels into order ready to be fed into the projectors, and

I put the odd reel in the feed, maybe the newsreels, now and again." His eyes were shining with excitement as he spoke; she could see his enthusiasm.

Then he realised that he was hogging the conversation, so he asked Grace if she was working. "I seem to remember you weren't at school very much – I heard you had to help your mam because she wasn't well. Is that still the case?"

"No, Mam is much better, and the kids are older, so they do more around the house too. I've been working for a couple of years; at first, I worked on the airships, and now I'm in the munitions shop." She was quite proud to say she was helping the war effort.

"Is your friend a munitionette too? The one who left you behind tonight?" he asked.

"Edna? Yes, she's on the same line as me. We're not good friends; she's just someone I work with who was free to go the pictures tonight.

"You like the pictures then? Do you go often?" Ned asked.

"Oh yes, I love it. I can be transported right away with some of the stories. It must be wonderful to be an actress like that Mary Pickford. I think she's terrific. And I love Charlie Chaplin. He makes me laugh."

By this time, the pair had reached Delhi Street and stopped at the street corner. "Thank you for walking me home," said Grace, "it was nice having some company."

"Think nothing of it!" smiled Ned, "perhaps I'll see you next time you go to the pictures. I daresay I'll see you around."

Grace turned to walk up the street to her house, and Ned watched her go. Then he turned and walked back the way they had come. Ned had lied about his home; he lived in Thomas Street in Barrow town centre, but he wanted a chance to talk to her, to see if she was as nice as their schoolmates had said, those years ago at Thwaite Street. He was glad to find they were right.

He'd developed a crush on her back then but had been afraid to make it known to her in the playground. He knew she wasn't the prettiest of girls or the most popular, but there was something about her that he wanted to get to know. She was tall and skinny and a bit gangly and didn't seem to bother about her appearance much. Ned guessed that was probably down to being the eldest girl with loads of brothers and sisters to take care of.

Looks weren't an issue for him. He wasn't exactly Douglas Fairbanks himself! True, he was still only fifteen and had time to grow, but at the moment, he was short compared to his friends. He was also fairly stout, and he lamented that his hair was very fine, not thick and curly like girls admire; lads like Grace's older brother, Charlie! Charlie was how Ned wished he could be – clever, sporty, and up for any challenge. He was tall and athletic, always picked for team captains and such, whereas Ned stayed in the background, preferring books and films to sports.

Oh well, he could but try to get to know Grace. He would have to look out for her whenever he was at Walney Cinema. Maybe he could get to walk her home every time she came to a showing! With a smile on his face and a warm feeling inside, Ned made his way back to town and home.

CHAPTER EIGHT 1917

Charlie had been desperate to join up as soon as the War had started, but he was far too young at only 15 years old. When he turned 16, he had tried to go out and serve with St John's Ambulance but again had been rejected because of his age. He had thrown himself into his work in the shipyard and his duties as a first-aider ever since. Nevertheless, he still longed for the opportunity to fight for King and Country.

Even though Charlie's was a reserved occupation, he couldn't bear that people might think he lacked courage and did not want to fight. When reading the lists of casualties and deaths pinned up at the Town Hall, he felt as if he wasn't doing enough, as if he was a coward. He dreaded one day receiving a white feather – the accusatory sign of cowardice, given by some women to able-bodied young men who weren't in uniform, to shame them into doing their patriotic duty. Many of the men who worked in Vickers were not even allowed to join up. Britain was better served by them using their skills to manufacture warships, submarines, and munitions.

So, Charlie was delighted when he arrived home one day to find the brown envelope that had finally arrived – he had been awaiting it since his 18th birthday – his call to the colours and adventure was here at last! As she gave him the envelope, Kate was in tears, but Charlie didn't notice as he tore it open and read the contents. It was only as he whooped with joy and whirled his diminutive mother around the kitchen floor with glee that he saw that she was crying.

He put her down gently – it was funny that it was only then that he noticed how small she was in comparison to him – like his father, over six feet tall. He bent over and took her in his arms, saying, "Don't you worry, Mam; I'll be all right. You know I live a charmed life – all those scrapes I got into as a kid, it's a wonder I'm still here at all!"

"Oh Charlie," Kate wept, "you'll never understand how it feels until you wave off your own son to war! No matter how big or old you are, you're still my baby boy – my firstborn son. I can't bear to think of you in the trenches and in such danger. It would kill me to lose you."

"I'll be fine, and I'll survive; I know I will. But I want to do my part, and I must. You don't know what this means to me. At last, I'm going to feel like I'm part of something; my actions will directly affect the enemy. It's not enough for me to know that maybe some part of a machine that I've made might be used in the fight. I need to be in amongst the action myself."

"Yes, I know that Charlie, I do. I know you have to go, and how much you've been waiting for your chance. You know I'll let you go – I have no choice in the matter – but I don't have to like it!" she wailed.

At that moment, the back door slammed, and Albert walked into the kitchen, "Now then, what's all this? Are you crying, Katie?"

Kate dabbed at her cheeks with the corner of her pinny, "Yes Bertie, I'm crying all right. Our Charlie is going away to war! He's just a boy, how can they do this to us?" she threw herself into her husband's arms and cried into his shirt front.

"No, Kate, you're wrong there, Love. Charlie is a full-grown, healthy and fit young man. He wouldn't be normal if he didn't want to test his mettle and join the front line. Whatever else he might lack, he doesn't want for courage. Good lad, Charlie, I'm proud of you!"

Kate pushed Albert away from her in disgust. "What is it with you men that you always have to prove to yourselves how brave you are and get into dangerous situations. You don't give a moment's thought to we women who are left at home to worry ourselves sick about whether you're alive or dead!"

"Aww Mam, don't be like that!" said Charlie, "surely you wouldn't want a son who was a milk-sop tied to your apron-strings; someone afraid of their own shadow who jumped when someone said 'Boo!'"

"No, of course not! I'm glad that you're brave and courageous – but you can't expect me to be happy that you might get killed at any moment and be away from your family in some god-forsaken hole in the ground for who knows how long?"

"Don't you worry, Mam," Charlie grinned, "you know it will be..."

"All over by Christmas?" Kate interrupted, "perhaps, but they don't say which Christmas!" Despite herself, she couldn't help but smile.

Given the option, Charlie joined the Liverpool Scots Regiment 'because I like the uniform', he replied when Albert asked. He had a couple of photographs taken, one in his regular uniform and one in his dress uniform and proudly presented them to his parents after picking them up from the studio. "There you are, Mam, something to remind you of me when I'm away."

"As if we needed any reminders!" his mother said, once again breaking down in tears. She sent Freddie to the shops to get two photograph frames and, when he returned, set both on the mantlepiece above the range.

"Coo," Freddie teased cheekily, "it's a wonder your ugly mug didn't break the camera! Having those up there will turn the milk sour! You're rotten, going off and leaving me alone with all these girls!" He pulled out his tongue at Charlie and ran out of the back door laughing before Charlie's slap hit its target. Once outside, he locked himself in the lavatory and cried as if his heart would break. He idolised his big brother and couldn't imagine life without him.

Charlie went off for basic training, and the next thing the family heard was that he was on his way to Belgium, to Ypres, where the conflict had been particularly hard and bitter with many casualties on both sides. Knowing how his parents would worry about him, Charlie wrote as often as possible. Still, he never knew what to write and knew it was heavily censored, with anything even remotely sensitive made illegible before it reached his family. In his turn, he welcomed letters from his family – even the smaller kids sent drawings – all of which brightened the gloom of the trenches.

His family read each letter he sent many times over, before being carefully stored away by Kate, in an old biscuit tin on the dresser. From time to time, when she was alone, which was admittedly not all that often with her large family, she would get out Charlie's correspondence and read each letter carefully. It was as if somehow Charlie might know that she was thinking about him and sending her love. In his turn, Charlie realised that his mother had been right – there was nothing noble or glamorous about this war. Just ordinary men like him on both sides, existing in the damp and cold and the mud in the trenches, facing each other over yards of barbed wire, trying to kill each other because it was their duty to do so on their government's orders.

It was Grace's turn now, when she went with her friends to the pictures, to search the Newsreels for a glimpse of her brother's cheeky grin amongst the many 'Tommies' that were filmed waving and smiling, knee-deep in mud and bullets. She could imagine Charlie hamming it up for the camera; he was such a clown. She missed her big brother very much and thought about him often.

Grace often went to view the Casualty lists at her mother's behest and was always relieved when she could return home to Kate with the good news that Charles Tunstall was not listed there; she dreaded the day when she might have to take home bad news. Kate was very emotional and constantly worried about her son. Albert and Grace did their best to reassure her that nothing bad could happen to their Charlie, but in their hearts, they prayed that their reassurance would bring him home to them safely and intact.

Grace had taken to going to the Walney pictures more and more often and usually alone. She would wait until almost everyone else had left at the end of the show before gathering up her belongings and making her way to the foyer. Then, with luck, Ned would be on his way out too, and they would walk home together, talking all the way.

She had become fond of him; she liked that he was shy and tried to draw him out in their conversations, finding out more about him. Of course, he was younger than her, but only by about six months, so they had plenty in common. He talked about his family, his parents and little sister, and their move to Barrow for his father to set up his business, and about the circumstances that had led to Edward being an auctioneer at Joseph Wood's. Ned had at first thought that his dad would resent that he had lost everything in the fire, but it seemed he was happy in his work and had become less careworn and worried than he had been when he had the business and all the responsibilities it entailed.

Like Charlie, Ned was waiting for his call up, but he was only 16 and must wait another two years before getting Lord Kitchener's call. When they talked about it, Ned was envious of Charlie being there already, but Grace wondered if his heart was really in it. He was such a gentle soul, quietly spoken and mild-mannered. She could not envisage him in uniform, armed with a rifle, much less using a bayonet on the enemy!

Besides, surely the war could not go on for much longer, could it? Maybe it would end before Ned had to go away. She wished with all her heart that might be so and she would not lose her friend and her big brother to the War Machine. The trouble with being a girl was that Grace felt so helpless. Had she been a boy, like Charlie, she could have gone to do her bit, joining the Army or the Navy, or even the Royal Flying Corps, which had come into its own during this conflict. All she could do was play her part by working as a Munitionette, which she had to remember was important. Without her and the thousands like her, there would be no ammunition with which to fight!

At any one time, munitions workers could be moved to a different part of the job if necessary. It meant that every person was trained in every aspect of the job. It also meant a constant turnaround of labour, especially in the filling sheds, where using the toxic TNT chemicals for long periods could greatly affect the workers' health. As soon as the skin started to become pigmented with the yellow colouring, the supervisors tried to move those workers to a different task. This led to the nickname 'Canary Girls' for a while until the effects had dissipated.

Grace had worked in most departments concerned with creating the finished product. She had recently been moved to the packing department, responsible for packing the finished shells into crates ready for shipment wherever the ammunition was required. It was dangerous work as the finished shells contained the detonators that would explode the chemicals contained within. One slip, one shell dropped, might result in the whole supply going up, the shed blown to smithereens and chances of survival would be minimal.

Grace and her colleagues were discussing the situation of women's work during their half-hour lunch break one day after one of the girls had been reading in the newspaper about the Royal Flying Corps. "Can you imagine being allowed to pilot an aeroplane, flying up into the clouds? The boys get all the fun!" Grace's friend, Sally said.

"Huh! Not so much fun being chased by a German plane and shot at with machine guns!" retorted Joan, the supervisor. She was an older woman, married with two school-aged children and rarely in a good mood. She worked in the Munitions shop mainly because the wages were better than most women's pay. Joan had been part of the suffragette movement before the War had started, and rumour had it that her husband had been about to throw her out. Instead, he decided that he would escape from her radical views under a cloak of patriotism when he joined up at the first push.

"I know that," wondered Sarah, "but do you think girls would ever be allowed to fly the planes, perhaps even afterwards, in peacetime?"

"I doubt it very much." answered Joan, "When all this is over, and the men come home – those that are left, that is – you'll see what opportunities there are for women then! The answer is NONE! Our menfolk will all want their jobs back, and they'll sack the lot of us without a second thought, you'll see!"

Knowing that Joan was about to start on one of her 'equality for women' rants, another girl, Marge, butted into the conversation. "I've heard that in some packing departments, the girls have been sending notes, writing to the lads who open the crates at the other end. Wouldn't it be fun if we did that?"

"Not likely," said Joan, "what's the point of that?"

"It's supposed to boost morale. So they know they're not forgotten. It's a great idea don't you think, Grace?" asked Marge.

"It's the first I've heard of it, but I suppose it would be a nice thing to do. I mean, when you're far away from home in some muddy trench, it must be nice to know that someone from home is thinking of you, even for just a minute!" said Grace. "The more I think about it, I think I'll do just that! It's nothing to me, but if it brightens some poor soldier's day, it can't be a bad thing."

When she got home that evening, Grace took some paper, ink and a pen and sat at the kitchen table, writing letters. After a few failed attempts, she had decided on the best thing to say. She copied it out ten times, then folded the sheets into envelopes and left them unsealed, just for now. She wasn't quite sure what to put on the envelope or in the letter, but she would see if anyone else had written and what they'd put before she sealed and sent them.

While watching her daughter writing away, Kate commented, "What are you doing, Gracie? It's not like you to write lots of letters! Who are you writing to?" In her younger days, Grace had missed so much schooling that she rarely put pen to paper, always finding it difficult. But tonight, she seemed to have a sense of purpose about her.

Grace explained to Kate what she was doing and offered her mother a copy of the letter to read:

26 Delhi Street
Walney Island
Barrow in Furness
Lancashire
24th July 1917

To Whom It May Concern

My name is Grace Tunstall, and as you can see from the address above, I am from Barrow though I was born in Hull. I work in the munitions shop here at Vickers, hence your receipt of this letter. We 'Canary Girls' decided to include some notes in the packing boxes of the shells we make so that when they arrive at the front and the soldiers, sailors and airmen unpack them, you might find our letters and take a little comfort from them.

It's just our way of letting you brave boys know that someone back home is thinking of you and is grateful for all your hard work and sacrifices in the fight to defeat the Kaiser, even if you don't have a sweetheart or a family of your own. I can't imagine how it must be for you – we see the Newsreels from Pathé at the Picture House, but I expect we are only seeing the best parts. It still looks very grim even so – it must be much worse for you being in the thick of it all, whether you're in the trenches, out at sea or flying dangerous missions!

There is not very much we girls can do in the fight, so we are keeping things running in Britain whilst you are away so that you can return when it's all over and find that we have not let you down and that 'Old Blighty' has not changed. I very much hope that it will be over soon and you can all come home as heroes.

If you would like to write back to me, if you have the chance, I would love to hear from you, if only to let me know my note has reached someone, somewhere over there. I promise I will write back to you too, perhaps we can become pen-pals. In the meantime, please take as good care of yourself as you can. We really appreciate the efforts and risks you are taking to keep us all safe.

Yours faithfully,
Grace Tunstall

"What a lovely idea!" Kate smiled, "I'm sure those boys will appreciate the gesture."

Later that night, Kate told her husband about Grace's letters. Albert thought for a moment, "You don't think the girl's being a bit fast, do you love? I mean, a young girl writing to lots of men she doesn't know, offering her friendship to them? What if we suddenly get a procession of young soldiers turning up on the doorstep when they get their leave, reading more into it than she imagines? Our Gracie doesn't know the ways of the world yet – what about her reputation? She doesn't want to spoil the chances of finding a husband, after all?"

"Oh, Albert – you would think something like that!" Kate rebuked, "All she's offering is a few words of comfort, not offering her body to them! I think it's a charming idea. And if it increases her chances of meeting some nice young men, I'm all for it – under the right circumstances, of course."

"If you say so, love. You're probably right. And to be truthful, if some poor lad is out there who doesn't have any family to write to or get letters from, it is a nice thing, I suppose."

"Of course, I'm right! Now, put out that lamp and go to sleep!" Kate kissed her husband and settled down as the room was suddenly in darkness.

CHAPTER NINE 1917 - 1918

The next morning, Grace showed one of her letters to Marge at tea break. "What do you think? Does that sound all right – I mean, does it give the right impression" she asked her friend.

Marge's eyes darted across the page. "I think that's perfect!" she said, "Much better than mine!" She handed an envelope to Grace to read. The sentiment was very similar to what Grace had written, and she was pleased that they'd had the same ideas about what was needed.

"Your handwriting is much better than mine, though!" Grace said, ruefully, "It looks like a drunken spider has crawled through a puddle of ink and across the page!"

"Never mind, Gracie," her friend said, "I'm sure whoever reads it won't care about that! I wonder who will receive them? Let's hope it's some handsome young man who doesn't already have a girlfriend. Just imagine if he fell in love with you, just through your writing? And then came home to find you and asked you to marry him! I think it's so romantic!"

"Don't be such a goose! That's hardly likely to happen. It's only a simple note, not a declaration of undying love." Sensible Grace laughed at her friend. When she'd written, she certainly had not contemplated the possibility of romance. "You read too many novels!" she grinned.

Despite the remark she had made to Marge, Grace had been watching the post every day since she'd slipped her letters into the packing boxes; she had been impatient to receive something back. She had decided not to expect too much too soon, to avoid the disappointment when nothing arrived. After the first week when nothing arrived, she realised that it might take some time. After all, the crates were shipped to some far destination, and they could be in storage even then.

Some weeks later, an envelope came through the letterbox addressed to 'Miss Grace Tunstall.' Kate picked it up and put it on the mantelpiece for her daughter to read when she came home from work. For once, she didn't worry that a letter with an army postmark might contain bad news about her son.

That evening when Grace came in, she noticed the envelope on the shelf straight away, even before her younger brother taunted her about it. "Ooh, Our Gracie has a love letter! I hope it hasn't got kisses on the bottom!"

She resisted the urge to give Freddie a sharp slap and excitedly picked up the letter. She put it in her pocket and started to help Kate dish up the evening meal. The rest of the children were already sitting at the table, waiting.

"Aren't you going to open it, Gracie?" Fourteen-year-old Faith asked her big sister.

"Not yet," Grace replied, "I'll wait until later when I'm on my own."

Once finished with the meal, Grace excused herself from the table. She went upstairs to the room she shared with her sisters, who were all downstairs or playing outside until bedtime.

Her hands were shaking as she carefully opened the flap of the envelope, wondering about its contents. She read the words with some difficulty – the writer had handwriting even worse than her own! – but nevertheless, she scrutinised the letter.

Dear Miss Tunstall,

Thank you so much for your note, which one of my mates gave me. He passed it on to me because he already has a sweetheart waiting at home that he's going to marry as soon as he gets the chance, whereas I am unattached. He didn't want his girl to think he was being unfaithful!

Anyway, you have no idea how much it meant to read your kind words. You're right – it is grim here, much worse than I could ever have imagined! I can't tell you the name of the place where we are – it's in Belgium, somewhere, I think, but I can't pronounce it, nor spell it, so I won't attempt to. Suffice to say, the tenements of Glasgow that I left behind to come here are looking like a much better place to be right now!

I've just realised that I haven't even told you who I am yet – I should start fresh, but paper and ink are pretty scarce, so I won't waste what I've written already. I am Pte Samuel Hutton or Sammy to my mates, and I'm 19 years old. As I've said, my family live in Glasgow. Dad works on the Clyde as a riveter in the

Shipyard. My Mam looks after him and my three little sisters who are still at school, but the eldest, Jeanie, will be leaving soon. I sometimes get letters from them, but Dad doesn't read or write very well, and Mam was never taught, so wee Jeanie has to write for all of them.

Anyway, I do hope you will write back to me, as you promised in your note. It would be good to have a friend to think of when things get bad here. I would like to hear about your family and where you live. I know they build ships in Barrow, too, so we have that in common at least.

Your new friend,
Sammy Hutton

Grace folded and put the letter back in the envelope. She was pleased that this young soldier was touched by her note. At the top of the letter, there was a return address to a Field Postal Office in Belgium. Grace decided she would write back to Sammy straight away and be as bright and encouraging as she could be. He sounded lonely and in need of a friend. It began a long-distance friendship that would give pleasure to both Grace and Sammy.

The weeks and months passed, and the family had a quiet Festive Season – they didn't feel it was right to celebrate whilst so many families were struggling, and people missing their loved ones, or worse, mourning those who would not return. Though not regular churchgoers, Kate and Albert took the children to St. Mary's on Christmas Eve for the midnight Carol Service. They enjoyed the hymns, especially Albert, who heartily boomed away in his tenor voice, almost putting the choir to shame. But Kate also wanted to be at church specifically to repeat the quiet prayers she offered up every day at home – being in God's house might ensure that her prayers quickly reached His ear. She knelt on the hassock and fervently prayed that the war would soon end and that her son might be kept safe and return home hale and healthy as quickly as possible.

On New Year's Eve, Albert kept up the tradition of 'first footing' around the houses of their near neighbours. The belief was that the first person who crossed the threshold in the New Year should be a tall, dark man to bring good luck. He should carry with him some bread, a lump of coal, a measure of salt, a coin and a little whisky to ensure the household would not want for food, warmth, flavour, prosperity and good cheer. As the whisky was then usually consumed to toast the New Year, Albert found himself quite tipsy by the time he had visited several of the neighbouring houses.

Well after midnight, he arrived back home to find Kate waiting up for him. He sat heavily in his chair next to the fire that Kate had banked up for the night and attempted to unlace his boots. Seeing him struggle, Kate knelt beside him and untied the knotted laces, finally removing his boots to reveal his big toe poking through a hole in his sock.

Shaking her head and tutting, she smiled, "Albert Tunstall, I have no idea how you manage to go through your socks so quickly! You're worse than the children!"

Returning her smile, he pulled her up to sit in his lap, "Oh my Katie! My sweetheart, the love of my life. My dearest little wife – what would I do without you? Have I told you how much I love you?"

She laughed, "Only every time you get drunk! But you won't hear me complaining. At least the whisky doesn't make you mean, like some folk I know. Some of my friends are scared to death of their men when they've had a drink, and with good reason! I've seen the bruises and scars on some of them. I'm so glad that you're not like them, Bertie. You're a good husband to me and a good father to our children, and I can't ask for more than that."

She nuzzled into his chest; she had always been grateful that her big man was no bully. She knew he loved her, and she felt the same towards him. Though sometimes life was a struggle and money was short, they had a good, happy marriage, and she was thankful for it. She heard his breathing start to deepen and moved, shaking him out of the stupor that was creeping up on him. If she couldn't wake him and guide him to bed, he'd end up sleeping in the chair and wake up in the morning stiff and aching.

Kate managed to rouse him enough that he stood up, and when she took him by the hand, he followed her like a lamb up the stairs to their bedroom. However, when he slumped on the bed, she knew she would not be able to undress him, so she covered him with the eiderdown and cuddled up next to him as his breathing turned to a gentle snore.

New Year's Day 1918 dawned bright and clear, a crisp cold morning that left a covering of frost over every surface, including the inside of the bedroom windows of the little house in Delhi Street. The family huddled under extra blankets, quilts and even coats on their beds to keep warm during the winter nights. Today was a holiday, so there was no need to rise too early, the rare luxury of a lie-in.

Grace was up first and stirred the embers of the fire, adding kindling, logs and coal to feed the slumbering glow. It was not long before the heat started to emanate from the range, and she began to make a large pot of porridge for a warming breakfast for the whole family to wake up to. She stirred the oats into the water, ensuring it was well mixed, with no big lumps, and set the pot onto the heat.

Between the frequent stirring, she sat in her father's chair near the fire and thought of the letters she needed to write today. Following Sammy's letter, more had arrived from other servicemen – in all, she had received replies to all of the letters she had initially sent out. They were mostly soldiers on the front, but one or two sailors too, though their letters came less frequently.

Fortunately, the letters didn't all arrive at once, so she could keep up with all her correspondents, but she found she was writing more or less the same messages to each. She worried that having little news to report to the boys might become boring. However, in every letter she received, reading between the lines, the lads were so grateful to receive word from her, no matter how mundane the content – it was just so good to hear from home.

Grace heard movement from the rooms upstairs; the family was stirring and would soon be joining her in the warmth of the kitchen. The porridge, thickening nicely, would soon be ready to serve up; she set the table with bowls and spoons and the sugar bowl, so each of them could sweeten the dish to their taste.

It wasn't long before the children hurtled down the stairs, bickering and laughing as they sat down at the table. Heaving the cooking pot onto the table, Grace ladled the porridge into the bowls and passed them around. Mam and Dad were obviously making the most of the holiday and enjoying the peace and quiet of their room whilst they had the chance, for which Grace couldn't blame them. She urged the others to keep down the noise and allow their parents to rest for a while longer. As soon as they'd finished their breakfasts and asked leave to move from the table, they settled down to their various pursuits. Faith and Joy sat together reading books, while the smaller girls, Hope, Connie and Prudence, sat together in front of the fire playing with their dolls.

Freddie asked to go and join his friends and donned a cap, coat and boots to go outside, where his little gang of marauders were waiting for him. They would take great delight knocking the ice from bushes and trees, showering each other with the cold droplets, then running and chasing about to keep warm.

Grace put the porridge back on the heat to keep warm for Albert and Kate, then boiled the kettle and put the dishes to soak for a few minutes before washing, drying and putting them away. Afterwards, she took her writing paper, pen and ink, and her collection of letters received and spread them out on the table to write some replies.

Her favourite was still Sammy, mainly because he was her first pen-pal. He had sent her a photograph of himself in his army uniform. He wasn't very handsome; quite ordinary-looking. She couldn't tell what colour his eyes or hair were, but he was presentable enough. Even if he weren't, though, she would still have favoured him. She knew what it was like to be passed over because she wasn't pretty or clever. She was just an ordinary girl herself, so she had lots of time for those the same as her. She didn't have any photographs of herself to send, but Sammy didn't seem to mind that. He was just happy to have some contact with home.

They corresponded regularly – at least once a week – which amazed Grace. She had imagined that it would take weeks and weeks for her letters to arrive at the front, but the postal service was a well-run machine. It was said that at the height of the war, the Post Office was delivering twelve million letters a week to the forces – it was quite a feat! The government was well aware that news from home and family boosted morale among the troops, and they did everything to keep lines of communication open and functioning.

Grace had her work cut out to keep up with all of her pen-pals, but it had certainly improved her writing skills. Her handwriting became much more legible, as did her spelling, because she asked her mother to read the letters before sending them. She didn't want her boys to think she was ignorant and ill-educated, though she supposed it wouldn't matter much to them, really. The important thing was to keep in touch and ensure they weren't forgotten.

CHAPTER TEN 1918

In her efforts to keep up with her correspondence, Grace had been much less frequent in her visits to the picture house. After the first couple of weeks, Ned noticed that she wasn't around so much, and he missed her. He wondered if he had upset her somehow, but having thought long and often about their last few meetings and searching his mind for possible offences, he couldn't put his finger on anything he had done. The last few times she had attended, Ned had walked home with her as usual, but she had been in a hurry to get home for some reason. Their usual stroll had been over too soon to get into a deep conversation. She also seemed distracted, as if she had something on her mind to which he was not a party.

The only thing he could think of that might have angered her is if she had found out, somehow, that he didn't live in Liverpool Street at all; it was an excuse to be able to spend a short while in her company. If she had discovered he had been lying all this time – well, that might be a reason for her sudden disinterest. He decided to leave it alone for a while, and wait until she turned up for a performance, then he would make a clean breast of it and tell her the truth. Then, she would either forgive him or have nothing more to do with him, but at least he would know.

The opportunity came in the Spring. The days were getting longer and warmer, and the fresh air blowing across the Island carried the scents of blossom as well as the salty tang of the sea.

Ned had seen through the projection room window that Grace was at the performance, which as usual, was a series of short films and newsreels. He was glad to see she was alone since he didn't like to interrupt because of his shyness when she was with friends. Girls of his age made him nervous, so he did not rush to finish his work to meet her on the way out on those occasions. But today, the young man was lucky – she sat a few rows from the front, the seats to either side of her unoccupied.

At the end of the performance, he asked the projectionist if he might leave straight away rather than help finish putting the spools back into their cans and cleaning down the projectors. He badly wanted to speak to Grace and was afraid of missing her on the way out. Mr Blake looked at him with a grin, "Girl trouble is it, lad? Aye, you get on your way; I won't stand in the way of true love. I'll finish up here."

Muttering his thanks, Ned grabbed his coat and cap and raced down the corridor to the plush foyer. The auditorium was still emptying, but he stepped out into the street to look in the direction she would take but could see no one. He correctly assumed that he hadn't missed her because when he returned inside the lobby, she was just exiting through the ornate double doors, blinking at the bright light.

"Hello Grace!" he said, "I'm glad to see you! I thought I might have missed you."

She smiled at him as she pulled on her gloves; although spring was well on its way, there was still a distinct chill in the air outside. "Hello, Ned. I wasn't sure if you were working or not. I haven't been here for a little while."

"I know! I've been looking out for you!" Ned coloured, realising that he sounded like a lovesick puppy. "I mean, I noticed you haven't been in and was worried you might be ill or something. Are you alright?"

"Oh yes, I'm fine! I've just been a bit busy lately, that's all. You've missed me, then, have you?" Grace teased him. The two young people left the cinema and began walking to Delhi Street.

"Not exactly 'missed'," he said airily, "but I hadn't seen you around and wondered if something had happened. What's been keeping you so busy then?"

"I've been spending a lot of time writing letters to some boys at the front."

"Oh, I see. I know your brother is out there, but I didn't realise you knew anyone else. Is Charlie doing all right?" Ned enquired. Not for the first time, he felt embarrassed that he was still too young to go and fight.

"I believe so. Mam had a letter from him last week, and he seemed in good spirits – at least that's what he said. But he didn't say much else – they're not allowed to in case they leak any information to the enemy. But, no, I don't know these boys." Grace explained how it had come about that she was pen pals with the young servicemen. "So, you see, I feel like I'm doing something personal to help. I know my munitions work is important, and I'm happy to do that, but I'm just a nameless, faceless body who inputs very little in the whole process. Although writing letters affects fewer people, at least I'm not contributing to the death count; I'm just trying to cheer up a few lads who are far away from home, doing their best to win this bloody war!" She blushed, having let slip the oath – it was a good job her parents couldn't hear her!

Ned laughed. "I've never heard you get so passionate about anything before – or heard you swear! I think you're doing a great thing, Grace."

By this time, they were nearing Delhi Street, and Ned debated whether or not to divulge the truth to her. As she wasn't already cross with him, perhaps there was no need to rock the boat just yet. They reached her corner, and she made to carry on walking up the street, as usual, when Ned said, "Grace, there's something I have to tell you!"

Puzzled, she stopped and looked at him. "What is it? Is something wrong?"

He had started but was kicking himself mentally. Why couldn't he leave well alone? "I have a confession to make. All this time we've been walking home together, I've been misleading you."

The puzzlement on her face grew more intense. "Misleading me? How?"

She could see him squirming inside as he spoke, "I don't live in Liverpool Street. I never have! I live in Thomas Street in town with my family. I just wanted you to let me walk with you that first time, so I made it up. I have a friend who lives in Liverpool Street, that's why I knew it was the next street along. But I just wanted the chance to talk to you and get to know you." By this time, Ned had blushed furiously red and was almost shaking. "I'm sorry if I've upset you, and I'll understand if you don't want to talk to me anymore."

Grace had a stern look on her face, "Have you lied to me about anything else? Is it all a pack of lies?"

"N-no! I promise everything else is absolutely true."

Grace had to put him out of his misery; he looked so forlorn. Besides, she was finding it very hard not to burst out laughing. Instead, she smiled and said, "You're forgiven. I don't get why you didn't say so in the first place, but it's all right."

"I'm so glad to hear you say that! I've been feeling rotten about it for months, but I was afraid you wouldn't let me walk with you anymore if you knew. I've wanted to get to know you ever since we were at Thwaite Street." His broad smile made her smile too.

"Why didn't you just talk to me then? Am I so scary?" she asked.

"No, not at all! But you always seemed to be in a hurry to be somewhere else – I suppose because of your family situation. You were always too busy to stop and play with the other kids.

And I'm not exactly an Adonis, and I'm also younger than you. I didn't think you would ever notice me; there were other bigger and better-looking boys in the class. You didn't even know I existed!" Ned looked downcast.

"The only boys I've ever had anything to do with are my two brothers! I never had time for those others, and anyway, none of them knew I existed either! They would always notice the pretty girls, not the likes of me! And I was taller than most of them too! Boys don't go out of their way to get to know me." She grinned, "Not till now anyway – and you've REALLY gone out of your way!"

They both laughed. Ned had only just turned seventeen, and Grace would be eighteen in October; he wondered if he dare ask, as their laughter faded. He would – so what if she said no? At least they could still be friends. "Grace, I know that we're both very young, but would you consider being my girlfriend? Can we be a couple?"

Suddenly flustered, Grace didn't know how to respond. No boy had ever asked her out before. She liked Ned; they got along well and always had something to talk about, but she'd assumed they were just friends, nothing more. But then, she might not get another chance! Making up her mind, she replied, "I don't see why not. Nothing serious, of course, we're both much too young for that! But yes, if you like, we can go courting together."

Ned thought his heart would burst. His face shone, and his smile could not be any wider. "I'm so glad! Perhaps we should have our first date soon. What shall we do?" he asked.

In unison, they both said, "Go to the Pictures!" and laughed.

Grace was pleased to find her mother alone when she got home, a rare occurrence in a houseful. "Mam, can I ask you something?"

"Yes, of course, our Gracie, what is it?" Kate smiled. She loved the mother/daughter talks with her eldest daughter. They had become more like friends than anything, and Kate was happy that Grace felt she could confide in her.

"How long did you know Dad before you started courting?"

"Ooh, now you're asking! I suppose it was quite late on – we were both in our twenties. Another chap was courting me for quite a while, and we were expected to marry, but he died in a road accident. Through the church, I was friends with your dad's sister, your Auntie Lizzie. A couple of years after Sidney died, we were all at a church picnic when your dad offered to carry my picnic basket. I hadn't noticed him before then, him being two years younger than me, but I suppose he'd always been around. Anyway, I let him carry my basket and the next thing I knew, we were walking out together, and Bertie asked my dad if we could marry. They'd known each other through work, and your grandpa liked him, so he agreed. To answer your question, I suppose I'd known him a long time, but only as an acquaintance.

We were only courting about two years before we got wed. I was glad I wasn't going to end up an old maid because I was nearly 27 by that time! Why do you ask, love?"

"Well, I have this friend, Ned. We were in the same class at Thwaite Street, but I hardly knew him then. Well, anyway, he works sometimes at the Picture House, and if he's there when I am, he usually walks home with me – well, to the corner anyway. We talk a lot, and I do like him very much, and – well – he's asked me to go out with him!" Grace was nervous and blushing as she spoke. "But I wondered if I'd be allowed? I don't know what Dad would say. What do you think?

"Oh Grace, that's lovely! I think you're old enough to make your mind up if you want to go out with him – as long as it's not too serious anyway. Why don't you bring him home to tea – perhaps next Sunday – so we can meet him. I'm sure you'll find out then exactly what your dad thinks!" Kate took her daughter's hand. "I hope he's brave enough to come under the scrutiny of the whole family! And you'd better warn him about Freddie too!"

CHAPTER ELEVEN 1918

As the year progressed, the news brought both good and bad tidings. Concerning the war, it seemed the Allied Troops were gaining ground and driving back the Germans. The Tunstalls were happy to hear that Charlie and his regiment were still pushing forwards and had engaged in some fighting, but he was uninjured and told them in his letters that morale was high, despite the heavy losses on both sides.

Closer to home, another, more virulent threat was making its presence felt, and there was no way to attack this new enemy – the Spanish Influenza. Thousands of people were ill or had died due to the virus, and there was little anyone could do. Government advice was to stay home as much as possible, but when one had to earn a living to support a family, there was no choice. All anyone could do was hope.

The Tunstalls had moved house again – their tiny house was becoming more cramped as the children grew and wanted more privacy, and Charlie would be coming home as soon as the war ended – sooner rather than later, they hoped. They moved to 12 Naiad Street - just a five-minute walk from Delhi Street - with another bedroom. There was a re-arranging of sleeping quarters for the children, all growing up so fast they needed more space.

No sooner were the family were settled in than Kate became very concerned when Connie complained of feeling ill. She said she was finding it difficult to breathe, and her head ached, and she felt hot. Kate felt her daughter's head and listened to her chest, but she sounded normal and was just warm to the touch – normal. Remembering the affinity between the twins, she called Hope down from the bedroom, but there was no response. Kate rushed upstairs, and sure enough, poor Hope lay on the bed, burning with fever and labouring to breathe, in between bouts of coughing, her chest rising and falling only marginally as she used every muscle to inhale and exhale.

Fearing the worst, Kate sent Freddie for the doctor. Dr Gray took some time to arrive, and while she waited, Kate sat at Hope's bedside, trying to cool her forehead with a damp cloth. She told Joy to boil a kettle and bring a bowl of boiling water and a towel up to the bedroom. She sat Hope upright and covered the child's head and the steaming bowl with the towel, hoping to ease her daughter's breathing.

Finally, the doctor arrived and went upstairs, directed by the children. "My apologies for taking so long, Mrs Tunstall, but as you can imagine, things are rather hectic at the moment. Now, young lady, what can we do for you?" He took his stethoscope from his bag and listened to Hope's chest and back, tapping at various points. "Hmm. I believe the situation is not quite as bad as we imagined, Mrs Tunstall. I don't think it's the Spanish Flu; I think we have a case of pneumonia. It's still serious but not quite as deadly, and we can treat her and hope she recovers fully. I see no reason why not."

The relief on Kate's face was almost palpable. She had always had a vivid imagination. In her mind, she had pictured all of her children sick or dying after infecting each other with the Spanish

Flu that was claiming so many victims both nationally and globally.

The doctor gave Kate some aspirin and his instructions; not to worry if Hope coughed up phlegm, it was good to get it up and out of her lungs, but Kate should let him know if the child coughed up any blood. Otherwise, it was just lots of rest, plenty of fluids, and a dose of aspirin once a day, and keep the other children away as much as possible just in case of contagion. He spoke to the child before leaving, "Hope, you do as your mother tells you! Lots of rest and take your medicine like a good girl. You'll soon be running about again." Kate thanked Dr Gray, and he left after checking the other children; fortunately, they all seemed healthy.

Kate moved Hope downstairs and made up a bed on the settee in the parlour to keep her separate from sharing a bed with her siblings, but Connie refused to leave her sister's side. Throughout Hope's illness, her devoted twin slept on cushions on the floor, next to the settee, so she could hold Hope's hand and be there should her sister need anything in the night.

Within a few days, Hope was feeling much better, and Kate could see she was on the road to recovery though she insisted on the child staying in bed for at least a week. Finally, the child had become bored with reading her books and drawing pictures. Hearing the other children playing in the kitchen, she begged her mother to let her get up and join them. Kate agreed but kept a close eye that Hope didn't overdo things and get over-tired with too much exertion.

The Armistice was declared on 11th November, and it brought much relief to the Tunstall household – at last, Charlie would be coming home! A week later, his letter said he had been in Villiers Notre Dame in Belgium when the news came. The local people had thronged the streets and had welcomed the liberating army with open arms. He wrote that he had been hugged and kissed by girls from 14 to 90 and enjoyed every single one. The conquering heroes had a whale of a time, but still, Charlie looked forward to coming home.

Unfortunately, though, his regiment was not among the first to be demobilised; they were sent to Antwerp. Finally, he was demobbed in December, almost a month after the ceasefire declaration.

Freddie wanted to throw a big party for Charlie's homecoming; he planned to paint a big banner saying 'Welcome Home Charlie' to hang on the front of the house so it would be the first thing his big brother saw when he entered the street. However, although she appreciated the young boy's enthusiasm, Kate felt she could not allow it this time. She took Freddie to one side to explain it was lovely to welcome Charlie home, and certainly, they would celebrate as a family. But they did have to remember those families whose sons would never come home again and be aware of the pain they might feel, seeing such a blatant reminder of their loss.

"I never thought of that. I'm sorry, our Mam," said Freddie, "I understand what you're saying, and it isn't fair on them." He was such a happy-go-lucky child, always cheerful; he had a good heart and appreciated that in many ways, he was lucky to have a large family that loved him. Never down for very long, after a moment, his face brightened; "Can I paint a smaller banner just to put up over the range instead?" His mother smiled and nodded her permission and after begging an old sheet to paint on, off the lad ran to locate the necessary paints and brushes.

The whole family was waiting for him as soon as Charlie arrived. Draped across the chimney breast Freddie's colourful banner – together with large drips of paint – echoed the ovation given him by the gathering. Cries of 'welcome home' and 'we've missed you' filled the air with a deafening clamour. Divested of his luggage, a glass of beer was pressed into his hand, and Albert quietened everyone else down to make a toast.

"To Charles William Tunstall, my son. A brave and patriotic young man, home from the wars after fighting to bring us all safety and peace. Welcome home, son; we're proud of you! To Charlie!" and everyone raised their glasses and echoed as Albert shook his son's hand, "To Charlie!"

Charlie woke early the next morning, hardly recognising where he was, as it was his first night in the new house too. Realising that he no longer had to answer reveille at six o'clock in the morning, he sunk deeper into the comfort of the bed. He luxuriated in the feel of a real mattress and proper pillows and the sweet smell of crisp linen and reminded himself that at last, he was home, safe. One of the lucky ones.

It took a little while for the young man to appreciate he was back at home; the cleanliness, the comfort and the quiet. Well, not exactly quiet, but as quiet as a house filled with children could ever be. It was certainly better than the deafening and invasive sounds of gunfire and shelling that had filled the trenches. The next thing was to restart his interrupted apprenticeship – settle back into some real work. And to pick up the threads of his old life – see the old friends he'd missed, those that had come back at any rate. Perhaps it was time to find a nice girl, settle down, make a life for himself. God, it was so good to be back home.

Grace was also very glad that the war had finally ended. She wondered if the correspondence she had with her pen-pals would cease once they all returned home to their families. There would be no need for her letters to cheer them up anymore. Perhaps one or two of them might still write, which would be nice – especially Sammy Hutton. They had exchanged letters for the longest time, and she felt they had a special bond; she hoped that perhaps he might still keep in touch. With him, it had been like writing to a real friend or a brother even. They'd exchanged information about their families and their homes. They had even written about their hopes and dreams about what would happen when the war ended. Sammy would go back to an apprenticeship in the Clydeside Shipyards, and she – well, she didn't quite know what she would do.

It was widely expected that as soon as all the men returned home, they would want their jobs back, which meant many women, including Grace, would be sacked to make way for them. Whilst she realised that these men needed to work, to provide for their families, it did seem unfair that she and her colleagues would be out without a backward glance; "without a 'kiss my arse nor bugger you'" as one of her more salty friends had said. They could at least show their appreciation in some small way – but that was the way of the world. Women just got on with whatever needed to be done and kept out of the way.

Anyway, she would need to find another job. Perhaps something in a shop or office, although she wasn't qualified for anything like that. Her lack of schooling made it quite difficult to think of anything she might be well qualified for except looking after a home and family. Perhaps that was the answer; maybe she could go into service as a maid, home-help, or even a children's nurse. She certainly had the experience of that!

She was brought out of her reverie when her mother called her down to the kitchen. There was a small brown paper parcel on the table, addressed to Grace. "The post-girl just brought this for you, our Gracie. What can it be?"

"I've no idea our Mam! I suppose I'd better just open it and find out!" she smiled – she liked surprises.

After fumbling with the paper and string, she opened it to reveal an envelope which lay on top of another paper-wrapped parcel inside. She opened the letter first, curious to find out who had sent the mystery package. She read the letter, then, to her mother's surprise, she suddenly dropped it on the table, picked up the parcel and ran out of the room.

Kate was confused. It wasn't like her sensible, calm Grace to behave this way. She wondered whether she ought to read the letter. Kate didn't want to invade the girl's privacy, but she had to know what had upset her daughter so much. She picked the paper up from the table and read:

'Dear Miss Tunstall,

I am sad to have to contact you this way, but my family thought you ought to be told our sad news. We heard a short time ago that my brother, Sammy, was killed in an accident on the way back from France. Apparently, the boat he was on collided with a German mine under the water, and Sammy was killed in the explosion as he had been below deck at the time. It's strange to think he survived the combat and the trenches, only to die on his way home to us. Thankfully only six of the men were killed, though many were injured, though it's hard to be thankful when our Sammy did not survive.

As you can imagine, my father and mother are devastated, as are my two little sisters and me. We have just received a parcel from the Army containing his belongings, and among them, we found this bundle of letters from you. He obviously treasured them, as they had a ribbon around them and were safely wrapped up in his waterproof cape. I hope you don't mind that we read them, firstly to find out where you live so we could return them to you, but also to find out about the kindness you showed him by being his friend. My family want to thank you for bringing a little light and comfort into his life during this terrible war. Your letters were obviously very precious to him. I'm glad they survived the explosion and were saved for you.

I'm sure you will be sad to hear this news, as you seem to think a lot of him and I'm sure he felt the same about you. Bless you, for your kindness.

Yours sincerely,
Jeannie Hutton

Kate went upstairs to find Grace sobbing her heart out on the bed. She put her arms around her daughter, stroked her hair and held her until Grace could cry no more.

Heartbroken in her loss, Grace was almost glad when the notice came that she and her colleagues were released from their jobs in Vickers' munitions shop. For a while, she could find no interest or enthusiasm for anything. The joy she'd found in her brother's return from the front had been dissipated by the news of Sammy's death. Somehow, it was so unfair to have survived the war and then die as peace came. It was such a waste of a young life, like so many who would not be coming home. Grace could not understand what it had all been for.

After more than a week of not seeing or hearing from her, Ned went to the Tunstall house and tentatively knocked on the door to ask if Grace was all right. He'd been for tea when he was invited a couple of Sundays ago and had met the family. They were all very nice to him, though he initially found Albert a little intimidating. Just standing between him and Charlie, Ned had felt awkward; they were both over six feet tall, with a lithe, muscular build, and he was only five feet six and a little portly. Somehow, he felt he couldn't match up to these two men. Not that they mentioned his physical shortcomings, but nevertheless, he felt he was lacking. But the tea had been a pleasant affair; Kate and Grace had both made a fuss of him, and the children had been lively and fun.

The memory of it made him smile as he waited for an answer to his knock. Although they had agreed that they were courting, it still felt strange to him to be calling at Grace's house. Eventually, he heard voices, and one of the twins (he could not tell them apart yet) opened the door.

Before he could say anything, she turned and called, "Grace! Your young man is here!" then turned back and said, "Hiya Ned. You'd better come in."

As he crossed the threshold, closing the door behind him, Grace appeared at the top of the stairs. She looked pale and red-rimmed round the eyes. "Hello Ned, what are you doing here?"

"I just wondered if you were all right. I know we hadn't made any arrangements to see each other, but I hadn't seen you at the Picture House either and thought something had happened to you, that you might be ill or something." Ned looked embarrassed, and the thought crossed his mind that he might not be welcome right now.

Grace smiled weakly and came down the stairs. She spoke to her sister, who was still standing watching this exchange, "Hope, tell our Mam that Ned's here, and we're going into the parlour to talk. And tell Freddie to stay out an' all!"

The youngster disappeared into the rear of the house, and Grace showed Ned into the front room. It was comfortably, if somewhat shabbily, furnished, but there was not a speck of dust to be seen. An upright piano stood against one wall, and the fire was laid, ready to be lit at a moment's notice. The chairs were covered on the backs and arms with colourfully embroidered antimacassars, and a rag rug lay in front of the fireplace. Family photographs and ornaments stood on every surface, and a small bookcase held some old leather-bound volumes that looked surprisingly well-read.

Grace gestured for Ned to sit on the overstuffed settee and sat next to him. "So, are you all right, Grace? I've been worried about you," Ned began.

Grace told him about everything that had happened and apologised for not letting him know sooner. "I'm sorry," she said, "I know it's not very flattering for you, but I've been so upset it never even entered my head about you. I just feel like I've lost a very good friend, even though I never met Sammy. I've never lost anyone before, and I just haven't felt capable of doing anything."

Ned put his hand over hers, "It's all right, Gracie, I do understand. I know that Sammy was special to you, and I also know how devastating it is to lose a friend. I don't want to bother you, but I'd like to help if I can. You know, maybe take your mind off it, take you out and try and cheer you up a bit. Only if you feel up to it, mind, if you're not ready, I can wait."

The tears welled up in her eyes, and she scrabbled up her sleeve to find an already damp handkerchief. Ned pulled his own hankie from his pocket, still folded and unused, and pressed it into her hand. "Here, take mine. I don't think yours can hold much more water!" he smiled.

"Oh Ned, you're so kind and understanding! Thank you." She dabbed her eyes and touched his cheek. She leant into him, and he put his arm around her. She rested her head on his shoulder, and they sat together quietly for a while. Grace found his presence comforting; she felt safe with him. For his part, Ned found himself feeling that he would protect this girl from every hurt if he could. If only that could be so! He wanted to take care of her and never let her be unhappy again.

Eventually, there was a light knock on the parlour door, and Kate came in carrying a tray with two cups and saucers and a plate of biscuits. "I thought you might like a cuppa. Talking is thirsty work!" she smiled as the couple jumped apart guiltily, Ned quickly standing up as she entered. "Sit down, Ned, make yourself at home. Well, I'll leave you to it. Grace, bring the tea things through when Ned leaves."

"Yes, I will, Mam. Thank you." Grace said as her mother left the room. The young couple looked at each other and burst out laughing. Not that there was anything to be guilty about, they hadn't even kissed yet!

CHAPTER TWELVE 1919

In the Summer, Grace found a new job. When she and the other munitions girls were sacked when the war ended, she was both sad and relieved. She had enjoyed being independent and having her own money – contributing to the family finances made her feel like a real adult. She also missed the companionship and camaraderie of the other women she had worked with. Grace knew they had done important work and had been an essential part of the British and Allied forces' efforts to end the hostilities. She was optimistic that the 'war to end all wars', as it was being called, was the worst thing that could ever happen, and now it was all over, Thank God.

She would be 19 in October. It was time to think about her life and what she might do with it. She knew that she was not qualified academically after the many interruptions during her schooldays, but she was not lacking in intelligence. She was happiest doing practical things, using her hands to create, although happily, she would never have to handle toxic chemicals and detonators again. She was a good cook and could bake bread and cakes to fill a family's bellies. She could sew – even her mother was envious of Grace's skill with a needle. Her embroidery on clothing and handkerchiefs was intricate and delicate with neat tiny stitches. But she wasn't a seamstress, even though she'd had experience sewing the fabric for airships.

She and Ned went for a walk one sunny Sunday afternoon up to Biggar Bank. The beach had reopened to the public, and lots of people were taking advantage of the fine weather. There were families with children, sitting together on the grass and playing. Couples strolled arm in arm along the front in their Sunday-best clothes, the men raising their hats each time they encountered another couple walking their way.

Ned and Grace walked to the edge of the grass, then sat and took off their shoes and stockings so it would be easier to walk along the pebble beach. The tide was on its way out, and the reflection of the sun's rays made the waves sparkle and flash as they receded. It left an expanse of wet sand and many rock pools which were like magnets for some of the younger children, who sat and dangled their feet in the cold brine, or searched for shells and pretty pebbles, or even crabs if they could find any.

After a while, the young couple walked back up onto the grass and replaced their footwear. They decided to rest for a while, and Ned walked up to the Pavilion to see if he could get them some tea to drink as they sat. When he returned with two cups, he settled on the grass next to Grace and handed her a cup.

"You know you said you were looking for another job?" he said, "I don't know if you'd be interested, but they've got a 'Help Wanted' sign up in the Café. What do you think?"

"It can't hurt to ask," she replied, "I'll take the cups back when we've finished and see what it's all about. I think I'm probably qualified for something like that, aren't I?"

"It probably won't pay very much, though," said Ned.

Grace shrugged, "Anything is better than nothing! We'll see."

The Café was about to close when Grace went to return their cups. A tired-looking middle-aged woman thanked her and took them into the back. When she came back out, Grace pointed at the notice and said, "Excuse me, but I see you're advertising for someone. Can you tell me about the job, please?"

"Just a minute, love, let me put the 'Closed' sign up, then we can sit and talk." She went across and turned the hanging sign around in the window, then returned and beckoned Grace to sit down opposite her at one of the tables, stacked with dirty cups and plates. "It's been a mad rush today – as soon as the sun comes out, so does the population of Barrow, it seems!"

She pushed a long strand of greying hair back under the cap from which it had strayed. "Now then, my love. Who are you?"

Grace introduced herself and explained that she had recently worked in Vickers but was looking for another job.

"Yes, there's a lot of girls in the same boat, I think," said the woman. "Oh, sorry! I'm Doris Dent, owner of this business – well, my family owns it, but I'm the one who runs it. My two daughters have been working with me whilst the war has been on, but their husbands are back from the front, and they're being good wives and looking after their men again. I can't say I blame them – being a wife and looking after a home is work enough without having a job. Besides, you know how proud men can be – they don't like people to think they can't provide for their wives and children, do they? Not only that, but both the girls are in the family way too, so they don't feel much up to being on their feet all day! Gertie is six months, and Freda is five months, so they're not exactly fit for squeezing between tables and chairs when the place is full either! So, yes, I need someone, and soon! I've got one girl who is starting next week, Sandra Robinson. She's a widow and has to sort out someone to look after the kids while she works, but she seems like a nice lass, and I hate to think of her and her poor fatherless children struggling. I've had a few others interested too, but none have struck me as someone I'd like to have around much. I want someone reliable, capable and experienced. Is that you, Grace Tunstall?"

"I think so, Mrs Dent!" Grace proceeded to tell her prospective employer all about herself and how she'd been brought up cooking, baking and cleaning for a family of ten. At length, she finished, "so that's me, Mrs Dent. Do you think I might be suitable?"

"Call me Doris, love; we don't stand on ceremony in this place. I keep thinking you're talking to my mother-in-law!" She laughed, once again trapping the stray lock of hair. "I tell you what; we'll give you a trial. Come tomorrow at nine o'clock, and you can start. At the end of the day, you can tell me if you think it's for you, and I'll tell you what I think of you. How does that sound?"

"That sounds fine, Mrs – Doris! Look, you look dead on your feet already. My young man is waiting outside for me – how about if I bring him in and we'll help you clear up this place. We can set him to washing the dishes. It'll be good practice for when we get married!" Grace laughed, then realised what she'd said and blushed. It was the first time she'd even thought about marrying anyone, and here she was singling out Ned without a thought of whether he wanted to marry her! "Ooh, please don't tell him I said that, will you, Doris? Please?"

Doris threw her head back and guffawed loudly, "I suppose he hasn't asked you yet, has he?"

"We've only just started walking out together!"

Well," said Doris, "I won't tell him if you don't. Bring him in, and let's get a look at the lad."

Grace stepped outside, where Ned was patiently waiting. The air was getting cooler as the evening approached. When she explained what she wanted, he was happy enough to go along with her. It was the first time in ages he'd seen her smile and laugh, and he realised then he would do anything – even dishes – if it made her happy.

The following day, Grace found that she loved the work. It wasn't very busy; being Monday, most people were at work, but plenty of ladies and children still took the air and got their exercise on Biggar Bank. Grace liked the work too – in the morning, she and Doris had been baking the cakes that would sell alongside the cups of tea in the Café. When the place opened, and customers started to arrive, she enjoyed taking their orders and talking to them.

When all the customers had gone, and they finished cleaning up at the end of the day, they sat again and talked together. "You've done well today, Grace, and been a big help to me. Have you enjoyed yourself?" said the older woman.

"It's been great, Doris. I can't think how I stood it, working in the munitions shop, standing all day concentrating for fear that a mistake might blow us all up. This hardly seems like work at all, though I must admit my feet are aching a bit. Still, I'll give them a soak at home, and they'll be right as rain." Grace took off the apron and cap she had been wearing all day. She had worn her second-best dress, navy blue and plain, with long sleeves and a small white collar.

"With that dress, the cap and pinny make you look like quite a posh waitress," said Doris, "I'll see if I can get something similar made up for you, me and Gloria when she starts. I think we'll have that as a uniform from now on; it'll give the place a bit of class. That is if you still want the job? I've just realised we haven't even talked about wages yet, have we? We can't pay munitions rates, I'm afraid. How does 12 shillings a week sound? Oh, and you and Gloria can take the leftover food home with you at the end of the day if there is any. How about that?" As good as her word, she picked up a paper bag and collected up the remaining cakes from the display case.

Grace thought about it for a moment. It wasn't good wages, but it at least WAS a wage. She'd still be able to contribute to the family, and that was what was important. She nodded, "Agreed,

Doris. I'm sure the kids will appreciate the cakes!" They shook hands and left together after Doris had locked up.

Back at home, Grace's siblings were thrilled at the treats she had brought home, although they had to follow the rules and eat all of their tea first. Over the meal, Grace described how much she had enjoyed her day and about her new employer.

"Mrs Dent sounds like a good woman, Grace," said Kate, "I'm glad you're working for someone so nice. Oh, who is that at the door? Joy, go and answer it, will you?"

They heard the sound of the front door opening, then Joy called, "It's Ned!"

"Well, bring him in then!" said Kate, "don't leave the poor lad standing outside!"

When he came into the room, Grace could see he was excited about something. "Mr & Mrs Tunstall, Grace – you need to come with me. And is Charlie here? You all need to come as soon as you can! The children especially!"

"Now then, lad, what's all the fuss about?" said Albert from his armchair. "We've only just had our tea, and I'm just about settled for the evening. What's so important?"

Ned had lost all his shyness in his excitement, "Oh, Mr Tunstall, please, trust me – you don't want to miss this. You need to be there or you won't believe it. But it's a surprise! Please, can you all get ready and come now?"

"All right, lad, keep your shirt on! Grace, you'd better round up your brothers and sisters. Joy, get everyone's outdoor clothes from the coat hooks for when they come in. And Kate, you'd better find yourself a hat – it looks like we're going visiting." Albert retrieved his boots and bent to tie the laces. "Now then, young man, this had better be worth it!"

They all walked up to Ocean Road and caught the tram into town, alighting outside the Town Hall. The children giggled and enjoyed the unforeseen adventure and followed Ned as he led the way to Forshaw Street.

Unable to hold her curiosity any longer, Grace grabbed Ned's hand and said, "Where on earth are we going, Ned? What are you up to?"

"Just a few minutes more Grace, honest! It will be worth it, I promise you." He slowed down as they reached the Tivoli Theatre and Cinema.

The children, excited, yelled, "we're going to the Music Hall! Or the pictures!"

"No," said Ned, shushing them, "not the Theatre. We're going next door."

"Joe Woods? The auction place?" said Albert, confused. "Is there a sale on or summat?"

Ned made them all promise to be silent and enter the building quietly, making as little noise as possible. When they reached the Auction floor, they saw that all the benches had been cleared to the edges of the room, leaving a big open space. Stealthily, they shuffled along and sat on a couple of the benches. They saw that only two or three lamps were lit, hanging from the ceiling in the middle of the room, leaving the rest in shadows. Nothing seemed to be happening, and all was quiet. Albert looked at Ned, who returned his gaze with his finger to his lips, reiterating the need to be quiet.

Suddenly, they heard the sound of wheels travelling across the wooden floorboards and looked to where the sound was coming from. To their complete surprise, a small man with dark hair was roller-skating across the room with such grace that it took their collective breath away. The man was like a ballet dancer, leaping and turning pirouettes. He skated round and round and displayed such art it was almost like watching a swan gliding across the park lake. The family watched, entranced, unable to look at anything but the figure performing in front of them.

He skated for about an hour, which seemed to fly by, as far as his audience was concerned; they could have watched him forever. Eventually, he came to a stop with a final pirouette. The Tunstalls couldn't help themselves – they burst into applause, showing their appreciation for the young man's artistic talent.

Surprised to hear the clapping, he called for more lights – suddenly, the room was bathed in light, and the family could see they were not the only ones who had been watching. On other benches across the room sat several people; two married couples and a few young people of varying ages. All were on their feet, applauding the young man who was bowing and smiling, blowing kisses and accepting their ovation.

"Come on," said Ned, taking Grace's hand and gesturing to the others, "let's go and see if we can be introduced to him."

"But who is it?" asked Grace, "introduced to who?"

Ned turned to face her with his eyes shining, "That's Charlie Chaplin, that's who!"

Disbelief crossed Grace's face, "that's not Charlie Chaplin! Where's his moustache?" Then realising, she said, "of course – that's just his character when he's acting – not the real person! How daft am I?"

The other audience members turned out to be Ned's parents and his sister, and Joe Woods, with his wife and their children. After all the introductions had been made, young Freddie looked disappointed. Mr Chaplin noticed and asked if there was something wrong.

"Well, I enjoyed the skating, Mister, and they say that you're Charlie Chaplin, but you don't look like him to me!" said Freddie.

"Freddie!" Kate was mortified, "Don't be so rude to the gentleman!"

"Ah, I see the problem," said the actor. "Well, if you can wait here a short while, I will go and make myself ready. I am appearing at the Theatre next door soon, and I will have to get dressed and ready. Then you will see, young man. Can you wait?"

Freddie looked at his parents for their consent (they wanted to see this as much as their children) and nodded. "Yes please, Sir!" Sure enough, after about twenty minutes, a door opened and using the famous walk, in came the 'little tramp' in his baggy trousers, jacket and bowler hat, sporting his bent walking stick, large moustache and eyebrows in place on his pale face.

The room erupted with delight as both adults and children whooped and cheered their hero. Sadly, he could not stay long as he was due backstage at the Tivoli before his performance. Waving goodbye, he chucked young Freddie under the chin and said, "Will that do, for now?"

"Oh yes, Sir! I'll remember this forever!" said Freddie in awe.

Once the movie star had left, the rest of the people finally dispersed. It had been an occasion they would never forget, and they would be reminded of it every time they visited the Cinema.

CHAPTER THIRTEEN 1920 – 1923

The country fell into a deep slump after the war, and many were hit hard in the industrial town of Barrow. Vickers laid off thousands of men, two of whom were Albert and Charlie. The orders for ships had dwindled, and there were just too many men employed to be used in the few contracts won by Vickers.

Albert worried for a time; his laying off had come as a surprise since he had been head foreman in the foundry for several years, but he took it with good grace. He was 49, and a lifetime of hard physical graft had taken its toll. He reckoned the family would manage well enough on what came in; he was well-known locally as a man who could turn his hand to anything. Little bits of work came his way; gardening, building. As long as the family was fed and clothed, that was the important thing. And Grace, Charlie and Faith made their contributions. It was a struggle, but then – life had always been that way!

Faith had been working since she was fifteen. In 1918 she was too young to work with Grace in munitions at Vickers. Instead, she took a job as a 'sorter' at Barrow Paper Mill; she put aside any marked or creased sheets of paper and squared up the remaining sheets into neat piles. These piles were then passed over to the 'tie-er uppers' who counted sheets into reams of 500, then wrapped up into parcels ready for despatch to customers. She worked from 7:45 am until 5:30 pm every day with an hour for dinner and from 7:45 am until noon on Saturdays. The hours were long, and she was on her feet all day, but she was lucky in that there was a good atmosphere; the girls were allowed to talk to each other, just as long as they kept working, and Faith had made lots of friends.

Her work at first had brought 10 shillings a week into the family coffers, of which Faith received 3 shillings as her pocket money. Then she had moved up to be a tie-er upper, and the wages were better – she earned 15 shillings a week and received 6 shillings allowance. At this, she was overjoyed – at seventeen, she had a small measure of independence. With her first week's increased pay, she took herself off to Hetherington's, the draper's shop in town, and bought herself some ribbons to decorate her Sunday best hat.

The financial situation became slightly easier when Joy and Freddie both left school within twelve months of each other. The aristocracy still had their stately homes to maintain, and Joy was taken on as a kitchen maid at Holker Hall near Cartmel in 1920 when she was fourteen. Being in service, especially in the lower orders, could be a hard life for a young person, but Joy soon settled in. She shared a room with two other girls; Daisy, a kitchen maid, and Polly, the scullery maid. They were fortunate in that they came under the rule of the Cook, and Mrs Dabney was a cook of the best sort. She was a large warm-hearted woman who took pride in her skills and kept a motherly eye on her charges. Yes, they worked hard, rising at 5:30 am and often not getting to bed until 10:00 pm, but Mrs Dabney did not believe in slave labour and ensured that her staff had rest breaks whenever there was a lull in kitchen activity. She instantly liked Joy, who was a lively girl, always smiling and cheerful and very willing to learn everything she could from her superior.

The Butler, Mr Jenkins, who had overall charge of every servant of the house, whilst strict, was fair-minded and agreed with Mrs Dabney that a house ran better with content staff. Mr Jenkins maintained discipline, and Mrs Dabney ensured they were fed and rested properly. So, Joy was happy with her lot, the only downside being that she missed her large family. Having only two days a month off apart from a half-day each week on Sunday mornings for church meant a fairly long journey to see them just for an overnight stay, but it was worth it. And being able to take home a goodly sum to help out made her feel very worthwhile – it wasn't a lot of money, but it would help.

She had been there for two years, when she heard that Holker's gardener was looking for a new boy to add to his team, Joy immediately thought of her younger brother and asked Mr Jenkins' permission for Freddie to come along and see if he would suit the vacancy. On her next visit home, she told her parents and Freddie about the job and the interview invitation.

Young Freddie was thrilled with the prospect. He had gone straight into Vickers on an apprenticeship with his father in the foundry and had been there two years when the shipyard started laying off men. Until they started getting more orders in, and with so many already skilled men out of work, it was highly unlikely that Freddie would get the chance to go back. The thought of working at Holker Hall in the gardens sounded like it might be a good plan.

When Joy returned to work after her days off, Freddie went along. As they reached the servants' entrance of the huge house, for once Freddie had no wisecracks or quips to offer, for which Joy was thankful. It wouldn't do if Mr Jenkins and Mr Hopwood, the Gardener, thought he was too cheeky. He was soon whisked off to the Butler's Pantry to speak in private to the two men, who were holding his future in their hands.

Joy was on tenterhooks, waiting in the kitchen. She wasn't due back on duty until the next morning, but she started preparing the vegetables for this evening's dinner, just to keep herself occupied whilst Freddie was being interviewed. How lovely it would be if he got the job! She wouldn't feel so homesick with her brother around, and perhaps they could even get their time off together to visit home.

When he came out, closing the door behind him, Freddie looked sad and upset. Seeing his face, Joy thought the worst and went to put her arm around him. "Never mind, Freddie, I'm sure you'll find something else." She hugged him and kissed his cheek.

"Aww, ger' off me, our Joy! Don't be so soft! Why would I want something else when I start here next week! I only blooming well got it!" his face was fixed with a huge grin.

He grabbed his sister and began to waltz her around the kitchen until Mrs Dabney clipped his ear. "That's enough of that, young man; this is a kitchen, not a dance hall!"

Freddie rubbed his ear, "Sorry, Missus! I was just so pleased!" Mrs Dabney grinned back at him, "I bet Joy is pleased too! Sit down both of you and have a cup of tea and a piece of cake.

You'll want something inside you before you go all the way back to Barrow."

So, that meant things were getting easier for the Tunstalls back at home. Kate was sad that two of her children would no longer be under her roof, but the extra money – and indeed the extra space – would be welcome. She couldn't help but shed a quiet tear when she found herself unusually alone one afternoon and was surprised when Albert caught her unawares.

"Now then, Katie, why so sad? You know it will happen sooner or later that all your little chicks will fly the nest in the end," he knelt beside her chair and put his arm around her. "And we can be thankful that they're both being treated well in their work too – there are a lot of people much worse off. We should be grateful."

"I know, Albert, I know. And I am grateful. We've been so lucky; all eight of our bairns grown-up or growing fast, all healthy. Charlie came back from the war, and Grace is walking out with that nice lad, Ned. So many women I know have lost their children through stillbirth, miscarriage, disease or war. I almost feel guilty about our good luck! I just wonder how much longer it can hold out!" She shook her head, scolding herself internally. "I'm all right – as you say, I was just thinking that before long, they'll all be away, working, married and having their own children. What will I do with myself then?"

"I know the answer to that already!" Albert grinned, "You can take care of me! Though I've no doubt, I'll have to fight for your attention again when the grandchildren start coming along."

"Away with you, Albert Tunstall! As if you're not spoiled enough already!"

Charlie had taken the loss of his job quite badly. Fortunately, he had finished his apprenticeship and had his skills to fall back on. If he could last it out, he would get back into Vickers with not much of a problem when things improved. In the meantime, he used the last of his Army savings and bought a boat – the *Isper Ann*. She was a small pleasure yacht, and with his best friend Rob Yates in partnership, they made a few bob ferrying people around the Island and up and down the coast. The English were a seafaring nation, and most people were fascinated with messing about on the water. It was a cheap and cheerful way of spending an afternoon when the weather was half decent in these grim times. At other times, Charlie cycled around the county, looking for any job he could find; he didn't mind what it was. He scoured the papers for 'Situations Vacant' and wrote off for any skilled positions but never heard much back. It was a case of keeping cheerful and not letting hard times get him down.

And he still had his St John's Ambulance to keep him busy. He had his family too – all nine of them! Three of his sisters were already earning their living, and the smaller children were growing up fast, not babies anymore. Even his younger brother had found work! Charlie missed him an awful lot. You couldn't stay miserable for long with young Freddie around, cheeky monkey that he was. It had been thoughts of his parents and siblings that had kept Charlie going in the trenches; thoughts of going home to them all kept him from wallowing in despair like some of the poor sods he had encountered over there. No, he was Lucky Charlie – something would turn up, it always did!

And something soon did turn up that would enhance Charlie's life. One evening at a local dance, he'd noticed a lovely, if very quiet girl at the outer edges of the ballroom. His friend, Rob, had wangled him an introduction to her; her name was Sarah Downs, and she was the most perfect girl Charlie had ever met – and he'd met quite a few. She was very slim and pretty with long dark hair, coiled into a neat chignon at the nape of her neck. When she overcame her shyness enough to look at Charlie, her eyes were dark brown, almost ebony, framed with thick dark lashes that gave her an exotic look. A small straight nose, with just a slight upturn at the end, and dimples each side of a full-lipped mouth, which revealed perfect white teeth as she smiled at him. Charlie was enchanted; he wanted so much to get to know her.

As a St John's Ambulance Brigade member, Charlie had an automatic invitation to the Ambulance Ball of 1922. Glad of the opportunity to dress up and offer Sarah a nice time, he'd gone to call for her at home in Windsor Street, which was fortunately just around the corner from the Victoria Park Hotel, the venue for the Ball. It was a very elegant occasion, and they had a wonderful evening; once Charlie had seen off the competition for Sarah's dance-card entries, that is.

As they whirled around the dance floor, he felt almost light-headed with this beautiful girl in his arms. Although she was shy, she answered his questions with a smile and somehow made him feel like he was the only man in the world. He felt so suave and sophisticated; he could have given Rudi Valentino a run for his money!

At the end of the evening, he walked her home. There was a light outside the front door, and Charlie noticed how her hair shone, reflecting glints of dark gold. He asked if perhaps he might call on her again. Maybe take her out for a walk on Sunday afternoon? She would love that, thank you. He took her hand in both of his and wished her a good night. She responded with a smile, then went inside, closing the door quietly after her.

Charlie's heart was so full he almost skipped down the garden path and took the gate in a single leap. Then he realised she might be watching him from a window and turned to look. Sure enough, he saw the lace curtain move slightly, so he waved and walked away, whistling happily.

Two days later, he was again on the garden path, having properly negotiated the garden gate this time. He pulled the bell and waited. He was surprised when it opened to find a tall man with the same dark hair as Sarah, standing on the threshold. The man reached out to shake Charlie's hand, "I supposed you must be Charles Tunstall? I'm Steven Downs, Sarah's father. Come in, young man."

Charlie followed Mr Downs along a short corridor and into the front room. Sitting waiting were Sarah and her mother. "You've already met my wife, Evelyn, I think?"

"Yes, Sir, we met a few weeks ago. How are you, Mrs Downs?" said Charlie, nervously.

"Nice to see you again, Charles," said Evelyn. "I'm well, thank you. I believe you and Sarah had a lovely evening at the Ball?"

"Yes, it was very nice, thank you," he hadn't expected this. Though he supposed it would not be right that he would just turn up and whisk their daughter away. Of course, they would want to know what sort of man she was getting involved with.

"Sit down, Charles, make yourself comfortable," said Sarah's father. "Unless you're in a hurry, of course?"

"No, Sir, not at all. We were just going for a walk. That's all," Charlie sat on the edge of the armchair.

"Well, you have a nice day for it," said Steven, "Anywhere nice?"

"I hadn't thought about it yet," replied Charlie. "I was going to ask Sarah where she would like to go."

"Dad," Sarah interrupted, "Charlie doesn't need the third degree!"

"No, of course not, love, I wouldn't dream of it. But you can't blame me for wanting to get a look at him, can you?"

"Dad! Please —!" Sarah was blushing now. When Charlie looked at her father, he saw a wide grin and was surprised when he winked at him.

"All right, all right. I'll put you out of your misery! Off you go, the pair of you, and have a nice walk."

Charlie stood up, hurriedly, "Thank you, Sir. We won't be out for too long, I promise." He held his hand out to Sarah, "Are you ready then?"

"I'll just get my cardigan; it's in the hall. Let's go! 'Bye, Mum and Dad. See you later on."

"All right, love," said her mother, "maybe we can have a cup of tea when you get back? But only if you'd like to, Charles — it's not an interrogation!" She laughed.

They heard laughter from the front room as they left the house, and Charlie took her hand as they ran down the path.

CHAPTER FOURTEEN 1923

After searching for a job everywhere he could think of, Charlie finally received word that he was invited for an interview in answer to a letter he had written. He had gone to Liverpool for the interview but had been dismayed to see so many applicants for the position. Charlie didn't hold out much hope of success. So it was to his great surprise that he eventually received a telegram telling him he had been selected. He then had to break the news to his family that the job was thousands of miles away in Ceylon, with a shipbuilding and engineering company called Hutson's.

The family were both thrilled and dismayed at his success but gave him their blessing. The worse part was telling Sarah; they had been courting for a long time and were in love. They understood that they would marry as soon as things got better, though it was not yet official. Charlie was too proud to take Sarah away from her parents and make her live on the breadline.

Now though, he spoke to Steven Downing, telling him about his prospects for the future. "So, I'll be working as an engineer for Hutson's in Columbo and will have men under me. It's a good job, and the salary is good too. I'll be able to give Sarah the sort of life she deserves. We'll have a house and servants, and she'll be treated like a lady. I love her, and I promise I'll take care of her. All I need is your blessing and permission to ask her to marry me. Will you give it, please, Sir?"

Sarah's father looked serious. "Sarah is my only child, Charlie, and you want to take her to the other side of the world. You'll agree that it's a big decision, I'm sure."

"Yes, I understand that. But we love each other very much, and this way, I can provide for her and keep her in – well, if not luxury, at least in comfort. I will do my utmost to make her happy. She's the only girl for me; I knew it the first time I set eyes on her. Besides, I won't be taking her away immediately. I'll need some time to settle there, find us a house and make it all ready for when she arrives. I'll be out there for a while before I can have some leave, but I'd like for us to be engaged before I go. So that she knows how serious I am; how committed I am to our life together. I'd just like to make it official, that's all." Charlie's heart raced. Was it possible that Steven would refuse? Was he hoping that they would forget all about each other; find someone else to love?

"I'll need some time to think it over, Charlie. I'll discuss it with my wife and give you my decision in due course. That's the best I can do for now."

"That's all I ask, Sir. Thank you." Charlie shook Steven's hand, and they both went into the sitting room where Evelyn and Sarah were waiting for them to join them for a cup of tea. Sarah looked quizzically at Charlie, then her father, but neither mentioned the result of their talk.

"Well, I'm ready for this tea!" said Steven, "What are you two to up to this evening?"

Sarah said, "We're going to Rob Yate's house – he bought a gramophone last week and has some new records that he wants to play for us, so we're having a musical evening."

Her father shook his head, "I don't know! The stuff that you young people call music these days! What sort of a song title is 'Yes We Have No Bananas' for goodness' sake? And what about that – is it Dixieland jazz? And who in their right mind calls themselves 'Satchelmouth' instead of their proper given name, Louis Armstrong? I'll never understand the youth of today." He was laughing as he spoke, joking with them.

Sarah laughed with him, "Dad, you're hopeless! It's 'Satchmo' he calls himself, not the full version. I suppose you'd rather we sat and listened to Bach or Beethoven all night long!"

"Well, it wouldn't do you any harm! I've heard some of those records by Enrico Caruso, though; I like him. Perhaps we ought to invest in a gramophone, Evelyn, what do you think?"

"I think I'd rather keep playing the piano if you don't mind!" retorted his wife.

Two days later, Charlie had another conversation with Steven and was delighted with his decision. He rushed to tell Sarah that they had his blessing. He did the traditional thing and went down on one knee as Sarah blushed. "Sarah, you know how much I love you; you're the only girl for me. I know that it will probably be a long engagement until I can afford everything I want you to have, but will you marry me? Will you wait for me to come back for you and take you to our new life in Ceylon?"

"Yes, Charlie, I will," she replied.

Charlie slipped a tiny solitaire diamond ring onto her finger, "That's the best I can afford right now, but I'll replace it with something much finer once I'm on my feet and settled into the job. Will it do for the time being?"

"It's just perfect, Charlie. I'll treasure it forever," she smiled as he stood and took her in his arms for a kiss to set the seal on their future together.

Charlie was not the only one getting romantic. Grace and Ned had been discussing the future, too, talking about their hopes and dreams. He had not asked her to get married yet, though he desperately wanted to, but felt the time wasn't right until he had saved enough money. Like Charlie, he wanted to provide for Grace, although she was happy working at the Pavilion Café and had been for some time.

Grace and Sandra, along with their boss, Doris Dent, had a great time at work. They enjoyed the visitors coming into the shop and café and worked well together. Having the three of them working meant that when things were quiet, one or another of them could take a bit of time off. Sandra loved that aspect of the job as it made things so much easier to get her children taken care of. Doris was easy-going as long as everyone pulled their weight and the three got along famously.

Ned had completed his apprenticeship some while ago. He had been fortunate enough to be kept on in Vickers as an electrician when so many other trades had been let go. He counted himself very lucky at having a full-time job and a wage coming in, as well as still helping out at the Walney Cinema some evenings. When Mr Blake occasionally left the running of the films completely to him and had a night off, Grace would join Ned in the projection room and was amazed at all the equipment that he controlled without a qualm. She was fascinated to watch him thread the celluloid film through the projector and get each of the tiny cogs in the right place, so the film ran smoothly. She sometimes had to remind him, though, that he must concentrate on the film and not on her when he got a little bit too romantic.

Ned had become part of the Tunstall family – he could even tell the twins apart, which was practically impossible, especially if they set out to play tricks and swapped their identities. He was a favourite with Albert too when he brought his violin around, and the two of them would make music whilst the rest of the family sang along.

When Kate and Albert decided to give Charlie a farewell party, they invited everyone they could think of – all the family and their friends, along with Ned and his family and Sarah and her parents too. Happily, Joy and Freddie had been allowed to come home for that weekend, so the entire family was there to wish Charlie well on his new venture. The house was full to brimming, but everyone found their own little space, and they even managed to clear a small place in the parlour for couples to dance if they felt like it. It was a joyous evening, full of congratulations on the engagement and best wishes for a 'Bon Voyage'.

The party went on until the early hours; at around three o'clock in the morning, Charlie and Sarah found themselves alone at last when Kate and Albert said goodnight and went upstairs. Before he left, Sarah was on the receiving end of a smacking great kiss from her future father-in-law as he told her he was looking forward to welcoming her into the family.

Charlie found Sarah's coat and put it around her shoulders. "It's time I walked you home," he said, "I promised your dad I wouldn't keep you out too late! I hope he won't be angry."

"No, he'll be fine; he enjoyed himself this evening. You know, Charlie, as an only child, I was always a bit lonely, having to rely on visits to and from cousins before I had anyone to play with. You're so lucky to have your family – all your sisters and your brother. At first, I found it all a bit overwhelming, but they've been so kind to me; I really do feel like part of your family." She linked her arm through his, "Do you think they'll mind if I keep on visiting while you're away?"

He laughed, "I think they'd mind a lot more if you DIDN'T visit! They already think of you as a daughter in law, and my mam said she's looking forward to helping you with the wedding arrangements."

"I think it won't be long before she's making arrangements for another wedding too. Did you see Grace and Ned together? They make such a lovely couple! He's so attentive to her and treats her like part of his dad's precious porcelain!"

"Yes, he's a nice lad – I like him a lot. I hope they'll be almost as happy as we're going to be. You don't mind the thought of living so far away from home, do you?" Charlie asked.

"I admit, I'm a bit scared, leaving my family behind and yours too. But it isn't like I have a vast number of friends to miss or who will miss me. Until I met you, I was so shy that I didn't mix well and spent most of my time alone. I'll be happy wherever I am as long as I have you to look after me, silly!"

A similar conversation was happening in the Naiad Street parlour. Ned and Grace had enjoyed the party; when he'd put down his violin from time to time, he and Grace had danced and created quite a stir with their rendition of the Fox-trot and the Charleston. Kate had been quite shocked – she and Albert and the other parents had performed a staid waltz, but that wasn't quite modern enough for the youngsters. People were still talking about the party for months after the event.

The following Friday, 13th September 1923, Charlie left Barrow on the night mail train to catch the *SS Dumana* from Tilbury Dock, bound for Ceylon on a four-year contract with Messrs Hutson and Co Ltd for the princely sum of £30 per month.

CHAPTER FIFTEEN 1926-1927

In 1926 Grace and Ned decided that it was time they settled down together. They had been courting for eight years, and everyone already considered them a couple, so it seemed natural to take the next step, now that the aftermath of the war had settled down and prospects for the future were optimistic.

By this time, the other Tunstall children had grown up and were making their way in life. Faith was 24 and still working at the Paper Mill as a supervisor. Joy was 21 and was the Cook's assistant at Holker Hall. She was walking out with a young man called Maurice Barker, a baker from nearby Milnthorpe. They had met when he made deliveries to the Holker Hall kitchens and discovered love over the bread rolls. Freddie, at 20, had left the Hall and was now in Accrington working with a dairyman. He had taken his gardening experience and set up a vegetable garden on the dairyman's land – they now supplied fresh vegetables to their customers on the daily milk round.

Hope and Constance, aged 19, had also moved to Accrington with Freddie; they had gone into nursing together and worked at Accrington Victoria Hospital. And lastly, young Prudence, the baby of the family at 17, was still living in Barrow with her parents. She had always been delicate, and although she would have liked to find work, Albert and Kate insisted that unless she could find some employment that would suit her delicate constitution, she should remain at home. Ned had been helpful in that he had suggested to the manager of Walney Picture house that Prue would be very suitable to work at the cinema.

She would be able to staff the Box Office and help out as an usherette if necessary. Although the work was only part-time, it was sufficient for Prue to contribute to the household and didn't stretch her health in any way, so she was happy too. It also instilled a love of cinema in her, which she shared with her soon-to-be brother-in-law.

But the dynamics of the family would soon change even further.

In truth, neither Grace nor Ned could imagine life without the other. By now, they knew each other so well, and they were best friends as well as being romantically involved. They had also become fairly intimate some while ago but had not yet gone the whole way. Grace had wanted to remain a virgin until her wedding day, and Ned had been patient, though both sometimes found it hard to stop when their kisses became more passionate.

They were sitting in the Tunstall's parlour one evening just after Grace's birthday in October. Finally, they were alone and could talk without the rest of the family hearing. Ned's arm was around Grace's shoulders, and they were smooching as they listened to records on Albert's new toy – a gramophone. In the kitchen, Kate and Albert heard the long delays between the records and smiled knowingly at each other. There was another long silence after Gertrude Lawrence had finished singing 'Do Do Do' before it was replaced by Henry Burr's 'I'll Be Loving You Always'.

"It's about time those two stopped messing around and got serious with each other," Albert said, "they've been walking out together for long enough."

"All in good time, Bertie. I think it won't be long before Ned wants to speak to you alone. Shush now, they're coming!" Kate heard the parlour door open and footsteps along the hall.

But it was Ned on his own who came into the room. "I wonder if I can have a private word with you, Mr Tunstall?" He was puzzled when Grace's father suddenly seemed to stifle a laugh.

"Yes, lad, come out into the yard while I have a smoke; it's a pleasant enough evening if a bit chilly." Albert tamped down the tobacco in the bowl of his pipe and struck a match on the side of the range before beckoning Ned to follow. Once outside, Albert sat on the upturned tin bath. "What can I do for you, son?"

Nervously, Ned began to speak, "Well, as you know, Sir, Grace and I have been seeing each other for a long time. We've been talking about our future and, if you'll allow it, I would like to take her for my wife. We love each other very much, and I promise I'll do my best to take care of her."

"Now then! It's funny you should ask because me and her mother were just talking about that very thing. It's taken you long enough, hasn't it? You haven't been keeping her waiting in case something better comes along, have you?" Albert kept his face straight but almost broke down at the dismay on Ned's face.

"Oh no, Sir! There couldn't be anyone better than Gracie for me. I think I've loved her since I first saw her at school all those years ago. No, we've just been waiting for things to get better. I've been saving for a few years and have a little nest egg that we might be able to use as a deposit on buying a house. And with my wages from the Shipyard and the bit extra I get from the Cinema, I'm sure I can provide well for her. And anyone else who might come along!" Ned suddenly stopped himself – had he gone too far?

"What's that?" said Albert, sternly, "you haven't got my Gracie in the family way, have you? You have to marry her – is that it?"

"No! No! Not at all!" Ned threw up his hands in horror, "we've not done anything more than a bit of canoodling, I swear! I wouldn't – she wouldn't – well, WE wouldn't dream of it!"

At this, Albert could no longer restrain himself, "I know that, I'm just having a bit of fun with you. Calm down, lad! Ned, if you want to marry our Grace, you're very welcome into our family. Come on back inside, and let's put her mother out of her misery! And Grace too, no doubt!" He slapped Ned gently on the back, and the two went indoors.

Albert announced, with a grin wide enough to split his face, "We were right, Katie! Our Gracie and Ned have decided to make a go of it. What do you think of that?"

Kate stood up, just as Grace came into the room, "I'm very happy! It's about time. When are you going to do the deed?"

The look of delight on Ned's face was enough to tell Grace there had been no objections to the match, and she looked at her mother, smiling. "I don't know – he hasn't asked ME yet! What if I refuse?"

Ned's face fell slightly, but Albert said, "Stop it, Gracie – we've teased the lad enough for one evening!"

"No, Sir, Grace is right." Ned fell to one knee and took Grace's hand, "Grace Tunstall, please will you marry me and make me the happiest man alive?"

Suddenly overcome, Grace got a lump in her throat and could do no more than nod at her new fiancé, who jumped up and took her in his arms. "Tomorrow," he said, "We'll go into town, to Story's the Jewellers, and find you an engagement ring!"

Kate dabbed her eyes with the edge of her pinny and said, "Just a minute, I need to get something from upstairs," and went out.

Grace looked at her father, puzzled. Albert shrugged, "Don't ask me, love, I don't know what she's up to."

After a few moments, Kate returned carrying a small velvet box. She gave it to Ned, "Here, use this. It was my mother's, and I'm sure she'd have wanted her eldest granddaughter to have it."

Ned opened the box lid to reveal an engagement ring, three diamonds set on a gold band. Grace caught her breath – "Oh Mam, it's beautiful! Are you sure?"

Kate nodded, "Yes, I'm sure. I have no need of it, and you deserve it, not only because you're the eldest, but because of everything you've done for this family through the years."

Grace hugged her mother and turned to Ned. He took the ring and gingerly placed it on Grace's ring finger – it fitted perfectly. "In that case then," he said, "we'll go and find an eternity ring to match it! I have to contribute something to this occasion."

After a long time on the doorstep saying goodnight to Ned, Grace returned to the kitchen. She couldn't help looking at her hand, delighting in the way the diamonds twinkled in the lamplight. Tonight, for the first time, she didn't feel like Grace, the ugly duckling sister among swans. Fittingly, she was the first of her sisters to get engaged, and if she had anything to do with it, she'd be the first to marry too!

Albert had gone up to bed, but Kate was waiting for Grace in the kitchen. Her daughter told her they had decided to get married just before her next birthday, on 8th October 1927, which gave them about a year to keep saving and organise everything. "On that subject," said Kate, "I have a surprise for you. You know it's traditional for the bride's family to pay for the wedding?"

"Yes, I know that, Mam, but we'll try to economise and keep everything to a budget. I don't want you and our Dad to have to worry about the money," Grace said. "I've got some savings put by from my earnings, and I know Ned has some money, so we'll both be able to help out with the costs."

"No, lass, you don't understand! You and Ned are going to need all the money you can get if you're planning on buying a house before long. But what I'm trying to say is that we already have the money for your wedding. I've been saving your keep ever since you started working on the airships all those years ago!" Kate's eyes shone with happiness, "There's more than enough put by to pay for your wedding, so you don't have to scrimp and save. You can choose whatever you want!"

As Grace went up to bed that night, she bubbled with excitement. Suddenly, the future was laid out before them for the next twelve months at least. Ned would buy a house, and they would furnish it, ready to move into after the wedding. She wondered if Ned would let her keep working after they married – at least until the first baby came along. She wanted to have a large family like her own. Grace could see herself surrounded by beautiful children, at least four. But she would see what could be done not to have a baby every year, like her mother – she had seen the effect that had had on Kate – so a new baby every two or three years would be much better. She would have to ask – maybe Doris would know – how one went about delaying pregnancy if it was possible.

Christmas 1926 came and went amid the usual festivities, and the New Year brought good news – Charlie would be coming home on leave in May! It had been a couple of years since he'd been home – this time, he would be back for about six months which meant he would still be here for Grace and Ned's wedding. He and Sarah had also named the day – their wedding would be a couple of weeks after Ned and Grace, a week before he was due to sail back to Ceylon. When he left next time, Sarah would be going back with him to start their new life together.

Sarah had apologised to Grace – she didn't want to take any of the shine off Grace's big day. Sarah still suffered from immense shyness, and the prospect of a large formal wedding was anathema to her. She and Charlie had decided to have a small affair, with just family and one or two close friends to witness the occasion.

But even had her brother decided on a big 'do', nothing could mar Grace's happiness. They would only do this once, so she and Ned went all out to plan their perfect day. Grace could hardly wait; she had never been so excited about anything in her life.

It was a busy summer, what with all the wedding preparations. But it was a very happy time, particularly for the ladies, giving them many opportunities to get together without their menfolk. Both brides prepared their *trousseaus*, more commonly known as the 'bottom drawer' in Barrovian working-class circles. This was a collection of the personal possessions a new bride would need after leaving her parents' home and included linens and household wares, crockery, pots and pans, ornaments and of course, her clothes. In Sarah's case, everything would be packed up and boxed, ready for the long voyage to Columbo.

Most exciting of all for the two brides-to-be was what to do about wedding dresses. Grace approached her future mother-in-law, who was an expert tailor and seamstress. Although many years before she had lost her business when the Parsons' shop had burned down, Florence had continued to sew, if not professionally. All of her daughter Florrie's clothes, were the envy of her friends, including Grace.

Florence happily agreed to make Grace the perfect dress and offered to make one for Sarah, if she wished, for which Sarah was very grateful. They all spent a lot of time together designing the dresses then shopping for the fabrics and trimmings. Grace chose beautiful ivory coloured watered silk. Her tastes were stylish; the dress had long, tight sleeves and a slashed neckline with a drop waist and handkerchief hem that was ankle length. The edges of the neckline and sleeves and the waistline would be trimmed with small seed pearls, and she would wear a long string of pearls around her neck. A bandeau headdress embellished with pearls and masses of tulle in a long veil would complete the outfit.

Sarah preferred a simpler style; she chose white lace laid over ivory satin in a sleeveless gown with a deep round neckline and the fashionable drop waist and long handkerchief hem. Rather than a veil, Sarah preferred a close-fitting cloche hat in ivory, decorated with a large flower accompanied by long kid gloves.

Ned and Grace spent a great deal of time searching for their first home together and had decided to rent until they could find their perfect house. They thought it was fate when they found a place in Delhi Street, just opposite where the Tunstalls had lived before they moved to Naiad Street some years before, so it was both familiar and new at the same time. There was decorating to bring it into the new couple's tastes and Albert made himself very useful for getting the house ready for when their married life would start.

There was a little uncertainty about whether those family members who had moved away from Barrow to work could attend both weddings. But they were able to give plenty of notice to their employers, so it was organised for other workmates and colleagues to cover their absences to the satisfaction of all concerned. That meant the entire family could see the elder sister and brother go off to their respective new lives and partnerships.

October soon arrived, and Grace and Ned's ceremony was held at St Mary's. They had asked Ned's sister, Florrie and her fiancé, Ray Thompson, to stand as witnesses not to offend any of Grace's many siblings. After the service, the whole wedding party walked down steep Church Lane, then up the Promenade to the King Alfred pub for their wedding breakfast. They had invited all their friends and relatives, and there was music and dancing until everyone had their fill of celebrating. They stayed at the Hotel for their Wedding night and took the train to Blackpool for a short honeymoon the next day. When they came home, they moved into their new house and started their life of marital bliss together.

In comparison, Sarah got her wish for a small celebration. Two weeks after the Parsons' wedding, Charlie and Sarah married at St Mary's, but this time with Rob Yates and his wife as witnesses and just the family present, which turned out to still be a sizeable number of people! Afterwards, Sarah's parents laid on a small celebration at their home in Victoria Road. As a wedding gift, they paid for the wedding night and stayed at the Victoria Park Hotel the rest of the week before the couple's departure for Ceylon. Evelyn Downs had thought this a romantic gesture since it was the venue of the couple's first date.

With the celebrations over, there was a tinge of sadness when Charlie and Sarah visited Naiad Street to say their goodbyes to the family. Ned and Grace had joined their parents, Faith and Prudence, but it was a depleted gathering since the others had returned to their various jobs. There were tears and laughter, joy and sadness and eventually, the couple left to catch their train to Tilbury for their voyage. Ned and Grace went home to their new house, and Faith and Prue went about their business, leaving Albert to comfort his wife after such an emotional time. "You know they're all going to flee the nest some time, love. But they'll visit from time to time. And think of all the peace and quiet we'll have. And time, lots of time, for you and me to enjoy ourselves without worrying about them all."

"Oh Bertie, you're such an old fool!" Kate sobbed into his chest, "they might be all gone, but that will never stop me worrying about them! Every last one of them!"

"I know, sweetheart, I know," he was glad she didn't see the tear that rolled down his own cheek before he dashed it away.

CHAPTER SIXTEEN 1928

With Grace and Ned married, Charlie and Sarah gone away and the others working away from Barrow, only Faith and Prue were left at home with their parents.

Faith had shared a bed with one or more of her sisters for as long as she could remember, and now, she missed the closeness. She was eight years older than Prue, and the age gap seemed much wider because Prue had lived such a sheltered life. At 25 and 18, a chasm yawned between the two girls, and they had nothing in common except their family. Faith had plenty of friends at the Paper Mill, even though she was now supervising some of the girls she'd worked alongside.

But it wasn't the same; no one knew her as well as Grace. So, Faith spent a lot of time a few streets away from home with her eldest sister; they had always been close and confided in one another. She missed the whispered secrets and sharing of dreams under the covers when the younger girls were asleep. And now Faith had a secret – she was desperate to tell someone, and the only person who would do was Grace.

Grace answered the knock at the door, wiping her hands on a towel. Ned had gone off to the Picture House to work, and she had just finished washing up the dishes from their evening meal. She had planned to spend the evening embroidering some handkerchiefs that she intended to give her mother as a birthday gift. When she saw Faith on the doorstep, she was glad to see her sister – at least they could gossip as she worked. It was still strange to live in such a quiet house with Ned, although she loved keeping their little love-nest spick and span. But there never seemed to be much that needed doing with only the two of them. Grace had found it even more difficult to cook meals for only two people. She continued to think in terms of a large family and was amazed that a pot of stew would last the couple three days at least. It was a good job Ned liked it!

"Why did you knock?" she asked Faith, "you could've just come straight in; the door's always open!"

"I didn't know if Ned was here; I wouldn't have wanted to walk in to catch the pair of you in a clinch, would I! That would be embarrassing." Faith enjoyed the look of guilt on her sister's face, "I know what you newlyweds are like!"

"Shut up! I'm glad to see you, anyway. Is everything all right? Mam, Dad and Prue – they're all well?"

"Yes, they're fine. Have you been working today? Was the Pavilion busy?" Faith asked.

"The sun always brings people out – it's lovely to see all the little children and their mothers out getting the fresh air. It wasn't too busy, though, but I expect it will be at the weekend if the weather holds up." Grace looked at her, her eyes narrowed, "Come on, out with it! What's with all the small talk? Is there something you want to tell me?"

Faith smiled, blushing slightly, "What do you mean?"

"I mean, what's going on? You're not normally bothered about my work. Has something happened?"

Faith nodded, grinning, "I've met someone!"

"Really? When? Where? Who is he? Do I know him?" Grace was agog at her sister's news.

"I hardly think so. He's only been in Barrow for a few weeks. He's from Derby, and he's started at the Mill as the new Production Manager!" said Faith.

"Ooh, that sounds interesting. Let me just put the kettle on, and you can tell me all about him."

Faith followed Grace into the kitchen, sitting at the table as Grace put the kettle on the hob and gathered the tea things. "His name is Harry Renshaw, he's thirty-two, so a bit older than me. I think he's very handsome; dark hair, brown eyes, almost as tall as our Charlie! And he's got a motorcar, a Morris Oxford or – I don't know what. He's asked to take me out at the weekend!"

Grace felt doubtful about her sister's news, "have you told our Mam? What does she say about it?"

"Grace! I'm 25 years old – a grown woman! I should be allowed to go out with a man without asking my parents first!" Faith complained.

"I know, I know! That wasn't what I meant. I mean, what does she think of the situation?" Grace asked.

"What situation?" Faith said indignantly, "A man has asked me to go for a drive on Sunday. He's respectable enough to be my boss, so where's the harm?"

"That's exactly my point! He's your boss. He shouldn't be getting involved with people who work for him; that's not right," Grace said, "and you shouldn't be getting involved with him either. What happens if you go out with him then it goes wrong? It's you that will lose your job, then what will you do?"

"I never said I was going to get involved. I just want to go out in his car, that's all; I've never been in one before. It's all right for you, with your lovely Ned, that you've been with forever. There aren't that many single men left that came home from the war. I'm going to end up an old maid if I don't meet someone soon." Faith put her head in her hands and started to cry.

"Oh Faith, please don't! You're not going to be an old maid – you'll meet someone soon, I'm sure of it!" Grace stroked her sister's hair, "You're too nice not to find someone, you'll see. And, I suppose there's no harm in going out for a drive – but you make sure that's all he takes you for!"

The following Monday evening, Grace went to her parents' house once Ned had left for the cinema. She was desperate to find out what had happened on Faith's date with Mr Renshaw the previous day.

Kate and Faith were in the Kitchen, Prue was reading in the Parlour, and Albert had gone to his allotment. Kate looked up from her sewing and smiled at her eldest daughter, "Hiya our Gracie, what a lovely surprise. I didn't expect to see you tonight."

"Oh, I just thought I'd come and see how you're doing. The house gets a bit too quiet sometimes when Ned goes to work. I'm just not used to it yet." Grace sat down and nodded at Faith, "how are you, love? Everything all right at work?"

With a blush and the biggest smile, Faith said, "Absolutely wonderful!"

Her mother and sister both looked at her strangely. "Wonderful?" said Kate, "working at the Paper Mill?"

"Well, it IS wonderful – I mean, at least I have a job that I like and friends there. It could be a lot worse!" Faith tried to backtrack and changed the subject quickly, "You know what, our Grace, if your house is too quiet, it's time you started making some babies! That would keep you busy!"

"Faith! Don't be so vulgar!" Kate admonished her, "Grace and Ned will have a family in their own good time."

Faith apologised, "Sorry, I didn't mean to be vulgar. It's just that they've been married quite a while; I'd have thought something would be happening by now. Sorry to upset you, Grace."

Grace grimaced for a moment, then smiled at her sister, "It's all right, love. I'd have thought I'd be expecting by now too, but it's just not happened yet. Tell you what, come round home with me and keep me company for a bit. Mam will be all right; Prue's here, and I daresay Dad will be home soon."

"That's a good idea – you go on Faith, but don't be too late home – you have work tomorrow!" Kate settled back to her sewing.

As the two girls went into the street, Faith started to laugh, "Phew, I nearly blew it then, didn't I?"

"Come on then, tell me all about it?" Grace linked arms with Faith as they walked the few streets to her home. "What was he like?"

"Oh Grace, he is so nice! He was the perfect gentleman. He picked me up on Ocean Road, then we drove to the Coast Road, all the way to Bardsea. We stopped for a drink at the Fisherman's Arms on the way back. We had a lovely time!" she sighed with pleasure at the memory.

As they reached Grace's house and she unlocked the door, she said, "Did you find out anything about him? What's his family like? How did he end up working in Barrow from Derby? Where is he living?"

"Oh Grace, you're like the Spanish Inquisition! We just chatted a little bit! We went out for a drive and had a nice time. That's it!"

Although she tried to make it sound matter-of-fact, Faith's eyes were shining with excitement.

"Are you going to see him again?" asked Grace.

"Yes, we're going out again next weekend," Faith smiled. "I can't believe that someone like him is interested in me, just an ordinary girl from Barrow! He told me that they just designated All Saints' Church in Derby as a Cathedral, which means it will soon be a city! It must be so exciting there."

"Has he said much about his family or what he's been doing until now?" Grace was curious to know how much Mr Renshaw had told her sister about his background.

"Not really. Not yet anyway. I'll tell you what, when we go out again on Sunday, I'll ask him. Make me a list of what you'd like to know... Honestly, Grace, how long did it take you and Ned to get to know each other? I can't give him the third degree on what will only be our second outing, now can I?"

"No, I don't suppose so," admitted Grace. "It's just. I can't help wondering why..."

"What, why he's taking notice of me? Am I so uninteresting and unworthy of a man like him?" Faith was getting upset. "I don't know why I bothered telling you. I might have known you would pour cold water all over it."

"No, please, Faith, you know I didn't mean anything like that! Of course, he'd notice you; you're a very pretty girl. But usually, that sort of man sticks to his own kind. You know, middle-class girls who've been well educated and such like. Not people like us." She tried to find the right words that wouldn't upset her sister any further. "I just mean like that old saying 'East is East and West is West, and never the twain shall meet', that's all. I'm not saying you're not good enough for him – you're good enough for anyone, but I can't help but wonder at his intentions."

"I don't think he has any intentions. He's just a man in a new town who doesn't know many folks and wants to spend the odd afternoon with someone agreeable, that's all. I think he's lonely. I feel sorry for him, in a way. Having a posh car and money doesn't make up for not having your family and friends around you." Faith was determined to get Grace on her side.

"You're probably right," said Grace, giving in. She knew her sister too well, and if she pushed it too far, it would just make Faith dig her heels in and become more determined to see this man. If he were a rogue, they would find out soon enough.

A few months later, all Grace's doubts were made certain. She knew that Faith had kept seeing Harry Renshaw. To be fair to him, he had agreed to come to meet her family, though he insisted that their relationship be kept as quiet as possible. This was because it might cause problems for either of them at work. If the management discovered their affair, they might both lose their jobs, which neither of them wanted to happen.

All of the family liked him, even Grace, once she met him, although there was always a lingering doubt at the back of her mind. But she put that to one side; her sister was happily courting, and that was good enough. Harry was charming and talkative and amusing, as well as being handsome. Albert thought he seemed decent enough, and Kate enjoyed it when Harry flirted with her. Prue developed a small crush on him, but that was natural enough, and she would grow out of it.

So, all was going well, until one evening Faith went to see Grace and obviously had something of importance to tell her sister as she drummed her fingers on the table. She waited impatiently for Ned to leave for the evening showing of the latest Herbert Wilcox film *'Madame Pompadour'* starring Dorothy Gish.

As soon as the front door closed behind him, she burst out, "Grace, I'm in such terrible trouble; I don't know what to do!"

Grace placed a cup of tea on the table in front of Faith, "Whatever's the matter? Are you alright? What have you done?"

"The worst thing that could possibly happen! And I know you're going to say 'I told you so', but that doesn't help at all! I think I'm expecting."

Grace was horrified, "What makes you think so?"

"Well, I haven't been 'unwell' for two months, and the last few mornings at work, I've been as sick as a dog. I just know that I'm pregnant. What am I going to do?" Faith's face had lost all colour, and she looked as though she was about to faint.

Always practical, Grace sat beside her and put her arm around her. "First of all, put some sugar in that tea and have a few sips. Sweet tea is supposed to be good for shock." As Faith did so, Grace continued, "Does Harry know? Does anyone?"

Faith shook her head, "No, I haven't told anyone until now. Dad will kill me, and Mam will be so disappointed. Their first grandchild is going to be a bastard."

"Faith! Don't use that sort of language! Let's not cross that bridge until we come to it. First of all, you have to find out if you are expecting – it could be something you've eaten that's made you sick."

"What about missing my monthlies, though? I'm always as regular as clockwork. That's not down to something I've eaten, is it? I can't believe it – it only happened once! One afternoon, we just got a bit carried away when we were in the dunes at Earnse Bay, where we'd gone for a walk. I remember it was unusually warm for early Spring; the sun was so hot out of the wind, and I'd taken off my stockings to go paddling and was feeling so free and wonderful. But the water was so cold, still freezing, and it took our breath away. We laid down in the sand together, cuddling to warm each other up, and we were kissing and getting passionate. The next thing I knew, we had done the deed. I was a bit worried that he might not respect me anymore – you know, might stop taking any notice of me, but he was a gentleman. He even apologised afterwards for going too far, but it wasn't his fault – it was mine just as much – we just couldn't stop ourselves. Oh, Grace, what shall I do? What's going to become of me?" she wailed.

"Well, the first thing, as I said, is to find out for definite. You're going to have to go to the doctor. I know he might tell Mam or Dad, but you'll have to hope they don't see him before you get the results. Then, if you are, you'll have to tell Harry. You'll have to find out if he's going to stand by you. If he does, at least then you can tell Mam and Dad that he's taking some responsibility. If not, then you'll have to throw yourself on their mercy and hope they don't throw you out. Honestly, though, I don't think that would happen. But you can bet they're going to be mightily angry if you become an unwed mother!" Grace hugged her sister, "I'll be on your side, don't worry. If the worst comes to the worst, I'll persuade Ned to have you here. You won't be on the streets or in the workhouse, I promise."

CHAPTER SEVENTEEN 1928

Grace went with Faith to the doctor to get the test result. When they got the news, all the blood drained from Faith's face, and she almost fainted. The doctor brought out the smelling salts, and she soon recovered. He suggested she should go home and lie down. He had called her 'Mrs. Tunstall' throughout the consultation, and when she looked dismayed at the news, he winked and said, "You're not the first, my dear, and I don't suppose you'll be the last!" Grace spoke to him quietly and asked that he not reveal anything to their father. "I can't promise, Mrs Parsons, but if he doesn't ask me, I certainly won't bring it up. That's the best I can do, I'm afraid." The two girls thanked him and walked back home to Grace's house.

"How are you feeling now, love?" Grace asked, "shall I make some tea?"

"How do you think I'm feeling? I'm scared to death! I don't think tea is going to solve this problem somehow. Oh, I'm sorry, I don't mean to take it out on you, Grace. I just have no idea what I'm going to do." Tears welled up in Faith's eyes, and she could do nothing to stop them from falling.

Grace pulled out a handkerchief from her skirt pocket, "I know it seems terrible at the moment, but we'll work things out, I promise. You just have to decide what you want to do. You're going to have to tell Harry and see if he will do the honourable thing and marry you. How has your courting been going – has he made any mention of getting serious? How do you think he feels about you?"

"That's just it," said Faith, "He's never spoken about us becoming an item or anything. He's never touched me, apart from kissing, that is, except for that one time. We've only been seeing each other for a few months. We've just been going out and enjoying each other's company, having fun. I don't know how he feels or if he intends to propose. I don't think he'll want to know."

"Well, you're going to have to ask him. You'll have to tell him what's happened and see what his reaction is," said Grace.

"I know. It's not going to be easy. I'll have to talk to him at work tomorrow – I'll pick a moment when his secretary isn't there and see him in his office. Oh, Grace, I'm dreading this!" The tears started to fall again, and Faith's eyes were red.

"Now come on – it's not the end of the world. As the doctor said, you aren't the first, and you won't be the last. It will be a blow to the family if he doesn't marry you, but as I said before, I don't think Mam and Dad are the sort to throw you out in your petticoats." Grace, always down to earth and no-nonsense, tried to raise her sister's spirits. "When you think about it, it's quite funny, you and me. Here's me and Ned, doing our level best to get me pregnant, and you go and do it without even trying!"

The next evening, Faith was round at Grace's again, and she could tell by Faith's expression that the news wasn't good. "You'll never believe what's happened. Harry's not working at the Paper Mill anymore – at least for a while! He's gone back to Derby to take over the family business because his father's had a heart attack! He wasn't in his office when I went to see him –

Miss Pritchard, his secretary, said he's already packed up and gone. I don't even know where he lives – and I can't ask because then they'll want to know why I'm asking, and I can't let them all know I'm in the family way! I'd probably get the sack myself, and I'd never hear the end of it from the girls. What am I going to do now?" she wailed.

Grace took her sister by the hand. "I'm not suggesting it, but there is another alternative, of course. Perhaps if we can contact him, Harry might pay for a – let's call it an operation? If you had considered getting rid of it, that is."

The shock on Faith's face was enough to reassure her sister that abortion was not an option. "Grace! How can you say such a thing? The thought hadn't even entered my head! I could never, never do something like that; I wouldn't dream of it. I'll live with the shame if I have to, but I won't kill my own flesh and blood."

"I'm very glad to hear it, and I would feel the same in your position. You poor thing. Look, you don't have to do anything straight away. The doctor said you're only a couple of months gone, and you won't show for a while yet. And even when you do, if you wear loose clothing, you can probably get away with it for a bit. Just keep it to yourself for now. We need some time to make a plan and decide what to do for the best. Let me find out a few things, and then we'll talk to Mam and Dad."

Grace continued, "There is one thing, I hope you don't mind, but I told Ned all about it last night. He noticed that I had something on my mind and when he asked me, it just slipped out. But that's not a bad thing because I told him my idea. That if Harry wasn't going to stand by you, that you could have the baby and then we'd bring it up as ours. We don't seem to be making any headway with our own, and at least you'll be able to see him and know how he's getting on. You don't want to have to give him to strangers and never know anything about him, do you?"

"Oh my God, Grace! What if Ned tells someone? How do you know he'll keep it to himself?" Faith was horrified.

"Of course, he won't say anything – good grief, he barely even speaks to me – what makes you think he'll blab to anyone else? You don't have to worry about Ned; I promise he will keep your secret." She didn't mention that her husband had become upset and blamed himself for not getting her pregnant. Grace had had to reassure him that she was sure there wasn't a problem and that nature would take its course before very long. She hoped.

Faith continued to work, hoping against hope that no one would notice her condition until, as the weeks passed, her belly started to show. As Grace had advised, she wore loose skirts, but eventually, there would be no hiding it. Some of her workmates had already mentioned her gain in weight, which she passed off with a joke.

Once again, in the Delhi Street house, Faith spoke to her sister, "It's no use, Grace. People are starting to notice. The other night in the kitchen, when I was standing by the fire to get warm, our Prue looked at me strangely. She didn't say anything, but I know she was wondering. I think I'm going to have to tell Mam and Dad, and soon!"

"I suppose it is time, and if there are arrangements to be made, we need to make them before it's too late. Now's as good a time as any. Let's go home and see what Mam and Dad have to say. Don't worry; I'll come with you." Grace held out her hand, which Faith grasped like a lifeline. "Get your coat on, love. Let's go and face the music."

When they entered the front door of their parents' house, they could hear their father singing while Prue played the piano. That boded well as if he was singing, he was in a good mood. They went through to the kitchen where Kate sat by the fire, her sewing in her lap.

She was smiling to herself when she noticed the two older girls arrive. "Hiya girls! I was just listening to your dad and remembering the old times. Now, what are you two up to? Faith put the kettle on, and we all have a cuppa. How are you, Grace? Any signs yet?"

Grace shook her head ruefully, "Not yet, Mam. Don't worry; when it happens, you'll be the first to know! No, I'm here to give Faith a bit of moral support. She's got something important to tell you and Dad. Do you think we should wait until he's finished, or can we interrupt him?"

"I would leave him be, while he's happy, love. What is it you want to say, Faith? Have you come to tell us finally that you're in the family way?" Kate looked sternly at her second daughter. Faith had stopped short, kettle in hand, and looked at her mother in shock. "What? Did you think I wouldn't notice? What sort of mother would I be to miss something as important as that?"

"But – how do you know?" Faith gasped, "I thought I'd managed to hide it."

"Maybe from other people, but I'm your mother. You might not think I notice things, but I do. When is the bairn due?"

"About another three months, I think. Around Christmas time." Grace took the kettle from her sister's hand and put it on the hob. "Sit down, Faith; I'll do that."

Faith sat in her father's chair, "Does Dad know?" she asked.

Kate shook her head, "Not yet – men don't notice these things like women do. He mentioned he thought you'd put a bit of weight on, but he was happy about that because he thought you were getting too skinny. Am I right in assuming that Harry Renshaw is the father? If so, what's he going to do about it?"

"Yes, he's the father. I promise, Mam, it only happened the once! We haven't been sleeping together, honest we haven't!" cried Faith.

"Well, that's all it takes for some people, as you now know! And here's our poor Gracie trying her best and getting nowhere. Isn't that just typical! Now, you didn't say whether Harry will take responsibility – what has he said about it? I assume you have told him?" Kate's face was still stern, and she held Faith's eyes with her gaze.

"He doesn't know, Mam. I was going to tell him, but he's left the Paper Mill and gone back to Derby. His dad was very poorly, and Harry had to go and look after the business until he recovers. He left without saying anything – I suppose he just didn't think about me because he was worried about his dad. Anyway, I don't know where in Derby he lives, so I can't even write and tell him. I've wanted to keep it quiet at work, so I can hardly go asking questions about him now. I'm sorry, Mam. I don't know what to do. Will you tell Dad? I know he's going to be really angry – do you think he'll put me out?"

"You're right, he is going to be mad, and no, I'm not going to tell him. You have to face up to the situation and tell him yourself. You're not a baby anymore; you're a woman grown. You have to take responsibility for yourself – and your child, when it arrives."

Faith nodded, "I'll go and tell him now." She left the room and went into the front parlour.

There was the sound of voices, and then Prue came into the kitchen looking puzzled, "What's going on? Faith just asked me to leave because she wanted to talk to Dad. What's wrong?"

"All in good time, sweetheart. Faith has something important to tell your dad, that's all. I daresay they'll both be back in here in a minute or two. Are you going to pour that tea, Grace? It'll be strong enough to stand a teaspoon up in it before long." Kate picked up her sewing and listened intently for sounds from the front room.

There was a slight murmur, which was Faith telling him the news, then they all heard him shout "What?" loudly, then his voice lowered again so they couldn't make out what he was saying. More murmuring from Faith, and then there was no sound at all. All was quiet for a few minutes, and then they heard the parlour door opening, and Faith followed her father into the kitchen. "Well, this is a fine how-d'ye-do, isn't it, Mother?" Albert sat down heavily in his chair. "What do you reckon we ought to do with her? I'm willing to believe that it was an error of judgement in the heat of the moment, but it has serious consequences. What do you think, Kate? The bairn will have to be put up for adoption, I suppose." He looked askance at his wife.

"If you want to know what I think," his wife replied, "I think Faith ought to go to Hull and stay with my sister until the bairn arrives. Grace has offered that she and Ned take care of the little mite as their own, and it will all be all over. Faith will have to find herself another job, but I'm sure she can manage that. And we'll all know that the babe is well-cared for and loved. I'm not going to have my first grandchild abandoned to the four winds, never knowing what might happen to it. At least this way, the poor little thing will still be our grandchild. Then it's up to you two girls to decide when it's old enough to tell it the truth." The hard look on Kate's face told everyone that was her decision, and she would brook no opposition.

In truth, Albert agreed with his wife. He was looking forward to seeing the next generation come along and was loath to lose this first one before it had even come into being. "You'd better write to your Annie then and make sure she's agreeable to take Faith until the baby arrives. We'll have to find some reason to tell folk why she's gone, though."

"That's simple enough," said Kate, "we'll just tell everyone that Annie's ill and needs someone to look after her. Nobody here will know any different. And over there, Faith can say that she was married, but her husband is away or has died or something. No one will be any the wiser, and if they think she's newly bereaved, they won't ask any awkward questions."

Albert shook his head in wonderment, "I never knew my wife had such a deceitful nature! I hope this is the first time I'm witnessing you telling lies, Kate Marshall!"

Kate laughed, "What you don't know doesn't hurt you! And I haven't been Kate Marshall in thirty years, you silly old fool!"

Albert rewarded her with a big kiss, then turned back to his daughters, all of whom were looking very relieved. "Right then, you girls. Your mother's right, and that's the plan. Anything you'd like to add?" he looked Faith straight in the eye, "But if I find that Harry Renshaw, he's going to know about it!"

Faith thought the better of defending Harry to her father at this moment. It was highly unlikely he would bump into Harry, so she didn't have to worry about retribution on Albert's part.

Two weeks later, the family saw Faith off on the train to Hull, where she would be met at the other end by her Aunt Annie. Everything was in place. She had given her notice at the Paper Mill, where she was told she would be welcome back when she was ready. Everyone they knew had been told of her visit to Hull, but not the real reason for it. The other siblings were aware of the situation, but they could be trusted to keep it within the family – no one wanted the shame of an illegitimate child to get out. All there was to do now was to furnish Grace's spare bedroom as a nursery, and at last, start collecting the layette for the little one, then wait for its arrival.

In December 1928, they received word from Hull that Faith had delivered a healthy bouncing baby girl. Everything had gone well, with no complications, and as soon as her lying-in period was over, she would be able to bring the baby home.

Grace talked to her mother one morning before going off to work at the Pavilion. The café was warm and cosy, and they had a good trade in winter walkers. Even in winter, they got some people in for some respite from walking in the bracing winds of Biggar Bank.

"There is one thing that I'm not sure how we're going to explain," Grace said, "and that is, how I am suddenly in possession of a newborn baby when there have been no signs of me expecting. What are we going to tell people?"

"I think we can get away with it, Gracie. I don't want to offend you, but you have put some weight on since you and Ned got married – I suppose it's down to contentment! But some women have babies and don't even know they're pregnant," Kate said. "Remember Mrs Walsh next door, when we all lived in your street? The same thing happened to her. She had no idea she was expecting and gave birth in the lavatory! She thought she'd eaten something that disagreed with her and ended up with another little boy!"

The two women laughed, "Yes," said Grace, "I do remember it, now you come to mention it. Oh well, let's hope I'm fat enough to get away with it!"

Faith arrived back home just before Christmas, carrying the tiny bundle that was her daughter. Albert was in love with his new granddaughter from the moment she clutched his finger in her small fist, "Hello, my little sweetheart," he whispered, "welcome to the family. I'm your granddad, and I'll look after you." He planted a kiss on the smooth forehead. "What's my new grandbaby called?" he asked her mother.

"Well, I suppose that's really up to Grace and Ned, as they'll be bringing her up," said Faith, "But if I were keeping her, she'd be Harriet, after her father; Hattie for short." Faith looked at the couple, "What do you think?"

"Yes, I like it," said Grace, "Hattie Parsons is quite a sweet name. All right, Ned?"

Ned, too was entranced with the little girl, "That's fine by me. Hattie it is."

Grace thought it a good idea if Faith stayed at her house for a short while; Faith was still breastfeeding the child, and it would take a little time to wean her onto a bottle, so Faith might as well be around until the baby was settled into a routine. She could sleep in the nursery, now painted a cheerful yellow and fitted out with a cot for the little one, but there was still a spare bed in there which Faith could use.

The family were preparing for Christmas, and the festivities would be held as usual, with Albert and Kate at their home. This time, Hope, Constance and Freddie would not be able to come, so it would be a smaller celebration than usual. Even so, there would be six of them around the table.

One evening in the week before Christmas, while they were all planning for the big day, there was a knock on the Tunstall's front door. Albert went to answer, wondering who could be calling so late on a cold, wet and windy night. A few moments later, they heard him say, "Oh, it's you. You'd better come in, young man. I want a few words with you."

Albert returned to the kitchen, followed by, to everyone's surprise, Harry Renshaw, who was in the process of asking, "Is Faith here?"

Shocked into silence, with eyes as round as saucers, Faith took in the sight of her errant beau following her father.

"Oh, thank God! Faith, I've been so worried! I went back to the Mill today, and they told me you'd left and no one had seen you for months, something about looking after a relative in Hull! I had no idea how to get in touch with you, so I thought I'd come round and ask your folks for an address to write to…" Harry suddenly noticed he was speaking into complete silence, and everyone in the room was watching him.

Albert spoke up, "You'd better sit, Harry. You have some explaining to do."

Harry pulled out a chair from the table next to Faith, who was still dumbstruck. "I know; I'm so sorry I couldn't come and explain. I just had to leave straight away because of my dad. He was so ill, and my mother couldn't cope on her own, not with the business and looking after him as well. There was no time for niceties; I had to go there and then, as soon as I'd heard."

"That's as may be, lad," said Albert, "But you could have written before now, once things had settled down a bit, couldn't you? My lass has been worried to bits about you; you could have been dead for all she knew."

"Yes, I know; I'm sorry about that too. But everything was such a mess. Dad had been feeling ill for ages and had not said anything. He'd been dosing himself up with some sort of Laudanum to ease his pain, and as a result, everything was going wrong. He'd left the plant's managing to some underling who had no idea what needed to be done to keep things going. I've had so much to do, as well as helping Mother with Dad, that I've barely had time to breathe. I have been thinking about you, though," he looked at Faith, "I've missed you."

She returned his gaze and said, "I've missed you too."

"That's all well and good, but things have been happening here too. There is a lot you need to know, but first, there's someone you need to meet," Kate spoke up. "Follow me, Harry."

Puzzled, Harry looked at Faith, who turned her face away. He got up and followed Kate into the Parlour, where Hattie lay sleeping in a Moses basket, warm and cosy. "You'd better say hello to your daughter, Hattie. Or Harriet – she was named for you." Kate announced.

Harry was stunned. He turned to Faith, who stood behind him, "What? I don't understand? My daughter? How – oh, I remember. From the dunes at Earnse Bay that day? Why didn't you say something? I didn't know…"

"I know you didn't. The day I went to tell you was the day you left for Derby, and I had no idea where to contact you to let you know. Nobody around here knows the truth. But everything is taken care of. I went away to Hull to have her and Grace and Ned are going to bring her up as their own. I'll just be her Auntie Faith, so you don't have to worry. It's all organised."

"What do you mean, it's all organised? Faith – don't you know that I love you? I came here tonight to tell you how much I've missed you and to give you this!" Harry reached into his pocket and brought out a ring box. "I want you to marry me – and given this news, you'd better say yes so we can bring up our daughter together."

Once again, Faith was stunned. "But, what about Grace and Ned? They've got a nursery and everything all ready for her."

Kate took charge of the situation and shepherded them back into the kitchen. "It looks like we have more talking to do," she said.

Gathered around the kitchen table once more, Harry once again asked Faith to marry him and placed the engagement ring on her finger. "I'm so happy. Oh, but Grace – the baby! You were so looking forward to… Oh, Grace, I'm so sorry!" Her face fell.

"Don't you worry about me, love!" said Grace. She looked nervous suddenly, "No, don't worry about Ned and me. I have a surprise for all of you. I'm expecting my own baby – and I'm due sometime in April or May! I was keeping it secret and going to tell Ned on Christmas Morning, but I suppose it will do as an early Christmas Present. What do you think, Ned?"

"I think this is going to be the best Christmas I ever had!" Ned replied as he took his wife in his arms and kissed her soundly. "Merry Christmas, everybody!"

CHAPTER EIGHTEEN 1929

In the Tunstall house on New Year's Eve 1928, there was an atmosphere of elation and optimism for the coming year. They celebrated the birth of 1929 and Harriet, and soon a child for Grace and Ned, after two years of trying. There was also a wedding to organise, as quickly as possible. In the event, Faith and Harry opted for a quiet Register Office wedding and a small family gathering afterwards, and they married the first week in February. Unfortunately, Harry's family could not travel; his father was still not well enough, and his mother would not come without him.

Faith was ill at ease that her new in-laws had not been present, "They'll think I've trapped you into making an honest woman out of me. They'll probably hate me; they certainly won't think I'm good enough for you – a mill-girl!"

Harry took her in his arms, "Don't worry about it, my love. My parents are happy if I'm happy, and I am definitely happy. They will love you, and they will especially love their granddaughter." As if to agree with her daddy, Hattie gurgled in her cot. For the time being, they were living in the rooms that Harry had first taken on his arrival in Barrow and had paid for upfront for a year.

Their landlady, Mrs Harrison, was the widow of a gentleman who had left the house but little else to his family, so she had had to find some means of supporting herself and her two children. The house was a large Victorian edifice at the top end of Abbey Road, much too large for her family's needs, so she had decided to rent rooms to gentlemen lodgers, and with a couple of housemaids to assist, it was a comfortable, genteel abode. The rooms were large and airy, and the furniture was overstuffed and plush. The Renshaws had a living room, a bedroom and a small kitchen. It also had its own private bathroom. Faith had been astounded at the indoor plumbing; she had never experienced such luxury.

But Harry had to explain to his new wife: "I'm afraid we won't be able to afford anything like this when we buy a house, Faith. My father's business has got into such a mess, and it's doubtful he will be able to keep it going and bring it back up to what it was. Even though he is recovering, he won't be able to run it as he did before. I am no businessman and have no interest in struggling to reverse the company's fortunes, so he'll probably sell up. Any money made from the sale will have to be used to keep Mother and Dad for the rest of their lives. They'll have to be careful and won't be able to afford the lifestyle they've been used to, but they'll be comfortable enough. But it also means that we'll have to live off only my salary at the Paper Mill, without any help from family money. So, I'm sorry, Darling, but the motor car will have to go, and our home will be much more modest than this. Do you mind very much?" he held Faith at arm's length, looking deep into her eyes for any sign of disappointment.

"Don't be silly, Harry! If anything, I'll feel more like myself if we're not so well off! As it is, I feel very odd whenever Mrs Harrison treats me like a posh lady. I feel like a fraud. I'm much more suited to below-stairs than being the lady of the manor. No, I'll be happy just as long as we're together." She picked up Hattie from her cot and cuddled her, "Daddy is silly, isn't he,

Hattie? As if we wanted to live anywhere grand like Abbey Road. I'll be happy with a little house on Walney, near my parents and sister. That will do us just fine, won't it, Sweetheart?"

The relief was visible on Harry's face as he embraced his wife and daughter, "As long as I have my two darling girls, I'd be happy anywhere too." So, the search was on for a Walney house, and one was soon found (including a bathroom) in Ocean Road, just a few streets away from both the Tunstalls and the Parsons.

In the meantime, that latter happy couple enjoyed the prospect of their child arriving into their lives. The short time Faith and Hattie had stayed with them had been good practice, and at least they already had the nursery prepared. Grace was busy replacing the layette since it was only right that Hattie took the things she had been given and used, but Grace was happy about that. She loved knitting the little matinee jackets and bonnets, and even hemming the towelling for the nappies seemed to give her pleasure.

Ned was proud of his wife and could not get used to the idea they had managed to create a baby at last. He treated Grace like Dresden porcelain, and when he was not at work, he insisted she rest while he carried out whatever chores were necessary.

"Ned, love, I'm not going to break if I fetch in a bucket of coal for the fire!" Grace protested when he'd scolded her for carrying the bucket from the backyard.

Ned replied, "If I'm here, I don't want you doing heavy jobs. We can't risk anything happening; it's taken us too long to get this far!" Ned guided her to the settee and pulled up the footstool. "Here, put your legs up, and I'll make you a nice cup of tea."

She laughed at him, shaking her head. This would soon wear off when they had a houseful of children if her dad was any measure. She'd seen it before, the first two or three, the parents watched their toddlers, eagle-eyed for any danger; by the time they'd had four or five, they would let the kids juggle knives! But she was also glad to see her husband so happy.

When she was five months gone, Ned had insisted Grace give up work at the Pavilion, and although she was sorry to leave her friends and customers, she was glad not to be on her feet all day. It felt like a luxury to visit her mother or Faith and spend leisurely hours gossiping.

She had been doing just that one Saturday afternoon at her parents' house when there was a tap on the front door; it opened, and a female voice called out, "Yoo-hoo, is anyone in?"

Kate replied, "Yes, we're in the kitchen!" She looked at Grace, shaking her head with a puzzled look on her face; they weren't expecting company.

Footsteps down the corridor, then the kitchen door opened and in walked Joy, and a very tall, slim young man with ginger hair. He looked embarrassed and shy, but Joy, as bubbly and cheerful as ever, kissed her mother on both cheeks then hugged Grace and Prue in turn.

"My, our Gracie, you are looking swell!" she joked, running her hand over Grace's growing bump, "You look wonderful, positively blooming! Aww, I was hoping Faith might be here, but I daresay I can pop round her house in a minute and bring her and the baby. Is Dad not home?" The 22-year-old young woman hardly took a breath as she chattered on.

Her mother held up her hand, "Stop talking a minute, Joy! I can hardly keep up with you. And you're being very rude; shouldn't you introduce your friend? Come in, young man, and have a seat. Prue, put the kettle on and mash a pot of tea, will you, love?"

"Ooh yes, I'm sorry! Mam, Grace, Prue, this is Maurice Barker. Isn't he a pet? We've been courting for a while now, so I thought it was time I brought him home to meet you all. We both got the day off, so it seemed like a good idea. Say hello, Sweetie!" As she spoke, she took Maurice's cap from his hand and darted into the hall to hang it on a coat hook.

Left to his own devices, Maurice blushed bright red and stammered, "Mrs Tunstall, Mrs Parsons, Miss Tunstall, it's nice to meet you at last. Joy has told me so much about you all."

Grace shook his hand, "It's very nice to meet you, Maurice. You don't want to let our Joy bully you, you know!" she laughed.

"She is a bit of a whirlwind, isn't she? You just sort of get swept along with her somehow!" he smiled indulgently.

Joy bounced back into the room, "I hope you're not talking about me behind my back, our Grace! Will Dad be home soon, Mam? Where is he?"

"He's down at the allotment picking some vegetables for tomorrow's dinner," said Kate, "will you be able to stay for it?"

"Yes, we don't have to be back until tomorrow night. There's an afternoon train, so we'll catch that. Is it all right for Maurice to sleep in the parlour, Mam? He'll be all right on the sofa, won't you, Flower?" Joy squeezed her young man's arm.

"There won't be any need for that. He can have Charlie and Freddie's old room, and you can bunk in with Prue," said Kate, "You don't mind, do you, Prue?"

"No," Prue laughed, "it'll be nice to have some company again; I've been a bit lonely since our Faith got married."

It wasn't long before they heard the backyard door slam and Albert's hobnails on the concrete yard. He opened the back door and shouted, "I'm home, love. Where do you want this lot?"

"Get your boots off before you come into this kitchen, Albert Tunstall! I didn't spend the morning scrubbing it just for you to muck it all up again," Kate ordered.

Albert grinned meekly at his wife and said, "Yes, my dear, whatever you say." After a few minutes, he came into the kitchen in his stockinged feet and dumped a big bag on the kitchen table. "Peeling that lot will keep our Prue going for a while, I think," he winked at his youngest daughter, who held out a mug of tea.

He took it from her then looked around, noticing the extra company. "Well, there's a surprise! Hiya Joy, come and give your old dad a love. And who is this?"

Joy ran over to her father and hugged him hard, then kissed his cheek, "This is Maurice Barker, Dad." For the first time, Joy looked shy, "He's my beau; we've been walking out for ages."

"Maurice, eh! Welcome young man!" Albert held out a muddy hand, "oops, I'd better give my hands a wash before I shake yours, hadn't I?"

When he had finished his ablutions, he dried his hands and face and then held out the now clean hand to shake Maurice's, who said, "I'm pleased to meet you, Sir. Joy's told me all about you."

Her dad laughed, "Well, she hasn't told us a thing about you, so you best had!"

"Dad, don't embarrass the lad," said Grace, "can't you see he's a bit shy?" She smiled encouragingly at Maurice, "don't worry, he won't bite you. At least, not hard, anyway!"

"Less of your lip, Mrs Parsons! You're not too old to get put over my knee, young lady!" said her dad, laughing.

"I can't remember you ever doing that, Dad; I hardly think it likely now – especially with this in the way!" Grace stroked her bump.

Maurice began to feel at ease. He'd been dreading meeting Joy's family. She'd told him there were so many of them, but these few seemed nice and very welcoming. They were obviously a happy and loving family, and it was great that the patriarch appeared to have a sense of humour. He wondered if he could summon up enough courage to ask for Joy's hand, whether Albert would give his permission. It was now or never if he wasn't to lose his nerve.

"Sir, I would like to talk to you, if you have a moment?" he said.

"Why, this is becoming a regular thing! Come along then, lad, let's go into the parlour for a man-to-man talk and leave all these squawking hens to it!" Albert led the way out to the front room, winking at his wife as he went.

Grace looked at Joy, goggle-eyed, "Is he asking to marry you? Already?" she asked.

Joy grinned, "I'm just so adorable; he can't live without me!" she said cockily. "Seriously though, we've been going out for over a year. He's the one for me, and he feels the same. What's the point in waiting?"

Grace couldn't think of a single reason. "I suppose you're right," she said, "When's the wedding?"

"Soon," Joy replied. "I want a spring wedding, and I don't want to have to wait another year. What do you think, Mam?"

"Well, he seems very nice and well mannered," said her mother, "It all depends how much of a fuss you want to make. Does he have any family?"

"Not really. He has a sister somewhere up in Cumberland, but his parents died years ago. That's how he came to be a baker. He was apprenticed out of the orphanage and taken on by Mr Reynolds. He's lived in Milnthorpe all his life, but I want to get married in Barrow. Would I still be able to if I'm not a parishioner here? Not that I'm a churchgoer there either, but all my family so far got married at St Mary's, and I want to as well," said Joy.

"You'll have to see the Vicar and see if he'll agree. I don't see why he shouldn't since you're from here and have family in the parish, but I should think you'll have to be there at least once to hear the banns called. That's how they used to do it anyway. Why don't you and Maurice go to the church in the morning and have a word? It'll fit in nicely before Sunday dinner."

At that point, Albert and Maurice came through from the parlour, "It seems this fellow wants to make an honest woman of you, our Joy. Should I let him?" Albert joked.

"Yes, please, Dad! You should be glad you're getting some of us married off – that's half your brood gone, anyway. There's only Hope, Connie, Freddie, and Prue left!" Joy kissed her father again on the cheek.

"Ah well, I don't see why not – if you're sure you want to take her on, Maurice?" he said.

Maurice ran his hands through his hair, making it stand on end, "Yes, Sir, I do indeed!"

"In that case, I'll give my permission. Welcome to the family, lad. It looks like you've another wedding to organise, Mother!" said Albert, slapping Maurice on the back.

The next day at Sunday dinner, the somewhat depleted family sat down for their meal. The two married couples were eating at their own homes, so only Kate, Albert, Prue, and the two lovebirds were present.

Joy told them about their interview with the vicar of St Mary's, the Reverend Mr Charles Williams. "He was ever so nice, wasn't he, Maurice? After the service, we stayed behind to chat with him, and he explained what has to happen before he can marry us. He said he's happy to marry us here, as although I work away, this is still my home, so that's all right." She paused to push a forkful of mashed potato into her mouth before swallowing it quickly. She continued, "he said that the banns have to be read for three weeks before the wedding, so if there are any objections they can be raised before the ceremony. The same at

Maurice's church, St Thomas', in Milnthorpe as well, even though we're not marrying there."

Maurice chipped in, "Yes, he was a very nice chap; he said he's only been your vicar for a couple of years. The congregation seemed to like him, though; lots of chatting as they left the service. He said he could marry us in about a month, so we went with him into the vestry, and he booked us in right there and then! It looks like you're going to get your Spring wedding, after all, my dear!" Maurice looked adoringly at his intended.

Both of them were beaming from ear to ear and chattering away constantly throughout the meal. "Will you tell the rest of the family, Mam?" Joy asked, "We probably won't see them now until the day."

"I will," said Kate, "though you can write to the twins and Freddie yourself. What are you going to do about the arrangements? And you'll probably have to give your notice at the Hall, won't you?"

"Mmm," Joy swallowed another mouthful, "yes. I can't stay in a live-in job if I'm married unless Maurice worked there too. But that's all right, isn't it, Love? Maurice already has his cottage where he lives now, right near the bakery. It will be a proper little love-nest when I've finished with it. It's lacking a woman's touch at the moment, but I've already started my bottom drawer, so I'll soon get it comfortable."

Maurice beamed with pride at his fiancée as though she was the eighth wonder of the world.

A few short weeks later, Joy and Maurice were married by Rev Williams; they settled for a small family celebration at the Tunstalls' home. The twins and Freddie had been able to attend, creating a houseful of well-wishers. Once again, Ned brought his violin, and he and Prue accompanied Albert as he sang the old popular songs. The food was plentiful, the beer flowed, and all had a good time. The couple spent their wedding night at the Ferry Hotel and the next day went back to take up residence together in their own little 'Love-Nest', proclaimed to all by a wooden plaque made by Maurice and affixed to the wall next to their front door.

Grace had taken it easy during the celebrations as she was by now heavily pregnant and feeling rather cumbersome. She sat in the Naiad Street parlour with her feet up on the footstool, nursing a small glass of beer and cuddling her bump as she watched the party. The birth couldn't come soon enough for her. She had her wish; a few weeks later, on 4th June, she and Ned became the proud parents of a beautiful baby girl named Thelma.

CHAPTER NINETEEN 1930-1932

It seemed that in 1929 the whole family had much to celebrate with all the marriages, births and christenings – and it appeared to be infectious. The next news was that Joy and Maurice had discovered only three months after their wedding that they were expecting their first child, due in January. Hard on the heels of that, Faith and Harry were overjoyed to find that they also would have a new baby in the new year of 1930.

There was some relief from the seemingly endless round of family events for the latter half of the year, and Kate and Albert were glad of the respite. They decided on a quiet festive season that year – all the new couples celebrated in their own homes and only gathered on Boxing Day in Naiad Street for an afternoon of family togetherness. It made a nice change for the older couple who, although they loved their offspring dearly, were beginning to feel their age and the lack of energy that came with it. Prue summed it up with a sampler she embroidered and framed for her parents' Christmas present: 'All of our Guests bring pleasure, Some when they arrive, Others when they leave!' Her father laughed uproariously when he read it and immediately hung it on the kitchen wall.

Albert did his usual rounds of bringing in the New Year for his neighbours and looked forward to the start of the new decade. The first good news was that Joy gave birth to Christine, who made her appearance at the end of January, weighing in at 7lbs 8oz. Maurice sent word that mother and child were both well, and as soon as her lying in was over, they would bring the newest arrival to meet her grandparents and family.

The older Tunstalls thoroughly enjoyed the role of grandparents, and it became usual on Sundays for various children, in-laws and grandchildren to visit for tea. At the end of one such day, when they had all left for their own homes, Albert settled in his chair by the kitchen fire with Kate in hers opposite. Prue had earlier drifted into the parlour to read; she found the passing around, feeding, cuddling and changing the babies exhausting, much though she loved them.

Albert lit his pipe with a taper from the fire and yawned contentedly, "You know, Katie, all those years ago when we moved to this town, I never would have guessed how true it would turn out that we would start a Tunstall dynasty here. Now the children are all grown and finding their way in the world, it's lovely to see them when they visit. I enjoy being a grandpa."

"Yes, I love it too. Being 'Grandma' instead of Mam is nice – especially when we can give them back!" she laughed, "it's all the fun and none of the responsibility! I'm looking forward to them growing a bit, though. Babies are lovely, but they get more interesting once they're walking and talking."

"You're right. Young Hattie is blossoming right well, isn't she? It won't be long before her little brother or sister arrives an' all. Have you seen our Faith? She should be popping soon, I think?" Albert blew out a cloud of pleasant-smelling smoke.

"Any day now, I expect. But I wanted to talk to you about Prue. She'll be twenty this year, but she shows no interest in getting out and about and meeting people. What can we do to help her? I'm sure she doesn't want to be a spinster aunt all her life!"

"Oh, just leave her be, Katie. The lass is bright enough. She might spend most of her time with her nose buried in her books, but she's still working part-time at the cinema with Ned. As the saying goes, 'what's meant for you won't go by you'; if she's meant to meet someone, it will happen regardless of what you or I do about it."

"I suppose you're right," said his wife, "for an old fool, you can be quite sensible at times. Oh, Bertie, look at your sock again! I can see your big toe poking right through!"

"Stop nagging, woman," he winked, "else I'll come over there and give you what you deserve!"

"What, a medal?" said Kate, laughing.

More happy news arrived from Lancashire. In Milnthorpe, Joy and Maurice were already expecting their second baby, only three months since Christine had arrived. In Accrington, after walking out with one or two lads, but not seriously, Hope had met a young man called Leslie Wilson, who was an electrician at Victoria Hospital. Connie had given her seal of approval to the match, which had been most important to Hope. She could not conceive of marrying someone with whom her sister could not get along. After this milestone, Hope wrote to tell her parents that Leslie had asked to marry her and accepted. They set a date for September that year, and the newly engaged couple would come to visit as soon as they could arrange time off work.

Faith gave birth to Caroline, another girl baby for her granddad to adore. Her doting daddy, Harry, talked non-stop about 'his girls' when he came to wet the baby's head with Albert, whilst Kate had been with her daughter throughout the process. She well remembered the experiences she'd had while having her children and was a calming influence whenever she could be with her daughters bearing her grandchildren.

It seemed the family had grown so fast in the last couple of years, and there was no stopping it now! The only sadness was that there was still no word that Charlie and Sarah had started their family after three years.

In addition to the nuptials within her own family, Grace and Ned had witnessed when his sister, Florrie, married her long-time beau, Raymond Thompson, at St Georges Church on 26th July. Not long afterwards, The elder Parsons and the newly-wed Thompsons had clubbed together and bought a house at 1 Warwick Street. It was a Victorian end-of-terrace house on three floors and was easily big enough for Edward and Florence to have several rooms to call their own for privacy. That still left plenty of room for any offspring the younger couple might produce. It also meant that in the future, the older Parsons would have a family to look after and support them in their old age if it became necessary.

On a larger scale, in Barrow, under new government legislation, the Workhouse at Roose was to be closed and converted into a hospital to care for the mentally ill, and responsibility for public assistance transferred to the local authority.

Nationally, in April, the BBC broadcast a unique message on April 18th saying, 'Good evening, today is Good Friday. There is no news', followed by a programme of piano music, which caused some amusement. More seriously, the Great Depression hit the country hard as demand for British products fell; unemployment figures would reach 2.5 million by the end of the year.

In August, the birth was announced of Princess Margaret Rose, a new baby daughter for the Duke and Duchess of York and sister to Princess Elizabeth, which added a brighter note to the news.

The following month, Hope and Leslie had a much pared-down wedding; money was very tight, and all were scrimping and saving to get by. However, they refused to allow the threat of unemployment and poverty to cast a pall over the celebrations. Although on a tight budget, the happy couple needed no elaborate party to seal their love. They were content with a Register Office ceremony and spent their first marital night together under the Tunstalls' roof. In what had been the sisters' bedroom, now solely occupied by Prue, she had made the old double bed up with her mother's best linens and decorated the room with ribbons and fresh flowers to celebrate their union. Prue happily moved into the boys' old room to share with Connie for the night. The following day, the couple, with Connie in tow, returned to Accrington and their daily lives.

In October, a second daughter, Louise, was born to Joy and Maurice. The whole family travelled to Milnthorpe for the christening of both Barker babies in St Thomas' Church. It turned into rather a loud occasion when Louise protested loudly at the holy water being poured onto her head. This then set off her sister, Christine, only nine months older. Joy was going to have her hands full!

Things had quietened somewhat in the ensuing months, which was something of a relief, not only to Kate and Albert but their children and assorted husbands and wives. The hiatus was not to last for much longer, though.

First, in August 1931 came the announcement from Hope and Leslie that they were expecting their first child in March the following year. The couple had been married for two years already and were thrilled that they had successfully conceived at last. Hope had continued her nursing after they had married, but she was now content to give it up, looking forward immensely to becoming a mother. Twin Connie was equally delighted and welcomed the news.

The next addition to the family came in the form of a young lady called Sally Dixon. She was a farmer's daughter from near Accrington and had caught Freddie's eye one day at the cattle market at Islington in Blackburn. She had been helping her father with some dairy cattle he wanted to sell, and Freddie had been there on behalf of Mr Skinner, the dairyman he worked for. Freddie had bought two of Farmer Dixon's cows and had met with him and his daughter after the sale. There was an instant attraction between them. Soon afterwards, Freddie kidnapped Charlie's old bicycle from the allotment when he visited his parents and became a regular sight, cycling the four or five miles from his home to the farm every weekend to meet his lady-love.

Eventually, he brought Sally home to meet his parents. They were quite surprised to find that it was truly a case of opposites attracting. Freddie, as always, a livewire, cheeky and funny, had fallen for a very proper young girl, not given to chatter or making fun. Freddie teased her, and she seemed to enjoy his banter, for she watched him constantly with adoring eyes, though her responses were measured and whispered in a quiet voice.

Freddie soon announced that Farmer Dixon had given his consent to their marriage, and they set a date for February 1932 to be married in Haslingden, near Accrington. As Kate watched the enjoyment at this announcement, she reflected, 'Only Connie and Prudence to get settled now. Then I can rest easier knowing they are all taken care of.'

Before that happy event, tragedy hit the family for the first time in a long while. In January, an accident at Victoria Hospital resulted in Leslie's death, leaving Hope a widow and seven months pregnant. He had been working on some wiring in one of the Operations Theatres when there was a sudden surge in the current, and he was electrocuted and killed instantly.

Leslie's boss went personally to break the news to Hope, but she was upstairs resting when he called at the house. When Connie answered the door and invited him inside (she lived with the couple at the time), the man had informed her of the tragedy, mistakenly believing her to be Leslie's wife. He had given his condolences and offered to help in any way he could, then left. Shocked into silence, Connie showed him out. It was now left to inform her sister that she was a widow. Once again, the affinity between the twins showed itself. It wasn't long before Hope came down the stairs, feeling the need to console Connie but not knowing why. Connie worried that the news might harm her unborn niece or nephew, but she had no choice other than to tell her twin what had happened. Naturally, Hope was bereft and inconsolable, despite Connie's attempts to comfort her.

Connie sent telegrams to the rest of the family, telling them the news. The first to arrive was Freddie, being closer than the others, then Joy and Maurice. That good man, while consulting Hope about her wishes, took over the necessary planning and spoke to clergy and undertaker and organised the entire funeral. This spared Hope any unnecessary sadness, for which she was grateful. Joy saw a new side to her shy, retiring husband and admired his compassion in his dealings with her sister.

The Barrow contingent of the family all arrived in due course, and the funeral was held at St James' Church, not far from Hopwood Street where the couple lived. After the sad and moving service, Kate insisted that her daughter go and rest in her room. She, like Connie, was worried about the baby and afraid that all the emotion might bring on the labour too soon. Kate decided to stay in Accrington for a while and sent Albert home with the family back to Barrow. Connie was grateful to her mother; she could feel what Hope was experiencing and was afraid for her sister.

After two weeks, when Hope started to feel a little stronger, Kate took her home to Barrow to stay until the baby arrived. Poor Connie still had her work to go to and did not want to leave Hope alone, so she was glad her mother prevailed against Hope's protests; she knew it was for the best.

With deference to his sister's very recent loss, Freddie and Sally suggested they postpone their wedding until the family had time to mourn properly; they felt it disrespectful to be preparing to celebrate. However, Hope would hear none of it. She insisted that Leslie would not have wanted such a thing, so the couple was persuaded to go ahead with their plans.

Freddie married his Sally at St James' Church, Haslingden. Farmer Dixon spared no expense on the wedding of his only daughter. The church was decorated with flowers, and the wedding breakfast was grand enough to impress all the family and guests. After the church service, Hope excused herself from the gathering; she had quietly sobbed her heart out during the ceremony. It had brought back so much the happy day that she and Leslie had celebrated their wedding, full of optimism and looking forward to a bright shiny future together. She could not face the party, knowing that her happiness had ended so swiftly. Kate had watched her newly-widowed daughter closely and offered to accompany her away from the merrymaking, but Hope wanted to be alone with her memories. Her mother's place was with her second son and the rest of the family.

Freddie and Sally would live in a cottage within the confines of the main farmhouse, to which they retired after the celebrations that were slightly subdued; the music, singing, dancing and laughter not quite so boisterous as it would have been under normal circumstances.

CHAPTER TWENTY 1932

The rest of the year passed somewhat uneventfully; no more offspring arrived, nor weddings planned, which was something of a relief to Kate and Albert. There had been much upheaval in the last few years, and they were both beginning to feel their age, although they never complained. They were happy enough with a quiet life, not that it was that quiet with having some of the family close by. The Parsons and the Renshaws were still within spitting distance, and Prudence was still at home.

It gladdened Kate's heart when her youngest daughter began courting at last. Prue had met Sidney Satterthwaite at the 'new' Central Library in Ramsden Square. People still referred to the 'old' Library, a building on Schneider Square, before moving to the Town Hall for a while. As the population of Barrow grew, it became necessary for a larger space to house the library; hence building the 'new' one had started in 1915. However, due to delays caused by the war, it was finally completed and opened in 1922. It was a purpose-built building, a magnificent edifice that created a sense of awe as soon as one entered.

Being the bookworm that she was, Prue spent a great deal of time in the library, even more so since the Museum had opened upstairs in 1930. She liked to wander among the exhibits, imagining the far-off places they had originated. She particularly liked the relics found at Furness Abbey and preserved in the large glass cases. The Abbey was another favourite haunt when the weather was nice; it was a good walk from Walney, but there was always a tram that would bring her home if she became overtired. She particularly liked to walk there when the wild garlic was out in the surrounding lanes – the heady aroma lifted her spirits, and she would bring home bunches of the leaves and flowers from which Kate would make a delicious soup.

Prue and Stanley were the only people in the museum when they met. The weather outside was unseasonably hot for even for Summer; the usual brisk sea breezes had not put people off spending the day out of doors. But Prue loved the quiet and coolness that the library always provided; being pale, she burned easily in the sun and preferred not to spend many hours in it.

She had noticed the tall, dark man with the trim moustache and dark-rimmed spectacles as he admired some of the exhibits of stuffed animals of which the Victorians were so fond. They weren't to Prue's taste. The glassy eyes used by the taxidermists always frightened her a little bit as a young girl, and she had imagined all the animals and birds staring at her, unblinking, perhaps waiting to attack her. She smiled at the memory of her fears, shaking it off as being silly.

"What is it you find amusing?" A voice from behind her made her jump.

"Oh! Nothing! I just remembered something from a long time ago," she stammered.

"I'm sorry if I startled you! You just looked so amused; you made me wonder. If I'm honest, I haven't found anything amusing up here. I think I prefer the books downstairs. I'm Stanley

Satterthwaite, by the way. I'm visiting here from Bury, near Manchester. Do you know it?" he held out his hand to shake.

"Prudence Tunstall. No, I don't know Bury, I'm afraid. Two of my sisters and a brother live near Accrington; is that anywhere near?" she shook his hand gently.

"Not too far, about fifteen miles as the crow flies, I think," he replied.

"What brings you to Barrow?" asked Prue.

"I'm visiting some relatives. I have a widowed aunt and her two children who live on Abbey Road. She is my mother's younger sister, and I promised to visit so I can report back to my mother," he smiled. "She invited Aunt Alice to move back to Bury after her husband died in the war, but she preferred to stay here."

"That's a coincidence! One of my sisters and her husband lived in rooms up Abbey Road for a little while, just after they married. Their landlady was a widow – a Mrs Harrison if I remember rightly. Then they moved to Walney, where they still live – they have two little girls now, Hattie and Caroline, who are so sweet." Prue loved her small nieces and loved to take them out whenever she could.

"Now, that really IS a coincidence," laughed Stanley, "My aunt is Mrs Alice Harrison! Isn't it a small world? What is your brother-in-law and sister's name? I'll remember them to her."

"They are Mr and Mrs Harry Renshaw. I'll be sure to mention your family to them too," replied Prue. They had been sauntering around the exhibits, not taking very much notice of anything, and suddenly found themselves near the Exit.

Stanley looked at his pocket-watch, "Oh dear, is that the time? I promised Aunt Alice I'd be back in time for afternoon tea! I'd better get a move on, or I'll be late."

They walked together down the stairs and out into the sunshine. "Well, it was very nice to meet you, Mr Satterthwaite. I hope you enjoy your visit to our town. I enjoyed our little chat. Goodbye."

"Likewise, Miss Tunstall, it was a delight to meet you. Good afternoon." Stanley turned and walked away up Abbey Road. Prue watched his long stride for a little while, then gave herself a little shake.

He remained in her thoughts all afternoon, and as she returned home, she met Faith just leaving after visiting their mother. "Oh, Faith," she said, "such a strange coincidence, this afternoon! I bumped into a chap at the museum, and we got talking. He's visiting from Bury. You'll never guess who his relations are?"

"You're right," said Faith, "I have no idea. Who?"

"Your old landlady from when you and Harry first married – Mrs Harrison! She is his Aunt Alice, on his mother's side."

"Good grief, Prue, you're a quick worker," Faith teased, "you've only known the man five minutes, and you've already got his family tree!" The two girls giggled together. "Are you going to see him again while he's here?" Faith asked.

"I doubt it," said Prue, "it was just a chance meeting, that's all."

"Oh well, never mind. Sooner or later, your prince will turn up, I'm sure! Oh, I've got to dash – Harry will be home soon, and I haven't even started to cook tea yet! I'll see you soon, love! Ta-ra!" Faith dashed off in the direction of Ocean Road.

As Prue let herself in the front door, she could hear voices in the kitchen and found her mother with Faith's two daughters. "Hiya, you two," she said, grinning at her nieces, "What are you up to?"

"They're waiting for their grandpa to come home. He went fishing and promised them some fish for their tea. I'll take them both home when they've eaten," said Kate.

"Ooh, lovely! Nothing like a bit of fresh fish! Do you want me to do the potatoes, Mam?" Prue took her library books into the parlour before returning to the kitchen and putting on her apron. As she peeled the potatoes, she told her mother about her interesting afternoon.

"Well, he sounds very nice," said Kate, "it's a pity he's only visiting. It's about time you found yourself a young man, Prue."

"I'm not too worried, Mam," her daughter smiled, "You'll need one of us left at home to look after you and Dad when you get old. It's beginning to look like that will be me! Unless I beat our Connie to it – it looks like she'll be single for a while yet too. But I'm glad she's stayed with Hope and the baby. Hope has needed to have someone around her since Leslie passed away." She changed the subject quickly; it was still too upsetting to dwell on Leslie's death. "Anyway, Mam, you've not done so bad – only two old maids out of the six of us!"

"You're hardly an old maid at only 22, love! I was nearly 27 before I married your dad, so there's plenty of time yet for you to meet someone. You perhaps just need to get out and about a bit more. Or maybe one of your brothers-in-law has a handy brother or cousin we don't know about yet?" Kate winked at her.

"You just can't wait to get rid of me, can you!" Prue laughed.

A week or two later, Faith opened her front door to find a tall, bespectacled young man standing on the step, turning his cap nervously in his hands. "Mrs Renshaw?" At Faith's nod of affirmation, the young man continued, "I don't mean to bother you, but I wonder if you can help me. My name is Stanley Satterthwaite, and I am an acquaintance of your sister, Prudence Tunstall. We met a short while ago at the library, but stupidly I forgot to ask where she lives."

A light dawned in Faith's memory, "Ah, you're the young man who is Mrs Harrison's nephew, is that right? How did you know where to find us?"

"Fortunately, your husband left your forwarding address with Aunt Alice, and she kept hold of it, so here I am," he said.

"You'd better come in for a minute, Mr Satterthwaite. I'll be going round to my mother's shortly, so you might as well walk with me. Prue still lives at home, you see."

Stanley followed Faith down the hall and into a light, airy front room. He liked the unfussy décor; there was not the usual clutter that adorned tables and shelves in many houses. The Renshaws had decorated with light coloured wallpaper and white paintwork. There was a settee in front and two armchairs on either side of the fire, which was laid, but not yet lit. Otherwise the furniture was minimal, which suited Stanley's tastes. There were a few family photographs, the usual wedding and baby pictures, but not so many as to be overwhelming. It was a comfortable and restful room, easy on the eye.

Faith came in, putting on her hat, "Right, we'll be off then. I hope you don't mind a bit of a mad house, Mr Satterthwaite, as my two daughters and my niece will be there. My mother likes to have them around in the mornings, which is a blessing for Grace and me – it means we can do our housework in peace!"

"That's all right," said Stanley, "I like children. I used to be one."

Faith giggled at his joke – it seems this young man had a sense of humour at least, which was helpful.

A few minutes' walk away, they turned up at 12 Naiad Street, and Faith let them in through the front door. There was much giggling, and no one heard them enter the kitchen. There, they found Albert on his hands and knees with four-year-old Hattie riding him like a pony around the Kitchen floor. Thelma, at three, was pretending to be the Ringmaster of her grandfather's make-believe circus and was using a long stick to urge him along quicker around the circus ring. Kate had Caroline on her knee, bouncing her as if she too was riding a horse.

"Good grief," said Faith to Stanley, "It looks like I was right about it being a madhouse!" She walked into the middle of the room and said, "Dad, what on earth are you doing?"

Albert emitted a passable whinny as he looked at his daughter and winked. On his back, Hattie cried with glee, "No, mammy, he's not 'Dad', he's horsey! C'mon Ganpa, faster, faster!"

Faith lifted her daughter off and said, "I think it's perhaps time 'horsey' had a rest. Come on, Dad, get up off that floor; you'll do yourself a mischief."

As Albert stood up and wiped the sweat from his glowing red face, he noticed the stranger in the doorway, "Oh, I see we have company. Don't mind me, young fella. I'm just trying to entertain my granddaughters. Who are you?"

"Dad, Mam, this is Stanley Satterthwaite. He's come looking for our Prue," said Faith.

"Oh, the man from the library!" Kate said, remembering the conversation. "Come in, Mr Satterthwaite – I'll just go and tell Prue you're here!"

She made to put Caroline down and stand up, but Faith gestured to her, "It's all right, Mam, I'll get her. Is she upstairs?" As her mother nodded, she said, "Excuse me a moment, I'll just run and fetch her."

Faith raced up the stairs and hurriedly knocked on Prue's door. "Prue, are you decent? It's only me! Your young man is here! The one from the library – he came looking for you. Quick, make yourself look respectable."

Prue looked astonished, "What's he doing here? How did he-?"

"Never mind that now, he's downstairs! Comb your hair and put a little powder on your nose; it's a bit shiny! Hurry up, he's waiting," Faith ordered excitedly.

Downstairs, Albert had taken Stanley into the parlour while Kate kept the children in the kitchen. "I believe you're from Bury, is that right, Mr Satterthwaite?"

"Please call me Stan, or Stanley, Sir – I keep thinking you're talking to my father! Yes, I'm from Bury. Your daughter might have told you that I have relatives here in Barrow?"

"Yes, she did mention something, I think – more her mother's domain than mine. I get to hear everything last around here!" Albert grinned. "What do you do in Bury, Mr – Stanley?"

"You may know Bury is a cotton town, Sir? I'm a manager for Lancashire Cotton Corporation and based at Pilot Mill, on Alfred Street. Do you know Bury at all?" Stanley asked.

"I haven't had that pleasure, son, not yet." Just as Albert responded, Prue walked into the room.

"Are you giving him the third degree, Dad? Hello, Mr Satterthwaite, how nice to see you again," she said.

"The pleasure is all mine, Miss Tunstall, but as I just asked your father, please call me Stanley. Mr Satterthwaite is so formal."

"Very well, Stanley, then you must call me Prue – everyone does. I think our mam is making a pot of tea, Dad. Do you want some?"

Albert stopped her as she prepared to leave the room, "It's all right, love, I'll get it. I'm sure you and Stanley have a lot to talk about." He nodded to both and closed the door behind him.

Entering the kitchen, he found his wife and daughter all agog. "What's happening? Did you find out much?" said Kate.

"Give them a chance, woman; he's only been here five minutes!" growled Albert, "are you mashing that tea, or what?"

CHAPTER TWENTY-ONE 1932-1933

Kate turned 60 in November, and the family got together for a small surprise party. The Accrington members came along, too, although Hope was still very much in mourning and not in the mood for celebrations. Little Hannah was beginning to take notice of her surroundings, and her grandmother spent a lot of time cuddling the smallest of the new generation.

During the party, Grace and Ned announced that although it was early days, they believed themselves expecting a new baby. Thelma was almost four, so this one had been a long time coming too, but Grace was grateful for that. She was happy with her life; she, Ned and little Thelma enjoyed good health in their nice little home in Delhi Street. Ned was working and bringing in a more than decent wage with Vickers and his part-time hours at the Cinema, which he still loved. He was a good husband, too; he rarely raised his voice and was usually happy to go along with whatever Grace decided. He spent a lot of time with Thelma and even helped around the house sometimes. Most of her family was close by, and although she grieved for the loss of her sister's husband, she herself felt blessed. Each morning when she rose, she looked in the mirror and counted those blessings.

Things could have been so much different for someone like her. She knew that not being a beauty often led to being discarded and demeaned, undervalued even. People without good looks went unnoticed and were left to bear the brunt of hard work and struggle. Whereas beautiful people were noticed and selected for opportunities, they were popular and could count on friends and family to adore them and ensure all their needs were met – usually by the disadvantaged ugly ones left behind.

But she had been lucky; she knew that her family valued her – her mother's ill-health had meant that Grace had taken great responsibility for her siblings. She had worked hard and earned their respect, as well as the love and gratitude of her parents. And Ned was possibly the sweetest man on earth – he never noticed her looks; in fact, he had often said she *was* beautiful, but it was an inner beauty that shone out from her very core.

Grace loved being a mother too. As Thelma grew into a lively, happy, little chatterbox, she kept her mother busy, always asking questions and wanting to help in the house. Grace hoped she would also want to help with the new baby too. It was certain there would be some jealousy; after all, Thelma was used to being the centre of her little universe; she would not want to share all the attention she currently received. But Grace and Ned would deal with that if the time came; there was no point worrying about something that had not yet happened if indeed it happened at all. She was very newly pregnant, if she was at all, as the doctor had not yet confirmed it. She had only missed one of her monthlies, but she *felt* pregnant and was almost certain that she was.

Anyway, it had been a nice extra birthday present for Kate, who had worried that Thelma might just end up being an only child, which was the worst thing imaginable for any kid as far as she was concerned.

Christmas came and went in its usual fashion, January dragged as it always does, and Grace couldn't wait for February to end; she hoped that perhaps Spring might come early this year. The first three months of her pregnancy had been hard this time. Morning sickness had taken its toll, and instead of gaining, she lost weight. She felt such a lack of energy it was hard to drag herself out of bed each morning. She'd been grateful that Ned had done as much as he could to keep Thelma occupied whenever he was at home. Otherwise, her mother and Prue had been a godsend too and taken the lively little girl off Grace's hands as much as possible. Faith had helped; her eldest, Christine was much the same age as Thelma and the two cousins played well together, often giving respite for both mothers.

In April, Grace turned a corner and began to feel much more like herself. She regained some of her energy, and it seemed like the Spring sunshine charged her like a battery. She felt well enough to take back some of the responsibilities that her mother and sisters had shouldered for her but was still very grateful to see Ned at the end of his workday. Then, he would take over and either keep their child occupied until bedtime or cook their evening meal and clear up afterwards. Once again, Grace felt blessed that she had her family nearby. It was too early to worry yet, of course, but she dreaded the thought that there might be complications with this baby. It never left her mind how her mother had suffered birthing Prue and the years that it had taken afterwards for her to recover fully. Only time would tell.

A long-distance courtship had developed between Prue and Stanley, which, due to his work, meant they could only meet at weekends. During the week, they wrote to each other; long letters which had started in exchanging opinions and news but eventually into which they began to pour their feelings as they grew closer. She had taken the train to Bury one weekend to meet his family after being invited by his mother. It had been nerve-wracking from start to finish. To start with, even though she was twenty-three, she had never travelled alone before and dreaded missing connections when she had to change trains. However, once she was settled onto the train, she began to enjoy herself and revelled in the freedom she felt at going towards this adventure alone.

Prue arrived in Bury without mishap and was met from the train by Stanley. She wasn't quite sure what to expect from Mrs Satterthwaite; with a plump figure encased in good corsetry, his mother obviously enjoyed the finer things in life; her well-coifed brown hair, perfect make-up and immaculate manicure gave a quite daunting impression. But, after a brief moment of being closely inspected and not found wanting, his mother - 'Do call me Dorothy dear!' – had turned out to be a kindly soul. She was very pleased that, at last, her only son was showing an interest in the possibility of presenting her with some grandchildren.

There were also two sisters, but they were younger than Stanley by some years, Beryl was seventeen, and Pearl was fifteen. Younger and slimmer duplicates of their mother, they giggled when introduced to Prue but seemed friendly and interested in their big brother's new 'friend'. Prue was led to believe that this was the first time he had brought a girl to meet his family, although Stanley had already told her he had courted one or two young ladies before he met Prue.

The Satterthwaites lived in a large Victorian mid-terrace house that had once belonged to a mill manager who was quite well-to-do. The rooms were large, with high ceilings and ornate plaster cornices. Large bay windows featured in the rooms at the front of the house; the 'drawing room' as Mrs Satterthwaite rather grandly called it, and the large bedroom above shared by her and her husband. There was a modern bathroom and water closet, which fascinated Prue, whose only experience of indoor plumbing was round at the Renshaws, which was much more modest. The house comprised four floors, including a large basement that contained the kitchen and scullery, and attics that had once housed the servants were spread along the top floor corridor. Now there was just one 'maid of all work' who lived in and helped Mrs Satterthwaite with the housekeeping, and a gardener, not resident, who maintained the gardens front and back, which completed the property.

When Mr John Satterthwaite arrived home, he was treated very much in the fashion of Lord and Master of the household. He was well dressed in a three-piece suit with the gold Albert chain of his pocket watch draped across his stomach. Mr Satterthwaite looked as if he had once been athletic, like his son, but as was the case with his wife, the good life had increased his waistline and his figure beginning to run to seed. He sported a large handlebar moustache, which was waxed and curled up at the ends, and made him look quite fierce beneath the horn-rimmed spectacles he wore. He looked like a fatter, older, and more pronounced version of his son.

Dorothy twittered around like a mother hen ensuring everything he needed was to hand: his slippers, warmed by the fire, the evening newspaper and a glass of whisky on the table next to his chair along with his favourite pipe and tobacco. This was plainly a nightly ritual, and Prue wondered if the man was some tyrant that everything must be 'just so' on his arrival. However, he shook her hand in the introduction and said he hoped she was enjoying her visit so far. He even gave her a little wink, so she assumed he was friendly enough.

Sure enough, the family gathered for dinner together in the evening – not formal enough to have to wear evening dress, for which Prue was very thankful. She had indeed brought her best Sunday dress but feared it was not fancy enough to double as an evening gown. Fortunately, Stanley reassured her that the rest of the weekend would be just as informal, so there was no need to worry. Nonetheless, Prue decided that once she got home, she must see if Ned's mother could make her something suitable for any future invitations, should things go well.

A very pleasant weekend passed without incident; Stanley had taken her on walks around the town and even inside Pilot Mill, which she found both fascinating and horrifying. It had been on Saturday afternoon, so the looms were still, and no one was working, but she could imagine the deafening noise and clatter of the machines, feeling grateful that she had never had to work in such a place. Afterwards, they had taken a walk beside the canal and had refreshments at a little tea shop Stanley knew.

On Sunday, the family went to St Paul's church for the Morning Service. Afterwards, Stanley took her on a walk around the churchyard, where he told her there were the graves of thirteen soldiers who had died in the war. Prue told him about her brother Charlie's brief foray into Belgium and said how glad she was he had come home unscathed. Typically, Stanley lamented that he had been too young to fight, but Prue told him she was glad since they might never have met if he had gone. It was at this juncture that they shared their first real kiss.

They joined the rest of the Satterthwaites back home for Sunday lunch before Prue took the afternoon train to Barrow. Stanley took her to the station, and they had time for a cup of tea in the refreshment room before the train was due to depart.

"Well," Stanley told her, "You were a grand success! My parents love you."

"They've been very kind," Prue replied, "and couldn't have been more welcoming. Please thank them again for me, will you?"

"I will. I'll come up to Barrow next weekend to see you unless you have other plans, that is?" He looked at her questioningly.

"No, I have no plans. It will be nice to see you again. If the weather is any good, maybe we can walk to Furness Abbey, or perhaps from Biggar Bank to West Shore?" Prue suggested.

"Let's see what happens and make plans then. It looks like your train is coming in. Maybe you'll come back soon?" he asked.

"I'll come if I'm invited!" she smiled, "Thank you for a lovely weekend; I really enjoyed myself." She wondered if he might kiss her again, as he had in the churchyard, but he simply helped her up the step into the train and passed her bag into the carriage. He closed the door, and Prue pulled down the window. "Bye, Stanley, I'll see you soon," she said as the train pulled slowly away from the platform.

CHAPTER TWENTY-TWO 1934-1935

In November 1933, Freddie and Sally were blessed with the arrival of a baby girl, who they named June, for no other reason than it was Freddie's favourite month. They arrived in Barrow to introduce the latest addition to her paternal family of grandparents, aunts, uncles and cousins just a week before Christmas.

At the same time, the romance continued between Prue and Stanley and began to get more serious. Prue, always of a romantic nature, had fallen for him the day they met in the museum but had never dared to believe that he could love her in return. She still felt the difference in their backgrounds and worried that, although they had always been very kind whenever she visited Bury, she was not the person his parents would want their only son to marry. Nevertheless, over Christmas, he approached the subject.

On Boxing Day afternoon, the couple took a walk in Barrow Park to visit the Cenotaph that was erected to honour the 616 Barrovians who died during the Great War, as it had become known. The memorial stood at the top of a hill and had a perfect view of the surrounding area. It was so cold, being open to the elements with no shelter from the biting December wind, they decided to descend the many steps to the bandstand, which was deserted that cold day. As they walked, he took hold of her hand. Despite wearing gloves, her hands had been cold, and she was grateful for the warmth seeping between them.

"Seeing all those names engraved up there," he gestured back up to the monument, "makes you think about how precious and delicate life can be. One moment, healthy, hardy young men moving from shipyard to battlefield; the next, nothing but a name on a plaque and a memory for those left behind. It makes you think that we all should appreciate what we have and do our best to protect it. I feel that way about you, Prue. I want to take care of you for the rest of our lives. Do you think you might accept a marriage proposal from me?"

She stared up into his dark eyes, her blue ones shining and beginning to well up with tears that weren't entirely due to the brisk wind. "Yes, Stanley, I think I might. But you will have to ask my dad first. I couldn't marry someone he didn't approve of, but I know he likes you, so I don't think that will be a problem," she smiled happily.

He bent to kiss her, "Then let's get out of this cold and go and ask him, shall we? Let's get the next tram that comes by and get a bit warmer – it's too cold to walk back to Walney. Besides, I can't wait to get his answer!"

Within the hour, they were back at Naiad Street, where Kate had just lit the fire in the parlour. "It's still cold in there at the moment," she told the two as they discarded their outer clothing onto the coat hooks in the hall, "come into the kitchen and get warm. You both look perished! I'll get the kettle on."

"We're all right, Mam, but it is freezing out there! Is our dad in?" Prue asked.

"No, I sent him up to the allotment to get him from under my feet, but I don't suppose he'll be very long. Unless one of his cronies drops by the shed with a bottle of something, that is!" Kate laughed. Then realising there was a purpose to the enquiry, she looked quizzically at her youngest daughter, "Why? Has something happened?"

"Not yet," said Prue, happily, "not until Stanley has spoken to our dad!" she grinned.

Kate returned the smile, if somewhat less than beaming, "Oh, I see! That's how the land lies, is it? Well, I'm sure he won't be that long. Come on in, and I'll get that tea mashing."

Eventually, Albert came home, taking off his muddy boots at the back door. "I'm home, Katie! I brought some veggies saved myself a job for tomorrow. Do you want them leaving out here or bringing in?"

"Bring them and yourself in, Bertie. Young Stanley here wants a word with you," said Kate.

After leaving the vegetables in the scullery, Albert emerged into the kitchen, removing his coat, cap and scarf as he came. "By 'eck, it's so cold out there I saw two brass monkeys looking for a welder..." he stopped as he saw the confused look on Stanley's face, "Hiya Stanley, how are you doing? What can I do for you?"

"I was hoping we could speak privately, Mr Tunstall," said Stanley, still confused about what brass monkeys had to do with anything. He would have to ask Prue's father to explain that one.

"Aye lad, come into the parlour; we can talk there. Fetch us a cup of tea, will you, Katie?" Albert led Stanley towards the parlour, giving Prue a big wink and a smile as they left the room.

"Sit down, son, and tell me what's on your mind," Albert stretched his legs out in front of the now blazing fire, then hurriedly tucked his feet out of the way before his wife could notice yet another big hole in his sock.

"Well, Sir, as you know, Prue and I have been seeing each other for quite a time now, albeit only at weekends, but we've come to know each other very well. I would very much like her to be my wife if you will agree?" said Stanley.

Albert took in a large breath, then blew it out again slowly, "My boy, I have nothing against you, but I'm not so sure. Our Prue is a delicate young lady and always has been, health-wise. I'm not sure how she would cope with the rigours of marriage and babies. I assume you want babies, that is?" As Stanley nodded in response, he continued, "I've always thought that Prue would stay at home with her mother and me, so we can take care of her, as we always have. I don't know that I want to let her go – especially as she wouldn't even be in Barrow and near to us."

As he spoke, Kate brought a tray in with the tea things, which she set down on a table next to Albert's chair. She noticed that neither man was looking particularly happy. "What's going on? Is something wrong?" she asked.

"Young Stanley here wants to marry our little Prue and take her off to Bury to be his missus. I'm not sure I can let her go. What do you think, Katie?" he looked seriously at his wife.

At first, Stanley had thought Albert was joking around as he knew the old man had a strange sense of humour and liked to tease, but as Albert had continued and then spoke to Kate, he realised that Prue's father was serious. "But Sir, I will look after her, take care of her, protect her for the rest of my life. I can provide her with a decent home and everything she might need. She'll even have a maid to do the housework. I wouldn't let her do anything that might harm her!" he exclaimed.

Kate looked from one to the other, "I don't know if you understand the circumstances of her birth, Stanley, but we very nearly lost our Prue in the womb, and she's been fragile ever since. She's never had to exert herself or do anything more strenuous than a bit of cooking or light housework now and then. I'm not sure how she would cope with running her own household.

"Having said that," she looked back at her husband, "I know what you're saying, Albert. But have we the right to prevent her from enjoying all that's good in being a grown woman? Stanley *is* able to take care of her and make sure she doesn't do anything to put her health in peril. The only thing that bothers me is children. I really don't know if she would have the strength or stamina for childbirth. It's certainly a dilemma."

Just then, the parlour door opened, and Prue stood on the threshold, "Don't you think perhaps I ought to have some say in all this? It is my life we're talking about after all!" It was the first time any of them had seen her angry, which was clearly denoted by the fire in her eyes and spots of high colour on her cheeks. "I wondered what was taking so long, you nattering away in here, so I came to find out. Now I find you're all making decisions for me, without even a thought for what I want! How dare you all!"

"Now Prue," began her father, "That's not –,"

"Yes, it is Dad, it's exactly that. I know that you love me and that you worry about me. But you can't protect me from life forever! I'm almost 24 years old and a grown woman, not the frail little girl I used to be. I need to make my own decisions about my future. I never expected you even to question that Stanley should be my husband – I only said to ask you because it's tradition and all my sisters have done the same. Dad, you need to let me go and experience whatever life has in store for me. Stanley," Prue turned to look at him, "yes; I will marry you."

Albert stood open-mouthed and stared, first at his daughter, then at his wife. "Well, I never! I would never have believed that my little girl had a temper and would put me in my place like that! Would you believe it, Mother?"

Kate smiled, "Actually, yes I would, Bertie! I've long thought that perhaps we were over-protective with her – it's just taken her a while to tell us so. Prue, sweetheart, of course, you must do what you think is best for you – your dad and I will just have to like it or lump it." She hugged her daughter and kissed her cheek, then did the same with her newest son-in-law to-be, though at the same time admonishing him, "Mind, you had better take good care of her, or you'll have us both to answer to, young man."

Now that she had vented her spleen, Prue looked worriedly at her father – had she upset him? Was he angry with her? She touched his arm, "Dad? Are we all right?"

He wrapped his arms around her in a huge bear-hug, "Of course, we are, little one! I just have to keep reminding myself that you're not my little cherub anymore!" Freeing himself, he turned to Stanley and offered his hand, "Well, it looks like congratulations are in order, whatever my opinion is!" He winked and heartily shook the young man's hand.

"Thank you, Sir and you, Mrs Tunstall. I promise I will take care of her. Only the best for our Prue!"

Later that evening, when they were alone in bed, Albert punched his pillows into a comfortable shape and laid down, "Well, our Katie – what did you think of that? Our little Prue with a fire in her belly! I would never have thought it!"

"I suspect there is a lot about our Prue that we underestimate. Just because she's always been the quiet one with her nose in a book doesn't mean she doesn't know what she wants. And he is a nice young man; they're well suited, don't you think?" she kissed her husband, "Well, that's only Connie left that's single, and though I'm glad she is staying with Hope and the baby and looking after them, I hope she doesn't end up an old maid. I imagine Hope will remarry eventually, don't you? She's too young for widowhood for the rest of her life."

"Aye love, you may be right, although it will be a special sort of man who'll take on a ready-made family – a widow, her child AND her twin sister! It's a lot to ask for." Albert reached out to douse the light.

And yet still the family grew; news came in that Joy and Maurice were expecting their third child in the summer. Christine and Louise would be four and three respectively when their new sibling arrived.

The planning went ahead for Prue's wedding, which was set for September; Autumn was her favourite time, 'season of mists and mellow fruitfulness' as she quoted to her mother from her favourite Keats poem, read long ago. She loved the colours of the trees as they started to turn into brilliant oranges, reds and browns, and the warm days growing shorter with the cold promise of winter.

Like her sisters before her, Prue married Stanley at St Mary's church, overlooking Walney Channel. The only one who could not attend was Joy, who was too heavily pregnant to travel, but who sent her love and best wishes in a telegram. Prue wore a floor-length, long-sleeved gown of white lace over satin, with a long tulle veil, and she carried a bouquet of orange roses, lilies and russet chrysanthemums. The newlyweds honeymooned in Blackpool before returning to Bury, where they would live with her in-laws until they found a suitable place of their own.

Two weeks after the wedding, Joy was safely delivered of her first son, Anthony, who weighed in at a hefty 9 lbs. At the news, Albert was heard to say, "It's about bloody time! I love all my granddaughters, but at last, I have a grandson!"

His joy was doubled in the first weeks of 1935 when Freddie and Sally produced his second grandson, Brian. The Tunstall dynasty was increasing apace and showed no signs of stopping.

CHAPTER TWENTY-THREE 1935-1936

Hope decided to move back to Barrow to be closer to her family. She had been in mourning for Leslie for three years, and although she shared living accommodation in Accrington with her daughter, Hannah, and her twin sister, she was finding it hard to cope. Connie had her own life, with her nursing, and was already a stalwart of St John's Ambulance Brigade, as Charlie had been in Barrow so many years before. She loved and was close to her sister and niece, but her commitments left Hope alone for much of the time.

So, Hope moved back to Barrow and found a vacant flat on Barrow Island, in Steamer Street. With two bedrooms, there was plenty of room for her and Hannah, and the rent was cheap enough for her to manage, provided she could soon find a job. She had been fortunate in that Leslie had been a responsible husband. On their marriage, he had taken out a life insurance policy, which had paid out enough money on his death for his widow and daughter to live on for a while. But the money would not last forever. She would have to find work to eke out her savings.

In the meantime, she spent a lot of time at her parents' house, which Hannah loved because she then got to play with her cousins, Hattie and Thelma, who were just two or three years older. This allowed Hope to look for work, leaving either of her sisters or her mother to look after Hannah.

It was Albert, though, in the end, who came up with an opportunity. He had never gone back into Vickers, and now at 62 realised that he never would – he doubted very much if he'd have been still capable of the job for which he was skilled. Neither did he want to return to the heat, the noise and the dangers of foundry work; he was happier out of doors fishing or doing the odd jobs that seemed to come his way without much effort. He spent a lot of time these days fishing, and with a couple of his friends had taken shares in a small fishing boat, which brought in money for the household. Thanks to Kate's thrifty ways, and now the children had gone, they managed well enough, and in just a couple of years, he would get his pension such as it was.

The prospect of work for Hope came about one afternoon when he had been out on the boat with Sid and Alf, his partners. The three were of an age and similar temperamentally, so they all got along. They enjoyed their forays out into the Irish Sea to land their catch. It was never very big, but big enough for the three to handle, and once the catch was sold, there was generally enough money to make it worthwhile. At the end of this particular day, they went to the Ferry for a pint and had got talking to the crew, with whom they were friendly, of another fishing boat. There was a lot of banter to start with, but then the conversation became a little more serious as they discussed their families. The other crew were younger men who worked for the owner of their boat, a Mr Barnard, an entrepreneur. His boat, the *'Marie-Christine',* was just one of his business interests, and his crew liked it because Mr Barnard did not interfere; he just let them get on with their work. However, in the conversation, it came up that Mrs Barnard, for whom their boat had been named, was looking for some domestic help in their large house at the Biggar Bank end of Ocean Road. Mr Barnard had asked if they knew of anyone who might be interested in helping out with the housework and the children.

At this, Albert's ears pricked up, "Aye, I know of someone. My daughter is looking for something. This might be right up her street."

George Bowman, the fisherman who had mentioned the subject, said he would be happy to take Hope to see Mrs Barnard and see if she might fit the bill. Albert agreed, and when he got home that evening, he was glad to see that Hope and Hannah were still at Naiad Street.

232

"Hiya love," Albert greeted his wife with a kiss on the cheek and addressed his daughter similarly, "Hello pet, how are you? I'm right glad to see you still here!"

"Hiya, Dad. Hannah had a particularly hard day playing and fell asleep over tea. Mam suggested that I put her to bed in Prue's old room and said I might as well stay over too. I have nothing to dash home for, after all." Hope explained.

"Well, luck must be running your way because I heard today about a job that might suit you if you're interested?" Albert sat in his armchair and unlaced his boots. "I was talking to a chap in the Ferry-"

"I thought as much," interrupted his wife, "Here am I keeping your tea warm, and you're boozing with your mates!" She smiled good-naturedly; she didn't really mind.

"Shut it, woman!" Albert grinned, "If a man can't have a pint after a hard day's work, there's something wrong somewhere. Anyway, Hope, this chap works for a well-off sort up on Ocean Road. It seems the boss's wife is looking for some home help. How would that do you?"

Hope thought for a moment, "Well, it sounds all right, but until I know exactly what's involved, I don't know."

"Of course, you don't. But George will speak to Mr Barnard tomorrow and arrange for you to see his wife and see how you get along. George said he'll take you to the house, if you like, and introduce you. He said she's a nice woman, not at all stuck-up, like some of them can be."

"Oh, well, that sounds reassuring. I wouldn't want to work for a snob! Thanks, Dad. Let me know where and when to meet up with this George, and we'll see what it's all about, eh?"

A couple of days later, George called at Naiad Street to pick up Hope and take her to the Barnard house. When he arrived, all three little girls were playing 'chase' around the kitchen table, and the noise level was high. "Quiet, you lot!" shouted Kate above the hubbub, "I can't hear myself think!"

"Hello Mrs Tunstall, it looks like you've got your hands full here! What's this, a day nursery?" George laughed.

"Not quite," replied Kate, "I'm just so glad they're my grandchildren, and I can give them back at the end of the day! Hope won't be a minute; she's just freshening up."

At that moment, Hope walked into the kitchen, patting her hair into place. "How do I look, Mam? Will I do?" As she spoke, she noticed the fair-haired man standing in the doorway, "Oh, hiya, you must be George? Sorry to keep you waiting."

"That's all right, Mrs Wilson, there's no hurry. If you don't mind me saying so, you'll do very nicely. You picked a nice day for it! The wind's dropped a bit, and it's very mild. At least you won't get soaked on the way to meet Mrs Barnard!" George smiled at the pretty brunette with the sparkling blue eyes. Albert hadn't said his daughter was a looker!

As they walked from Naiad Street to the Barnard's house, the conversation flowed, which surprised Hope as she tended to be a little shy with people she didn't know. But George was easy to talk to; he had asked politely how she liked Barrow and what had brought her back from Accrington. Hope had explained about Leslie's death and the loneliness she'd felt at being widowed so young. But now, she was ready to put it behind her and make a life for herself and little Hannah.

"Which was Hannah? To be honest, the three little girls looked very much alike to me! They're certainly a lively bunch!" said George.

"Oh, Hannah is the littlest one. The other two belong to Faith and Grace, my sisters. Our mam loves to have them around, even though she complains about them all the time," Hope laughed.

"Well, here we are," George announced as they reached an imposing house on the wide avenue. He rang the bell and was surprised to see Mrs Barnard answer the door.

"Oh, hello George, and you must be Hope. Please come in!" The lady of the house was a plump, smiling woman with just a slight air of harassment about her. "No, you too, George, you don't have to wait outside." Mrs Barnard ushered George and Hope into the large airy vestibule. "You can go and see Mrs Bell in the kitchen; she'll make you a cup of tea, and I believe she's been baking this morning, so you might get lucky with a cake or a scone! Would you ask her if she would bring some tea up for us? We'll be in the front room."

A few moments later, Hope found herself in a pleasant, comfortable room. A fire was laid, but not lit, in the marble hearth, which was flanked either side by comfy armchairs upholstered in dusky green velvet. Mrs Barnard waved Hope into one of these then sat opposite. They chatted inconsequentially for a few minutes until a well-built older woman wheeled in a tea trolley furnished with delicate china and a large teapot, milk jug and sugar bowl.

"There's your tea Mrs Barnard. Just to let you know, Mr Barnard telephoned while you were out. He said he would be a bit late home for dinner and would you wait until he arrives."

"Thank you. Of course, that's fine. Oh but, will that impact your plans, Mrs Bell? Do you mind staying a little later this evening?" said her employer.

"Makes no odds to me; I've got nothing to rush home for." The older woman turned and left the room, her corsets creaking as she walked.

"That, as you have probably gathered, is the cook, Mrs Bell. She comes across a bit brusque, but she's a kindly soul once you get to know her. Now, about the work. We need a general assistant really – someone who can turn her hand to anything, whether it's housework, looking after the children, helping Mrs Bell in the kitchen, or waiting at the table when we have company. Another girl works in the same capacity so that the hours would be divided up between you. Sometimes you'll work together, other times by yourself. You have to be flexible; you see – a sort of 'Jill of all trades' if you will. Would that be a problem?"

"Well, there is my little girl, Hannah. She's nearly four, but I'm sure my mother or one of my sisters would be glad to have her when I'm working. They all live on Walney, so it's nice and close; Hannah and I live on Old Barrow, so not far away at all." Hope replied.

"And what sort of experience do you have?" Mrs Barnard asked.

"Well, I've never been in domestic service, but I trained as a nurse before I married, so I'm used to expecting the unexpected. And of course, I come from a large family, and we were expected to help out at home, so I'm sure there isn't anything I can't handle." Hope willed herself to sound confident while she was feeling anything but. This was the first time she'd gone into anything by herself – she'd always had her twin close by to depend on before.

"I think you sound perfect for the job," said Mrs Barnard, beaming all over her face. She had taken to this girl and had felt sorry when she heard about her background. To lose one's husband within a couple of years of marrying and still pregnant at the time! The girl must have some character to have got through all that. "How do you feel about starting on Monday? Just come in the back door to the kitchen at 8 o'clock, and Mrs Bell will get you fixed up with a uniform and tell you what needs doing. I think Deidre will be here then, too, so she can show you the ropes. How does that sound?"

Hope's face was wreathed in smiles. There was a happy atmosphere in this house, and she felt sure she would enjoy working here. Now she just had to talk her relatives into childcare, and she would be set. Mrs Barnard insisted she finish her tea then rang a bell fixed to the wall by the fireplace. Mrs Bell creaked her way back into the room.

"Mrs Bell, you'll be glad to hear that Hope is going to join our happy little crew. No more having to drag yourself from your kitchen to serve tea! Now, would you take her to wherever George might be?" she turned to Hope, "and we'll see you on Monday. It was a pleasure to meet you, Hope."

"Thank you, Mrs Barnard. I'll try not to let you down." Hope followed the Cook to the rear of the house where George sat at the kitchen table, an empty mug and a plate of cake crumbs in front of him.

"Mrs B! That cake was delicious! I'm very fond of a bit of Victoria Sponge! Thank you." He stood and took the cook's hand and kissed it as though she was a great lady and he a gentleman.
The old lady blushed and giggled like a schoolgirl. "Get along with you! You're a right charmer, George Bowman, and no mistake. Well, Hope, the missus seems to have taken a fancy to you. It's a nice house, this,

and we all get along. I'm sure you're going to fit in. See you on Monday – 8 am sharp now!"

"Thank you, Mrs Bell; I won't be late," Hope said.

As she and George walked back to her parents, she told him about the interview and how well it went, "And I can't thank you enough, George. Dad said it was you that told him about the job. I'm grateful."

"You're welcome, Mrs Wilson. You'll be all right there. They take care of their people. Mrs Barnard is kind, and Mr Barnard is an all-right sort of chap too," he said.

"Please, call me Hope, George. Otherwise, I shall start calling you Mr Bowman whenever I see you!" Hope smiled.

"Very well, Hope. Now I know that you're a respectable widow, but I was wondering if perhaps you might let me take you out to celebrate. Perhaps I can take you for tea at the Pavilion tomorrow afternoon. And Hannah too if you think she'd like it?"

Hope was taken aback; she hadn't been expecting that. She had been so wrapped up in her mourning for so long that the thought of entering a relationship with another man had never occurred to her. However, it was only tea that he was suggesting, and she couldn't see anything wrong with that, so she agreed.

George became a frequent visitor to Naiad Street, ostensibly to see Albert and talk about fishing, but more and more he appeared when Hope was there, usually collecting Hannah on her way home from work. Eventually, after many months of this, they found themselves alone one day. Kate was at Faith's with Hannah, and Albert had not yet arrived home, so George took the opportunity to ask her if there was any possibility she might consider him as a suitor.

"I know it's only a few years since your husband died, and you've told me how much you love and miss him still. But Hope, you're still a young woman. Surely you don't intend to spend the rest of your life alone. You don't have to take an example from Queen Victoria!" He took her hand in his, "I would be so good to you. And Hannah, of course. I can take care of both of you. I know I'm only a fisherman and not wealthy, but I'm not poverty-stricken either."

"George, you've taken me by surprise!" Hope had shocked herself by not removing her hand, which he still held tightly in his coarse, weather-beaten one, "I hadn't even thought that we might be more than friends."

"I have; I've thought about it often. You, me and Hannah would make a lovely little family. But that's in the future; I'm not asking you to marry me now! Just to think about us courting together, that's all." He pleaded.

Just then, they heard the front door open, and Hope snatched her hand away from his. "I'll think about it. I promise," she whispered as her daughter came running into the room and flung her arms around her mother.

"Hello, Georgie!" the little girl smiled at him.

"Hiya, sweetheart!" He lifted her high onto his shoulders, making her squeal, "how's my best girl today? Have you been good for your grandma?"

"As good as she ever is," laughed Kate, taking off her coat. "Pop the kettle on, Hope, let's have a cuppa. I'm parched!"

Hope disappeared into the scullery to fill the kettle, hoping that the blush that suffused her face and neck would disappear before her mother noticed.

"Well, I'd better be off. I'll see if I can catch Albert at the Ferry – and I'll send him home, I promise, Mrs T!" said George, placing Hannah firmly back on her feet. He winked at Hope as she came back in, "I'll see you very soon."

In January 1936, the nation had been rocked by the death of the King, George V. The Tunstall household well remembered when the King had acceded the throne from his father, Edward VII, in 1910. On the day that Barrow had celebrated his coronation, they had received news that they must hand their home in Cameron Street back to its owner, Miss Muncaster. Albert's revenge for her treatment of his family had passed into folklore, often remembered and enjoyed.

The King had been popular; there had been many achievements during his reign. One of which was the change of the Royal Family's name from Saxe-Coburg-Gotha, to Windsor, after the castle of that name that had been the home of English royalty since William the Conqueror. It had been a change much approved of by the population, as it showed that the King wished to distance himself from Germany, in a patriotic gesture, during the Great War.

His son, the Prince of Wales, became King Edward VIII and Emperor of India. He had been popular with the younger generation in the 1920s as something of a playboy man-about-town. He loved parties and gatherings, which gave rise to the popular song '*I Danced with a Man who danced with a Girl who Danced with the Prince of Wales.*' As a single royal prince, he was probably the most eligible bachelor in Europe, having also acquired a reputation as a 'ladies' man'. The most notorious rumours suggested he had frequent affairs with aristocratic ladies such as Lady Thelma Furness. He had recently taken up with an American divorcee, Wallis Simpson, who had still been married to start with but was now seeking a divorce from her second husband.

Albert and Kate had been following the scandal in the newspapers and had sided with the traditionalists in the Government who decreed that marriage between the King and his paramour was impossible. As head of the Church of England, which at that time did not allow divorced people to remarry in Church whilst the former spouse still lived, he could hardly be allowed to break one of the Church's rules. And especially as the prospective wife was someone of 'dubious morals'. However, Edward had insisted he would marry Mrs Simpson and fully intended to do so as soon as she was free.

Meanwhile, as the furore continued, love and marriage were also very much in the minds of one of the Tunstall girls. Hope had agreed to see George as her suitor, and they had been 'walking out' together for several months now. The rest of the family were happy for her, particularly her mother, who worried about her. Hope had only been married to Leslie for two years before his death, and she was still only 28 years old. George had brought a twinkle back into Hope's eyes, and she seemed happy with him.

The two lovebirds married in a small ceremony at St Mary's church in April, with only the immediate family present. George had few relatives, and they mostly lived in Fleetwood, near Blackpool. He had come to Barrow originally to work in Vickers but had taken to fishing when he was laid off and had made his living at that ever since. He moved into Hope's Steamer Street flat, a far cry away from the lodging house he had lived in until now.

Sadly, the new King did not have such a happy ending to his own romance – his love of Wallis Simpson cost him his crown. He left his younger brother, now King George VI, with his wife Queen Elizabeth and their two daughters, Princess Elizabeth and Princess Margaret Rose as the reluctant heads of state in the United Kingdom.

CHAPTER TWENTY-FOUR 1937-1939

In January 1937, Hope gave birth to her first child with George Bowman, a baby girl named Angela, half-sister for Hannah. The number of grandchildren for Kate and Albert was steadily rising, including the new baby they now had twelve, with only Prue and Connie yet to become mothers. Connie joked that she didn't need to get married and have children. Since she had already suffered the labour pains twice on behalf of her sister, she had no wish to experience them in real terms! Kate worried that perhaps this long-shared affinity between the twins might be why Connie showed no interest in settling down or marrying. She seemed to be much more interested in her nursing career than finding a husband.

Connie was a regular visitor to Barrow since Hope had moved back and married George. Although Connie still saw a lot of Freddie and Sally, she now lived alone in Accrington and missed her twin and niece after living with them since Leslie died. It was good that she was able to stay at Naiad Street on these visits; it allowed her to see more of her parents and her other sisters still in Barrow. They all seemed to be surrounded by little children, and while Connie loved them, she didn't see what all the fuss was about. She was happy with her independence and didn't see the necessity of adding a man to the equation, which was very worrying for her mother.

There was a lull in baby production for quite a while, not surprisingly, as there was so much going on in the world to cause distractions. 1937 was the year that saw the former King Edward VIII become Duke of Windsor, and the new King George VI and his queen crowned. May 12th had been the date of Edward's proposed coronation, so the new King decided to keep the same date – the only difference was that changes had also to be made to crown Elizabeth as his consort at the same time. Of course, there was much celebration – street parties and parades went ahead as previously planned. For the first time, the coronation was filmed and later shown in cinemas as a newsreel, which gave everyone the opportunity to watch the ceremony.

At the end of May, Neville Chamberlain became the new Prime Minister of the Coalition government, and the following week, news came in that the Duke of Windsor had finally married his Wallis at the Chateau de Cande in France. Although she was now entitled to be addressed Duchess of Windsor, the King decreed that she was *not* allowed to use the title of 'Royal Highness'.

Rumours of a possible war were beginning to abound due to the policies of Adolf Hitler. He had been Chancellor of Germany since the early 1930s and was now ruling as Dictator. Hitler completely controlled the country through the tactics of his National Socialist Party, known as the Nazis. Racism, eugenics and antisemitism were ideological features of the regime, and since 1933, concentration camps had been established to imprison Jews, Romanies and other races classed as 'undesirables' by *der Fuhrer*. Even the mentally ill and disabled were targeted, and it was later revealed that thousands had perished in asylums and hospitals on the orders of Hitler and his cohorts. Anyone was in peril who did not fit his ideal of the Aryan Nation, i.e., pure-bred Caucasians with blond hair and blue eyes.

Back at home, marital law changed, in that insanity and desertion joined adultery as grounds for divorce. Albert read that newspaper article out loud to the assembled family members, to which Kate commented, "You'd better watch your step then, Bertie!" which made them all roar with laughter.

On a much more sombre note, 'In Parenthesis', an epic poem by David Jones, was published that year, which described in great detail the experiences of an infantryman, John Ball, during the battle of the

Somme during the Great War. Ned had borrowed it from the library and had read it aloud to Grace and her parents each evening for a week, as it was divided into seven parts. They were all moved to tears at various parts of the poem. It gave Grace an insight into what her beloved older brother Charlie had gone through but never talked about when he returned. He had just considered himself lucky that he had come home, at least physically whole, unlike many of his comrades who came back maimed, psychologically scarred, or didn't return at all.

Taking note of the rumours of a possible war, Freddie and Sally moved their young family back to Barrow after deciding that he would prefer to do something concrete that might become necessary for the war effort. He applied to rejoin Vickers. As a semi-skilled brass moulder, he could finish his training on the job and become fully skilled. The Company were happy to take him back, as they would soon be working full-tilt to build warships and submarines for the – it now seemed inevitable - coming conflict.

With some financial help from his father-in-law, Freddie and Sally could buy a brand-new house. Amphitrite Street was a road that ran from Ocean Road as far as Bristol Street before becoming Southampton Street which finally ended at Central Drive. Number 23 was a brand-new semi-detached house at the bottom of the hill down from the Ocean Road end, in a row of others built the same. The semis were attached at one side and shared a wide drive with the other, in this case, number 25. Upstairs, it had two bedrooms, a boxroom and a bathroom, and downstairs was a hall just inside the front door, with what was called a 'Sunshine Lounge' in that the living room stretched from the front to the back of the house with large windows at each end and a kitchen with a built-in pantry. There was a small front garden, but the garden at the back was 100 feet long. Freddie loved the idea of being able to grow his flowers and vegetables – not realising that in the not-too-distant future, every available plot of ground would be turned over to growing food.

Britain was becoming increasingly aware of the actions of the Third Reich. After the Great War, Europe was re-drawn, resulting in three million Germans living in several other countries, including Austria and Czechoslovakia. An Austrian German himself, Hitler aimed to reunite all Germans into one nation. It would also benefit Germany to be in control of Austrian assets, such as raw materials and labour, the products of the iron, textile and machine industries, and gold and foreign currency reserves. Hence, the 'Anschluss Osterreich'; the annexing of Austria, in March 1938.

In the British Parliament, Chamberlain made a speech against the Anschluss, but the Government, desperate to avoid another world war, followed a policy of appeasement. This included the Munich Agreement in September 1938, which allowed Germany's expansion into part of Czechoslovakia.

Despite the apparent policy of appeasement, it seemed the powers that be were already making plans should war become unavoidable. In 1937 a contract to produce 38 million gas masks had been won by a factory in Blackburn, Lancashire after the government decided that every man, woman and child in Britain must have a gas mask for protection. In July the following year, the gas masks were issued to the civilian population. A cinema newsreel showed a government official opening the factory, then demonstrating the use of a gas mask.

Gas had been a major weapon during Great War. Those who had previously served remembered well with horror, the mustard- and chlorine gas attacks in the trenches that had left some men blind and others with breathing difficulties that would last the rest of their lives. With the very real possibility of bombing attacks on towns and cities coupled with the release of chemical agents, this presented a very real threat of disruption to British lives. Civil defence workers were issued with football-style rattles to warn the public of an attack and trained to deal with casualties. Telephone boxes were painted with bright red paint that would turn green in the event of an attack within its vicinity.

On 4th April 1939, the Royal Armoured Corps was formed, and later that month, the Military Training Act came into force which meant that every man between the ages of 18 and 21 must register for six months of military training. Also, in April, the Women's Royal Naval Service was re-established since being disbanded at the end of the Great War. In June, the Women's Auxiliary Air Force was created, which incorporated the ATS, then in July, the Women's Land Army was formed. It seemed that women were going to be much more proactive than just filling in for men in 'ordinary' jobs, this time. Although they would never actually go into combat, women in the forces would still be essential to the war effort should there be another conflict.

In March 1939, Hitler violated the 6-month-old Munich Agreement when Germany invaded the whole of Czechoslovakia. Albert read the news with disgust. "You mark my words, Katie; there'll be another war before we're very much older."

"Oh, Bertie," his wife replied, "I do hope not! For the first time, I'm glad we're old! At least I know that you won't be called up to fight, but what about all our boys, our sons and sons in law? They're all young men!"

"I wouldn't worry too much, love – not at first anyway. They'll take the young single lads first like they did last time. They've all had to register already for that six months' military training. All our lot are married with children, so they won't be in the first intake," but as he was reassuring his wife, Albert kept his own secret worries to himself. Ned and Freddie would be all right; working in the Shipyard, theirs was a reserved occupation, same with Ned's brother-in-law, Ray. Charlie, still out in Ceylon, was now forty, so hopefully safe enough.

The only good news, which was in itself somewhat worrying, was that in April, Prue wrote home to say that she and Stanley were expecting their first child, due in November. Whilst she was happy for the couple, Kate could not help but worry that her youngest daughter was not robust enough for childbirth. Kate had written to her, sending congratulations from the rest of the family and enquiring after Prue's health. Prue had soon written back, knowing how her parents worried about her:

'Dear Mam and Dad, there is no need to worry about me! I'm feeling very well indeed, not even any morning sickness yet! The doctor has said that as long as I don't try to do too much, there is no reason why I should not be able to carry the baby to term and give birth naturally. However, he will keep a close eye on me, and should he think it necessary, he has assured me that the latest techniques in Caesarean births have meant that it is much safer nowadays. Closer to my time, we will discuss whether or not he thinks that is the better option.

In the meantime, Stanley and my in-laws are treating me like a piece of Dresden porcelain – I'm barely allowed to lift a finger!

So, you see, there's no need to worry, I'm being well taken care of...' the letter went on to routine family matters, giving her love to everyone in the family before signing off *'... your ever-loving, and completely spoiled and happy, Prue'.*

On 1st September 1939, Germany invaded Poland. Also, starting on that day, 1.5 million children were evacuated from British towns and cities to rural areas that were deemed safer from German bombing raids. Being the home of one of the most important ship- and submarine builders, Barrow was naturally high on the Luftwaffe target list. But all of the Tunstall girls, including Freddie's wife, Sally, had decided not to allow their children to evacuate.

Grace had announced solidly, "My Thelma and Audrey are staying at home. I couldn't bear to think of them being farmed out to strangers for months or even years on end. If we're going to die, we're all going to die together."

Faith agreed, "I feel exactly the same, Grace. Poor little things being herded away like sheep, not knowing where they're going or if they'll ever come home again. No. I'm keeping my children here with me."

The rest of the family were in agreement. The Tunstall Dynasty would stick together, come hell or high water. And if God forbid, any of the children were left orphaned, there were enough aunties and uncles that could take them in and bring them up with their own.

The Army was officially mobilised, and Blackout was imposed nationwide. This entailed that all windows and glass must be covered sufficiently to prevent even the tiniest glimmer of light that might be visible to the German air force, enabling them to target strategic objectives such as railway lines, shipyards, factories etc.

Prime Minister Neville Chamberlain broke the news at 11.15 am on Sunday, 3 September 1939. In a five-minute broadcast on the Home Service, he announced, *"This morning the British ambassador in Berlin handed the German government a final note, stating that unless we heard from them by 11 o'clock that they were prepared at once to withdraw their troops from Poland, a state of war would exist between us. I have to tell you now that no such undertaking has been received and that consequently, this country is at war with Germany."* Later that day, France also declared war on Germany.

Once again, Britain was at war.

CHAPTER TWENTY-FIVE 1939-1940

It seemed unbelievable that war could be happening again. "I thought that the last conflict had been called 'The War to End All Wars,'" said Kate to her husband, "How can it be – only twenty years after the last lot? Why does that madman in Germany think he can conquer the world like this?"

"I'm with you, my love," replied Albert, "It's beyond belief. But I can see he does need to be stopped. And you know our lot – we own half the world, so we always have to go and sort it out. Those poor beggars in Poland need our help. We have to make a stand somewhere."

The Government seemed to have plans well in hand this time. National Service was introduced for men aged 18 to 41, who had to register for service. Those medically unfit were exempt, as were those in key occupations, which happily included the men working in Vickers as well as bakers, doctors, and farmers.

Charlie would be safe in Ceylon, as he was an engineer in Shipbuilding, and in any case, he would be 41 on his next birthday. Not that he would not have gone to war if he could, but the Far East was suffering already from the Sino-Japanese Conflict that had started in 1937. Emperor Hirohito's attempts to invade China were causing major problems throughout the Pacific region. Charlie began to make plans for himself and Sarah to leave and go to Australia until the situation was resolved.

That Britain was at war began to sink in when the news came that HMS Courageous was sunk with the loss of 519 souls. The introduction of identity cards struck even closer to home. The National Registration Act ordered that on Friday 29th September, every householder must fill in a registration form listing each member of the household, similar to the Census. That would be followed on the Sunday by a visit from a government enumerator who checked the details of the form and issued identity cards for every member of the family. This caused a little difficulty for Freddie and Sally when Freddie had filled in the form. Then his wife had given birth to their son, Kevin, on the day the enumerator called round. In all the excitement, Freddie had forgotten to amend the form, and poor Kevin very nearly missed getting his ID card – not that he knew anything about it.

Kate laughed when Freddie told her this. Trust him – her younger son was always the one to cause trouble or get into mischief. It appeared that he hadn't improved any in growing up. Fortunately, he was safe from conscription too – now he was back in the Yard. Kate counted her blessings; her sons at least would not be going to the front line.

Of her sons-in-law, Harry was already 43; although he was too old for conscription at this time, he volunteered to join the Civil Defence and became an ARP Warden. Ned did the same; although not too old to join up, he was in a reserved occupation in Vickers and thus exempt from call up. George was a fisherman and in a reserved occupation; the country still needed feeding, especially as the Germans would attempt to cut off any supplies to Britain, so it was necessary to become as self-sufficient as possible. There was danger out there on the seas from the German U-boats, even for a fishing smack, which meant Hope worried every day until he got home. For his part towards the war effort, George joined the reserve Coast Guard and spent many nights on coastal watch to try and spot the enemy's approach from the sea. Finally, as a baker, Maurice was also safe from front line duties. Only Stanley was not in a reserved occupation, but his eyesight and a childhood bout of rheumatic fever that had resulted in damage to his heart (although mild) meant he was not classed fit enough to serve in the forces. He, too, joined the Civil Defence in the Home Guard in Bury. In November, Kate travelled to Bury to Prue during her confinement. Stanley picked up his mother-in-law at the railway station, and she was pleased to find Prue, sporting her enormous baby-bump, sitting with her feet up on a chaise-longue with a pile of books next to her.

"If it weren't for your bump, I would feel like I'd gone back in time!" laughed Kate, "this was always your 'position normal' from being a bairn, never happier than when your nose was in a book!"

"Well, Mam, Stan won't let me lift anything heavier!" Prue grinned, "How was your train journey?"

"It was fine, love; I like to watch all the scenery passing by through the windows. Do you know, though – that was the first time I've travelled on a train by myself? It was a bit nerve-wracking at first, but I quite enjoyed it!" She took off her gloves and overcoat, which Stanley solicitously took from her. "Now, where's the kitchen? I could do with a cup of tea – I feel like I'm spitting cotton!"

Kate soon made herself at home and was comfortable in the bedroom next door to Prue's. For the time being, Stan had removed himself to the other guest room so that Prue would be more comfortable in their double bed; she had worried about keeping him awake at night as she tried to find a comfortable position.

Two days after Kate's arrival, in the early hours of the morning, she heard her daughter's moans as the contractions began. Instantly, Kate was up and dressed and went in to find Stanley already sitting by the bed, holding Prue's hand.

"Have you sent for the midwife?" Kate asked her son-in-law.

He nodded his head, "Yes, and the doctor. Just in case."

"Well, you've done your bit, Stanley; I'll sit with her now. You go and wait downstairs so you can send the midwife up when she arrives. You can start by boiling up a few kettles and pans of water and getting out whatever towels you can find. And bring up a bowl of cool water and a flannel so we can keep her comfortable."

"Yes, Ma. Is there anything else I can do?" Stanley was white as a ghost and looked terrified.

"Aye, have yourself a large whisky or something! It'll calm your nerves. Don't worry; everything will be fine," Kate tried to reassure him.

The day had dawned bright, crisp and clear. Unable to stand the sounds of his wife's pain any longer, Stan had put on his overcoat and was standing in the garden, smoking. The labour had been going on forever, it seemed, and with every moan and scream, he swore he would never put Prue through this agony again.

Above him, the bedroom window opened, and Kate put out her head, "There you are, Stanley! I've been shouting down the stairs for you! You'd better come up here and meet your son!"

Without a word, Stanley discarded his cigarette and raced back into the house, taking the stairs two at a time. He stopped outside the bedroom door and quickly shrugged off his coat, draping it over the newel post at the top of the stairs. He opened the door gently, and then all he could see was a vision – his wife, exhausted and white as a sheet, but beautiful in her happiness as she gazed intently at the tiny baby, swaddled in a white shawl, in her arms.

She looked up at her husband with a beatific smile, held out the small bundle towards him and said, "Look what we made, Stan! Isn't he so absolutely beautiful?"

Kate stayed in Bury for the two weeks following her latest grandson's birth. She had been surprised how well Prue had managed, insisting that she wanted to give birth without an operation. But it had all gone surprisingly well, and Prue had astonished everyone by recovering so quickly and completely. Now, she was ready to get up and start mothering her new son properly, though Kate was glad that Stanley had employed a nursemaid, so Prue had help when it was needed.

Albert met his wife from the train, looking forward to news about the newest addition to the family. It wouldn't be long until Christmas, though now the war was on, there wouldn't be any extravagances this year. Before then, there should be the arrival of yet another grand-baby to look forward to; Freddie and Sally were expecting the imminent birth of their second child, due in December.

Sure enough, the week before Christmas, another grandson, Kevin, joined the ever-expanding Tunstall dynasty, the first child born to Freddie and Sally in their new home. Freddie was glad to have had another boy – there were so many girls already in this family! He felt it was up to him to preserve the Tunstall line since it didn't look like Charlie and Sarah would oblige.

Sadly, though, in January, Maurice wrote to Kate and Albert from Milnthorpe, unhappy to have to ask them to break it to the family that Joy had given birth in January to a stillborn baby girl that they had named Alison.

On a brighter note, Hope and George had a new arrival – their first son, Gerald, was born in March. Hope was thrilled at George's reaction! He was so proud that he took little Gerald to meet his partners and his boss, Mr Barnard, as soon as Hope allowed. Mrs Barnard was very pleased to hear that Hope was well; although she hadn't worked at the Ocean Road house for very long, Mrs B had become fond of the family.

She presented George with a silver teething mug as a birthday present, which Hope was proud to display on the mantelpiece in the flat.

In May 1940, Neville Chamberlain resigned, and Winston Churchill became Prime Minister of the Coalition government, announcing in his first speech to Parliament; '*I would say to the House, as I said to those who have joined this Government: "I have nothing to offer but blood, toil, tears and sweat.*"' His speech was to prove correct as, within the next two weeks, the evacuation of Dunkirk began.

The Wehrmacht had surrounded the British Expeditionary Forces in the Port of Dunkirk. Tens of thousands of Allied Forces had retreated and were trapped on the beaches; they needed to be rescued imminently or risk the loss or capture of thousands of souls. As time went on, it became apparent that the vessels currently carrying out Operation Dynamo, as it had been named, would not be sufficient to retrieve all of the men in time.

The news went out all over the country – vessels of all types were needed to assist the evacuation. On hearing this, George and his colleagues aboard the *Marie-Christine* set off immediately for the English Channel to aid in the rescue. Theirs was one of the hundreds of civilian vessels which flocked to Dunkirk, thus alleviating what might have been a disastrous massacre.

On the 4th of June, the Prime Minister broadcast his famous '*We shall fight them on the beaches*' speech, reminding the population that, although the evacuation of Dunkirk was an event to cause pride within the nation, it was not a Victory. There was still a war to be fought – and won – before the world could be safe from the Third Reich.

At the beginning of August, Ned and Grace announced that they were moving house. They had finally been able to buy the home of their dreams, and even better, in Grace's eyes, they had bought the house right next door to her brother Freddie, at 25 Amphitrite Street. When they had visited Freddie and Sally in their new home, Grace had been very envious, so when they realised that next door was available, Ned immediately took steps to secure it for his family. The house was perfect for their needs and just a stone's throw from their old home in Delhi Street, so there was no need to make new friends as their old neighbours were so nearby.

Later that month, Albert took a trip to Hull to see his siblings. His brother, Walter, had become an Alderman of the City, and Albert went to attend the ceremony, proud that one of his older brothers had achieved such an accolade. While he was there, he visited his sister, Lizzie, who lived in Inglenook, near Ellerby, about 20 miles from Hull. One morning, Lizzie had called him down to breakfast, and he replied he would be down shortly.

After about twenty minutes, and not hearing any movement from upstairs, Lizzie went again into the hall to shout, "Bertie! What's keeping you? Your breakfast is getting cold…" but as she looked upwards, she saw him sitting on a stair near the top of the staircase. "What are you doing up there, Bertie? Are you alright?" she asked.

Albert did not respond, and as Lizzie ascended the stairs, she could see there was no movement, no breathing, not a flicker of an eyelid. She immediately sent for the doctor, who, when he arrived a short while later, confirmed it. Albert was dead.

Not wanting to upset Kate with the news long-distance, Lizzie sent a telegram to Freddie, being not the oldest but the only son near Kate. On receiving the telegram, Freddie – serious, for once in his life – first went next door to Grace to enlist her help in going to inform their mother. Grace took the news very hard. As the second oldest sibling, she was close to her father, knowing he was especially proud of how she had stepped into the breach for several years as a young girl to help the family when her mother was trying to recover from complications while giving birth to Prue. Her relationship with her father had always been very precious to her; she had been the very first 'Daddy's Girl', and he meant the world to her.

Eventually, Grace felt strong enough to accompany her brother to walk the few blocks to Naiad Street, where their mother waited completely unaware and unprepared for such a shock. Kate, feeling a little lost at home alone, was overjoyed at the unexpected visit of her son and daughter but realised by their demeanour that something was wrong.

"Mam, you probably need to sit down," began Grace, "there's some bad news."

"What is it?" said Kate, "Not the children? What's happened?"

"I'll put the kettle on," said Grace, "Freddie…?"

"Well, Mam, it's like this," said Freddie, taking his mother's hand, "I just got this telegram from Auntie Lizzie in Hull. It's about our Dad." He handed her the telegram, crumpled from being grasped so tightly. "You'd better read it."

Kate took her reading glasses from her apron pocket and placed them on the end of her nose, then took the paper from Freddie. She stared motionless at the words for several minutes, unable to take in the dreadful news. Grace brought her a cup of strong tea, sweetened with a couple of spoons of sugar and put it on the table next to the armchair, then got similar for herself and her brother.

Kate eventually raised her head, her gaze unseeing as tears welled up and ran down her cheeks unchecked. "Bertie..." she whispered, then collapsed in a heap backwards in the chair.

"Mam! Freddie, find the smelling salts; she's fainted!" Grace yelled as she patted her mother's hand and stroked her face. A few minutes later, Kate came to, looking around her as if she had just had a bad dream. Then as she looked at the woebegone faces of her children, she realised it was not a dream at all. Her husband of over forty years, her best friend, the love of her life, was gone forever.

Freddie went to Hull to bring his father home. There had been a post-mortem, and the cause of death was established as *Angina Pectoris*. He must have been suffering chest pains for years and had not told anyone about them, not even his wife. All of his family had believed him to be a strong, hearty man, full of life and looking forward to a long old age, and here he was, dead at only sixty-seven. Freddie had sent a telegram to Charlie to let him know, but everyone realised that he would not be able to come back in time for the funeral.

Albert was buried in the first week of September 1940 in the graveyard at St Mary's, where he had seen most of his children marry and begin their adult lives.

Grace and Ned, with their two daughters, moved into Naiad Street to be with Kate. They had made the excuse that their new house was not yet ready for them to move into but had already given notice on the Delhi Street rented house, so it was a good stop-gap for them.
Kate wasn't fooled for a moment, but she was glad of the company. The house was so empty without him, and every moment she expected his footsteps across the yard and his cheery greeting as he came home. She had slept alongside him for forty-two years and now missed his presence where she had previously needed to keep

elbowing him in the ribs to stop his snoring. Never again would he come in and joyfully pick her up and swing her around the kitchen when he had good news or had an unexpected windfall. She had always been able to rely on her 'big man' to comfort and cheer her through all of the ups and downs of their large family. The Tunstall Dynasty had lost its patriarch.

CHAPTER TWENTY-SIX 1940-1943

After a month, Kate insisted that the Parsons move into their new house. She knew she would mourn Albert for the rest of her life, but that was no reason why his children should put a stop on theirs. Albert himself would always say 'Life goes on!' and 'This too shall pass' when any misfortune befell – and she must carry on his policy.

Reluctantly, Grace and Ned did as they were bid and were soon comfortably ensconced in their perfect home.

In September 1940, Churchill made another historic speech, *'Never in the field of human conflict was so much owed by so many to so few'*, a tribute to the RAF fighting the Luftwaffe in the skies over southern England, which lasted until 15th September when the RAF claimed victory over Germany in the Battle of Britain. The London Blitz began in earnest from September 7th; for 57 consecutive nights, the Luftwaffe bombed the capital city, causing mayhem and destruction.

The entire country had been on alert since 4th September when Hitler had announced that Nazi Germany would invade Great Britain; however, on 17[th,] he postponed the invasion indefinitely. Finally, in October, the cryptographers of Bletchley Park confirmed there would be no invasion. The bombing continued around the country, and in November, the City of Coventry was destroyed by more than 500 Luftwaffe bombers. It was reported that sixty thousand of the 75,000 buildings in the city were levelled, and the death toll was 583, with 863 injuries. The following week other parts of the Midlands, including Birmingham, were bombed, followed by the Blitzes of Southampton, Liverpool, Bristol and Sheffield. The bombing campaign carried on well into December. Just before the New Year dawned, on 29th December, heavy bombing caused the second Great Fire of London, destroying many buildings, including the Guildhall. The number of deaths and casualties throughout the campaign was horrifying.

However, as proof that life does go on regardless of the circumstances, a new baby girl named Theresa was born to Freddie and Sally in March 1941. Later that month, another baby girl entered the family, this time to Hope and George, a sister for Hannah and Angela, to be christened Maisie.

Back in 1936, when the German airship Hindenburg was supposed to be carrying passengers on a luxury trip and had flown slowly and quite low over Barrow, many believed it was on a spying mission to allow photographs to be taken of the town.

The Luftwaffe prioritised a bombing campaign attempting to destroy or disrupt the prolific production of submarines and ships being built by Vickers. The first bombs to hit Barrow had been in September 1940, but did little damage compared to the bomb strikes in April and May, which became known as the Barrow Blitz. Other important targets were the Steel and Ironworks, which had been the largest in the world in former years, and the railway lines that were the main artery for distribution of goods and munitions in and out of the town.

On 7th May, Barrow Central Station was hit and heavily damaged. The blast from this attack hit Ned's family, living in Warwick Street, leaving every window smashed and damaging the gable end wall at the end of the terrace. The house was designated dangerous, and the family, Ned's parents, Edward and Florence, and his sister Florrie and her husband Ray, had to move out until the building could be repaired.

Ned and Grace discussed this problem and then confronted the elder Parsons and the Thompsons with what they saw as a solution. "Now then, Ma and Pa, and you two," said Grace, nodding to her sister-in-law as she poured tea for everyone, "there's only one thing to do. You must move in with us until your place is ready, which might take a while, the way things are going! It will be a squeeze, but we'll manage!"

Florrie began to protest, "No, Grace, it can't be done. You've not enough room for all of us; especially now you've had that nice fireman billeted with you. And I believe Fred and Sally have two other night watchers billeted with them too!"

"No," Grace insisted, "me and Ned have worked it all out. It's not Buckingham Palace, but we'll be alright as long as we make an effort to muck in and all get along together."

Ned laughed, "Even Buck House got bombed last year, remember? But I think they probably have a few more rooms than us! Grace is right, though. We've worked it out, and it will be alright. Mam and Dad can go in the back bedroom our girls have been using. They're only young, so they can top and tail in the boxroom, but you and Ray," he looked at Florrie, "will have to make do with a mattress on the floor down here, in the living room."

Ray took a sip of tea, then asked, "But what about your fireman?"

"Oh, Herbert? Fortunately, he's on nights, so once the girls are up, he can sleep in their bed. It'll be interesting, to say the least, but we'll manage. Everyone's got to put up and get on with it if we're going to win this damned war! Keep Calm and Carry On, as they keep telling us," said Grace.

Despite the attempts of the Coastal Defences on Walney in the shape of Hipsford Fort and Walney Fort to defend the town from enemy attack, 300 incendiaries were dropped on Salthouse, the first victim of the bombing was a five-year-old child. The worst bombing was from mid-April until May 1941, and finally, the last bomb was dropped on Barrow in January 1942. The entire campaign resulted in 83 fatalities, 330 injured, and around a quarter of the town's housing stock destroyed.

In December 1941, the government brought in a new National Service Act, conscription for women to do 'war work'. At first, only single women and childless widows aged between 20 and 30 were called up, but this was later expanded to between 19 and 43 years old. Florrie got a job driving cranes in Vickers, alongside Freddie, Ray and Ned, who were all working all the hours possible in the Shipyard.

Having Naiad Street to herself, Kate opened her doors to give lodgings to various girls who had come from elsewhere in Northern England to work in the Yard. They were now filling in for what had always been considered 'men's' work; riveters, platers, welders, and munitions workers. She enjoyed their company when they were there – as with most of the Yard employees, they worked all the overtime possible to get ships and submarines built. It was good for Kate to have a houseful again – although it was hard work at 70 years old, with all the cooking, cleaning and laundry to be done. But keeping busy kept sad thoughts of missing Albert at bay, and she was thankful she had something to keep herself occupied.

In December 1941, the news shocked the world about the attack by the Japanese Air Force on the US Naval Base at Pearl Harbor in Hawaii. The raid was completely unexpected, and there were many fatalities and casualties. Having been a neutral country, America now had no choice but to join in what had become World War II.

Kate was pleased to receive a letter from Australia, where Charlie and Sarah had gone to wait out the War. The Japanese invasion of so many

Eastern territories had made Charlie think that, especially since the British Eastern Fleet was based in Colombo harbour, sooner or later they would come under attack. Sarah and Charlie upped sticks and left just before an attack from a Japanese Aircraft Carrier came on 5th April 1942. Fortunately, due to information from military intelligence, the Eastern Fleet had been warned and the harbour vacated. There was damage to the port, and some ships sunk or damaged, but the Japanese did not find the bulk of the Fleet. It was a relief for the family to know that Charlie and Sarah were safe.

There was sadness for Ned and his family in July when his mother, Florence, died at the age of 65. She had been unwell for some time but without a specific diagnosis, and she died peacefully in her sleep. Fortunately, the family were still staying with Ned and Grace at the time, so Edward had his son and daughter there to comfort him through his loss. Like Kate, he found it very hard to cope with living without the woman he had loved and shared his life with for over forty-two years.

But in that strange way that the world sometimes has of balancing things, the loss of one of the family was filled by the birth of another. In October, Malcolm Bowman made his entry into the world, a second son for Hope and George and Kate's nineteenth grandchild.

Around the same time as this happy news, more of the same arrived when Prue wrote that she was pregnant with her second child, due in April. She wrote that she hoped that she and Stanley and little Stan Jr would be able to visit, perhaps at Christmas, before: *'...I blow up like one of those awful barrage balloons floating about everywhere...'*.

Unknown to the rest of the family, as Prue had not wanted to pass on the bad news, she had suffered three miscarriages since having her son, who was now three years old. Now she had managed to carry the baby to the third month, which had made her believe that this time, please God, the baby might survive to full term, and she was optimistic enough to inform the family about her pregnancy.

Sadly, the visit never happened. The doctor deemed it unsafe for Prue to travel and recommended complete bed rest for the remainder of her pregnancy as the only way to ensure safe delivery. Once again, she wrote home about being spoiled and cosseted and said that Stan and the other Satterthwaites were not allowing her to lift a finger. She had a stack of books by the bedside and was thankful that she wasn't easily bored as long as she had her novels in which to lose herself.

When April arrived, Kate left her lodgers to look after themselves and went to Bury on the train to stay with Prue until her next grandchild arrived. Studying her reflection in the window, she was shocked to see the old lady with grey hair and more than a few wrinkles staring back at her. She had never been a vain woman, and with a houseful of children, there had been no time to preen or take more than the minimum care of her appearance, but when did she get so old?

As she watched the changing landscape, she pondered on whether her other daughters wondered why their mother insisted on being with Prue during the birthing procedure when she never had with them. Certainly, there didn't seem to be any animosity or complaints of unfairness from them. Kate didn't even know herself why she felt she should be there for her youngest, except that Prue's delicate health all her life had perhaps made her mother more protective. The other girls seemed to be healthy, strong young women, who hardly needed their old mother on the scene, and none of them, except the loss of Joy's baby Alison, had had any problems bearing their children.

Stanley picked Kate up at Bury station again, with Stanley Jr bouncing along beside him. The little boy didn't remember 'Grandma', but nevertheless, he refused to miss out on going out with his daddy in the car and going to see the trains too! It was an exciting adventure for a three-year-old. When Kate saw Stanley standing on the platform, she knew immediately that the little boy standing on the luggage trolley a little way away was her grandson – he was the image of Bertie, with the same tousled mud-coloured hair and startling blue eyes. For a moment, it took her breath away, but then, gathering her thoughts, she waved to her son-in-law.

When she went into Prue's bedroom, Kate was immediately worried by her daughter's appearance. Always pale, her skin had become almost translucent, and dark circles under her eyes belied the wide smile as she greeted her mother. "Mam! It's so good to see you! You look so well! Of course, I haven't seen you since Dad's funeral, have I? But you look like you're doing all right?"

"Yes, love, I'm fine. You can't keep the old girl down, you know. I might be 71, but I'm not past it yet! But enough about me – how are you? If I'm honest, pet, you really don't look very well."

"I know; I look worse than I feel, though. I just have no strength; the baby seems to be draining all of my energy! We'll be fine, though. Everyone is being so kind and thoughtful – and now you're here! I'm so pleased to see you, Mam." She held out her arms as Kate moved closer to hug her. As Kate held her, she could feel the lack of flesh on Prue's bones; she felt so fragile and brittle that Kate was almost afraid of holding too tight and breaking her.

A few nights later, Kate awoke as she heard Prue coughing, trying to clear her throat. She sat up in the single bed that she'd insisted on having moved into Prue's room so that she could be with her daughter constantly. With the blackout, the room was pitch dark except for the one lamp on Prue's bedside, which was covered with a scarf during the night to dim it further but left a little light by which to see.

Kate swung her legs over the side of the bed and felt for her slippers. Finding them, she then put a shawl around her shoulders, as the room had gone chilly since the fire had died down to a few small, glowing embers. She slipped quietly to Prue's bedside and placed her hand on her forehead. Prue was burning up, as if with fever, and had been sweating so much that her nightdress and bedlinen were soaked. Kate poured a glass of water from the jug on the bedside table and gently lifted her daughter's shoulders, raising her enough to take a sip. She then soaked a flannel in the cool water and pressed it to Prue's forehead and face, trying to cool the fever and wipe away the sweat.

Having heard movement in his wife's room, Stanley opened the door quietly and stepped inside. Seeing Kate standing over Prue, he whispered, "Is she alright? Has something happened?"

"I don't like the look of her. She's baking hot and doesn't seem to know what's going on. I'm going to try and change her nightdress; it's soaked! I'll try to keep her cool and comfortable. I think you had better call the doctor and the midwife. And hurry!" Kate turned back to Prue, "Alright, love, your old mam's here," she whispered.

The doctor and the midwife arrived quickly and almost at the same time. The doctor examined Prue as best as he could, but she was far from responsive. He looked around at Stanley, "I'd have liked to get her to hospital, but I don't think there's time. I will have to do an emergency C-section, but I have to warn you that the prognosis isn't good. The baby is in some distress, and your wife is beyond being able to push, even if she were having contractions and was dilated enough. I think you and Mrs Tunstall had better go downstairs; this isn't going to be pretty. Can you organise lots of boiling water and as many towels as you can muster, please?" he gestured at the midwife, "Mrs Taylor will come and get them from you. I'll do everything I can for both of them, I promise."

Mrs Taylor ushered Stanley and Kate from the room, "Mr Rodgers knows what he is doing; your wife is in the best hands. We'll take care of her. Now, where are the towels?"

Kate pointed in the direction of a large linen cupboard in the corridor, "You should find what you need in there. I'll go and get the water boiling." She held the midwife's hand for a moment, "Please take care of my daughter?" Mrs Taylor nodded and gathered an armful of towels.

"Come on, Stanley, let's get that kettle and a few pots of water boiling. I could do with a cup of tea. I think you could probably do with something a bit stronger, though!" She took Stanley by the arm and guided him down the stairs. He seemed to have gone into a daze, the worry about his wife and baby filling his thoughts.

The April sun had risen on a fine if windy day. Stanley gazed out of the dining room window onto the garden that Prue loved. He had fitted it out with a gazebo and tables and chairs dotted about the lawn so that she could sit outside and play with Stanley and read her books. How he wished she was sitting there now, waiting for him to bring out her morning cup of tea and their chat about what the day would bring.

He looked at his pocket-watch; "My God! It's been hours! What are they doing up there?" he turned to see that his words had roused Kate, who had nodded off in the armchair. "Sorry, Ma, I didn't mean to wake you," he apologised.

"No, that's alright, love, I was just dozing. There must be some news soon, though – like you said, it's been a long while. What time is it?" Kate asked.

"It's only six o'clock, but that's still four hours since the doctor arrived! What can be taking so long? The rest of the house will be up before long. What do I say when Ginny brings little Stan downstairs? He'll be wanting his mummy!" Stanley's eyes had bags from his lack of sleep. "I'll need to send a note to work too; I don't think I'll be going in today."

Just then, they heard a door open upstairs and footsteps coming down the staircase. There was a brief tap at the dining-room door, and the doctor popped his head round. "Ah, there you are, Mr Satterthwaite." He looked exhausted and beaten down. "There's no easy way to say this to either of you. I'm afraid we've lost them, both mother and baby. I'm so, so very sorry."

"What? How can that be? I don't understand..." Stanley screwed his eyes up and rubbed them with his fists like a child denied his favourite plaything. He sat heavily on a chair and looked at Mr Rodgers. "You couldn't save either of them?"

The doctor shook his head, "I'm sorry. Believe me when I say I did everything I could, but sometimes there is just nothing you can do. Sadly, this is one of those times. I believe Mrs Taylor is tidying up; you should be able to go up there in a few minutes if you wish." He turned his attention to Kate, who sat rocking her body quietly, both arms hugging herself, trying for some comfort as the silent tears fell unchecked. "Mrs Tunstall, are you alright? Is there anything I can do for you?"

Kate shook her head, sobbing. She felt every one of her 71 years – oh how she ached to have Bertie with her, to hold her. Her last baby girl was dead, and her grandchild too. How could she bear it alone?

But bear it, she must. "I want to see her. Will it be all right to go up now, do you think?" As Mr Rodgers nodded, Kate touched Stanley's arm. "Are you coming with me, Stanley?"

Stanley got to his feet with an enormous effort, as if all the life at been sucked out of him. They went upstairs together, and as they reached the bedroom door, Mrs Taylor came out carrying a large bundle of towels and linen. Kate spoke, "Thank you for your help. It would probably be best to take that lot and burn it. I can't imagine for a minute that they can be laundered properly, and even if they could, I don't think I'd want to keep them. Is that all right with you, Stanley?"

Stanley looked bewildered at his mother-in-law as if she was speaking a foreign tongue, "Yes – yes, whatever you think, Ma." He stood outside the door, almost afraid to go in.

"Don't worry, dear," said the midwife softly, "there's nothing bad to see. They just look peaceful now."

Kate opened the door and went into the room, but Stanley stilled hesitated on the threshold. When eventually he gathered his courage, he entered and was glad to find Mrs Taylor was right. Prue lay under the covers, and next to her, in her arms, was her baby. Both looked as though they were in a deep, content and peaceful sleep. Stanley stumbled to the side of the bed and fell on his knees, sobbing as he took Prue's cold, pale hand and kissed it. "Oh, my darling," he whispered, "why did you have to leave me?"

Kate placed her hand on his shoulder as her tears fell like rain, "She was never meant to live a long life, Stanley. But you made what little time she did have on this earth the happiest. Thank you for that. Thank you for making my little girl happy."

The funeral was held at St Paul's church in Bury, and Grace remarked that although every loss was sad, this was probably the most painful. "I'm glad though that they had allowed Prue and little Albert John to be buried together in the same coffin. It would have been so dreadful to see such a tiny coffin alongside his mother's. At least we can believe that the poor little mite will be with his mam for all eternity."

CHAPTER TWENTY-SEVEN 1945-1949

Following Prue's untimely death, things remained calm in the Tunstall clan for some time. Each of the offshoot families worked their way through the war years, as did every other household in the country, 'making do and mending' and 'digging for Victory', somehow managing to survive through all the hardships.

But although the war had brought hardships to almost everyone, it had also brought about a great 'pulling together' and community feeling among the population. Yes, times were hard, but they were hard for everyone, so they all made the best of whatever came along, supported one another and made an effort to enjoy every good thing as if it was the last.

25 Amphitrite Street became a popular venue for parties and get-togethers. Grace wanted hers to be a happy and sociable home for her two girls, Thelma and Audrey, now aged fifteen and eleven. She encouraged them to bring their schoolfriends home often. It might just be a bit of bread and dripping for tea, but they would gladly share it. It was a sadness Grace never mentioned that she and Ned had not had more children; she would have loved a big family like the one in which she'd grown up, but it just wasn't to be. Which, given the current circumstances was probably a blessing – it was hard enough to manage for just the four of them!

Grace would often organise a 'knees-up' for the neighbours and family who lived nearby whenever she felt things were getting too serious or depressing. They would all donate part of their rations, enabling her to bake enormous potato pies with a little meat if it was possible and huge pans of mushy peas. Ned would get out his violin, and Grace or Florrie play the old upright piano. Everyone would sing along to the day's popular songs, and the two girls would demonstrate the dances they had learned at dancing class. Grace felt like it was a poke in the eye for old Adolf – he would find out soon enough that he couldn't keep the British down for long!

The war was gradually drawing to a close, thank God. The bombing attacks on the United Kingdom were dwindling as the Allied Forces began the push to liberate the countries that the Wehrmacht had occupied. There was a mixed reaction to the news in February that the RAF had bombed Dresden in Germany – it was good that the Germans were heading towards defeat, but the firestorm caused had killed tens of thousands of civilians in the act.

On the 8th May 1945, just over a week after Hitler's suicide, the Germans finally surrendered, and the nation celebrated Victory in Europe Day. There was music and dancing in the streets all over the country, and later, newsreels showed the celebrations in London. The Capital was thronged with people both in and out of uniform. Masses gathered in front of Buckingham Palace, calling to see the King and Queen and the two young princesses. Everyone hugged and kissed each other, climbing the streetlamps and dancing together, the true spirit of rejoicing. At last, the war was over!

In Accrington, Connie decided she needed a change. She was 36 years old, still single, and still spending her life working as a nurse at Victoria Hospital. She had seen so many war casualties, soldiers returning maimed from the front, families suffering when bombing raids had injured or made them homeless. She still wanted to be a nurse but wondered how she might continue in the profession that had grown slightly stale for her.

The answer to her prayers came when she worked on the women's ward for a while. One of her patients, Emily Whiteside, had been in for an operation. She had had a cancer which the surgeons had tried to remove and was now well enough to be discharged, but would need nursing care for some while before she fully recovered. Her husband, David, had noticed how well his wife had got along with Connie on the ward and how much care Connie had devoted to her. He had asked if there was any possibility of her becoming a live-in private nurse to look after Emily for as long as was necessary.

Connie accepted immediately. It was perfect for her, and even if it turned out to be not long term, at least there would be a few months to give her time to decide what she was going to do. She packed her belongings, moved out of the flat she had shared with Hope and Hannah, and moved into the Whitehead family home in Baxenden, a village just outside Accrington.

The Whiteheads didn't have any children, and at 47, it was highly unlikely, even if she did make a full recovery, that Emily would start a family now. Even more unlikely, considering that David was more than ten years older.

When Grace received the letter from Connie, telling her about her change in circumstances, she wondered why her sister had informed her, and not their mother or her twin. Then she realised that she was expected to let her mother down gently that Connie still intended to remain single. It wouldn't be likely that she would meet any eligible bachelors while she lived with the middle-aged couple.

When Grace went to Naiad Street to see Kate, she casually brought up the subject in conversation. "It sounds like our Connie is very happy where she is, Mam. She says she's settled in with the Whiteheads, and they treat her more like family than an employee. She does say, though, that it looks like Emily is on a very long road to recovery – she doesn't seem to be making much headway. But Mr Whitehead – David – seems to be devoted to her, all the same."

Kate sighed, "It's such a pity and a waste. Our Connie would make someone a lovely wife – and I've seen how she is with Hope's little ones; she'd be a great mother too. Still, I suppose only one out of the eight of you unmarried is not bad going. I'd have loved to see you all settled before I go to join your dad, though."

"That's enough of that sort of talk, our Mam!" Grace scolded. "You're not going anywhere if I have my way! And to think when our Hope delivers their new bairn in a couple of months, you'll have twenty grandbabies, so you're going to be needed for a good long while yet! Now then, I've made you a nice rice pudding for after your dinner. Do you want me to put it in the oven for you?"

"After my dinner?" Kate smiled, "aye, love, it will probably BE my dinner. Since my lodgers have all gone, there doesn't seem much point in cooking just for myself. But there's plenty of goodness in a rice pud, so thank you for that!"

When Ned came in from work that evening, Grace told him what Kate had said, and she revealed that she was a bit worried about her mother. "All that talk of joining our dad! Do you think she'll be all right?"

"I'm sure she will. It's only natural. When she's lost her husband and one of her children in recent years, she's bound to be feeling it a bit. She and your dad were so close and had such a good marriage, she must be feeling lonely without him, and it'll take her a while to get used to being on her own. At least my dad has Florrie and Ray living with him to fill the emptiness a bit. You're doing the right thing by visiting her often. And maybe you should start asking her round here for meals a bit more now that we haven't got such a houseful!"

Grace nodded, "you're probably right. Things are much easier now your family have gone back to their own house. I know the girls are much happier to be out of that box room! Did I tell you we'd had a letter from Herbert? He's marrying that girlfriend of his – what was her name, Rita or something? – now that he's back in Hull?"

Towards the end of 1947, Hope and George produced another baby girl they called Kathleen, their seventh child.

There was news from Connie too. She wrote to say that sadly, after two years, Emily Whiteside had passed on; she had never recovered from her operation but had gradually just wasted away. Her last words to Connie were to look after David and to David, "look after Connie", the two most precious people in her sad short life. Her words became prophetic – Connie found she had developed feelings for David, although she kept them well hidden. She had stayed to help with the funeral arrangements and support David in his loss, but after a month had passed, she began to feel awkward about her position.

Connie had heard that gossip about herself and her employer was doing the rounds – how disgraceful that Mr Whiteside should still have his wife's young nurse still living at his house – and him more than twenty years older than her! And not only that, his wife of 30-odd years barely cold in her grave! Connie was ashamed. She knew how she felt about David, who she thought was the kindest, gentlest person she knew. She did not want his life ruined by a scandal caused by any behaviour on her part.

One evening, after she had cooked their meal, they sat at the kitchen table, and David had asked her what was wrong. He had noticed something on her mind was troubling her, and could he help her at all?

This was the perfect opportunity for Connie. "Yes, something is bothering me, David. I'm afraid I will have to give notice and find another job, and somewhere else to live. I've heard there is gossip going around about our situation, and it's the only way to stop their chattering tongues. They're quite right, I suppose – it isn't done for you and me to live under the same roof and not be related, even though we both know it's perfectly innocent. I'm worried that the next thing suggested is that something's been going on between us since even before poor Emily died. I don't want your name to be blackened because of me. So, I must find something else to do with my life. I'm sorry, but that's all there is to it."

"Well, Connie, you and I know that for as long as my darling Emily was alive, everything was proper and above board." David glanced at the framed photograph of his and Emily's wedding, which stood on the mantelpiece. "And I've realised since she's been gone that eventually you will probably leave and find your way in the world. You're a young woman with your whole life ahead of you, and I wouldn't want to hold you back from that. It's nice of you to think of me, but you mustn't worry because a few chatterboxes have found something to witter on about! I don't give a hang what people say. If it's up to me, I don't want you to leave, I want you to stay on here. I know I'm an old man compared to you, but I've found that I care for you very much. And I think Emily would approve; she would take it as a compliment that my life with her was so good that I find I don't want to carry on alone. Especially when there is already someone here that I know and care about, and she did too.

"If what you want is to leave, then, of course, you must go and follow your heart. But if you'll have me – for however long I have left on this earth – I would like very much for you to stay, not as my nurse, but as my wife. Of course, we shall wait for a decent interval, but I would love for us to get married sometime in the not-too-distant future. What do you think?"

Connie was astonished. She had not allowed herself the luxury of contemplating a relationship with David, despite her fondness of him. To find that her feelings were reciprocated threw her off balance.

David noticed the confusion on her face and said, "I can understand if you want to take some time and think about it. So, take as long as you need and have a good think about what you want. I'm happy to go along with whatever you decide. But please don't let those tittle-tattlers influence you with their nattering. You and I will soon become yesterday's news when they find a new scandal. Now, let's get on with this lovely dinner you've cooked; it's a shame to waste it!"

It didn't take long for Connie to make up her mind. David was right; why should she let the gossip bother her? She was stronger than that.

The next letter Grace received with an Accrington postmark had her running straight to her mother's house. "Mam, you'll never believe it! Our Connie's gone and got married! Here, look what she's written!"

She handed the letter to Kate. *'Dear Gracie – and Mam, because I know you'll pass this straight on to her! You can finally rest easy – David and I got married yesterday at the Register Office in Willow Street in Accrington. I know it's been a bit sudden, but with Emily's death so recent, we didn't want to make a song and dance about it. It's bad enough the gossips have been trying to make out something was going on before she died, but honest to God, that's not true, I promise.*

It's just that we both realised after she'd gone that we cared for each other very much, and David insisted that we get married so that no one can make me out to be some sort of scarlet woman, living in sin with a man old enough to by my father and so recently widowed. We both sincerely believe that Emily would have approved, so neither of us feels any guilt.

I know he is much older than me, Mam, but you'll like him when you meet him. At my age and his though, I don't think it likely we'll start a family – I'd be 40 before any child was born, and that's much too late in my opinion to have a first baby. In any case, I think Hope is taking care of my share – I certainly know that I feel her labour pains every time, so I think I've done my bit already!

But I just wanted you to know and to tell all the rest of the family that at last, the spinster aunt is now a respectable married woman. We'll come for a visit before too long, and you can all meet 'my husband' – it still seems strange to write those words!

Yours, as always, Connie aka Mrs David Whiteside.'

Tears of happiness rolled down Kate's cheeks as she read and re-read the letter. "Oh, my goodness! What a surprise!" she exclaimed, "Who'd have thought it?"

"Well, you've finally got your wish, our mam, all of your children married off at last!" said Grace, hugging Kate and kissing her cheek. "Isn't that the best news?"

Kate remained a strong matriarch over her husband's prophetic 'Tunstall Dynasty', who all of her children and grandchildren adored. She continued to live in Naiad Street for some years after Albert's death; then, in 1953, she went to live with Connie and her husband David in Accrington. She came back to Barrow in 1956 for a little break because Connie was ill in hospital with pneumonia. It was then that Kate died at the home of her daughter Faith. She was 84 years old. At last, she could go and meet her beloved Albert, which was all she had ever wanted, once her children were all taken care of.

Grace took over the reins where Kate left off, becoming the Matriarch of the family. From a very early age, her siblings had come to respect their eldest sister's wisdom, and this continued in later life when her siblings would still seek her advice. Sometimes, of an evening when Thelma and Audrey were out or in bed, Grace and Ned would talk long into the night about their lives and experiences. Apart from the brief period before her marriage when she had worked in Vickers and at the Pavilion Café, she had spent her entire life caring for different generations of her family and her own children. She had never been ambitious for success at work and had been only too happy to follow the time-honoured tradition of women as the bastion of home and hearth. And that, Grace believed, was nothing to be sniffed at.

Continue reading the Tunstall Family's story in the next volume: Monday is Washing Day Book Two: Audrey – Escape and Surrender Coming Soon!

Acknowledgements

I am indebted to Michael Heppell and his 'Write That Book Masterclass', amazing people who offered support, advice and encouragement, particularly Norman Hill, Anne Anderson and her partner Derek. My best love and thanks to my sister, Mel Royle, and Helen Hyde, who kept my nose to the grindstone. Many thanks to Leasil Burrows and Frances Brown for a mine of information about our antecedents, the Turners. Special mention to Fran Taylor for allowing the use of her family history: the Woods family of Forshaw Street. To Matt Elks, who made a wonderful job of my website and answered all my stupid questions without swearing at me (at least in person!). Much love to my long-time BFFs from Risedale, especially Sue and Barnie Cleasby for their infinite hospitality and Angie Downing, who has encouraged me to write for so many years and also supplied her crafting services. Also, my love and gratitude to my wonderful friends, Ann Marie Gale and Sheri Wardell, for looking after me so well and encouraging me every step of the way. Last but not least, my cat Toni, for her companionship and constant interruptions for cuddles.
Liz Hughes – 2022

About the Author

Elizabeth Hughes was born in Barrow in Furness in 1958. She married young, often referred to as an adolescent mistake, after which she relocated, alone, to the South of England where her 'real life' began. She worked in hospitality and customer service, eventually remarrying and living in various locations, making a few lifelong friends along the way. When that marriage ended, Liz studied for a BSc at Lancaster University, then met and lived with author and poet Glyn Hughes in Sowerby Bridge, until his untimely death in 2011 after eight years together. She now remains in God's Own County, living alone with her elderly cat Toni, reading and writing to her heart's content

Keep up with the latest news, blog and gallery at
www.lizziehugheswriter.com